GHOST TRAIN:
The Lost Gold of the Nazis

The Crypt Trilogy: Book Three

Bill Thompson

Published by
Ascendente Books
Dallas, Texas

Published by Ascendente Books

ISBN 978-0996181686

Printed in the United States of America

Books by Bill Thompson

Brian Sadler Archaeological Mystery Series
THE BETHLEHEM SCROLL
ANCIENT: A SEARCH FOR THE LOST CITY
OF THE MAYAS
THE STRANGEST THING
THE BONES IN THE PIT
ORDER OF SUCCESSION
THE BLACK CROSS
TEMPLE

Apocalyptic Fiction
THE OUTCASTS

The Crypt Trilogy
THE RELIC OF THE KING
THE CRYPT OF THE ANCIENTS
GHOST TRAIN

The Bayou Hauntings
CALLIE

Middle Grade Fiction
THE LEGEND OF GUNNERS COVE

DEDICATION

I dedicate this book to Dick McGrew, a man whom I came to admire greatly in the short five years I knew him. He was a savvy businessman, a great conversationalist and a frequent gin rummy winner even at age 89.

I'll miss our stimulating conversations, Dick. If there's an information booth in Heaven, please find a way to let me know if aliens built the pyramids.

———

I also want to honor the memory of the millions who perished in the Holocaust. Let these atrocities be forever etched in the hearts of mankind so they may never happen again.

ACKNOWLEDGEMENTS

As always, I thank my beta readers Bob, Peggy, Jeff and Ryan. Thanks also to my wife Margie, who patiently listens to every word read aloud, a process critical to my reviewing.

AUTHOR'S NOTE

To keep things simple, I used U.S. dollars for most of the monetary transactions in this book.

Prelude
Piedras Negras, Guatemala
One year ago

Paul Silver lay trapped under a pedestal in a crypt filled with ancient technology. Although he didn't know it, the archaeologist was in a similar predicament, ten feet away beneath a pile of rubble. Paul could move his hands and feet and he could see faint daylight above him. Clearly their last shot, meant to open the huge stone door that held them captive, had instead caused a massive cave-in

"Mark! Mark, can you hear me?"

Paul thought he heard a muffled response but he wasn't sure. He tried to dislodge himself using his hands but the heavy pedestal remained securely on his upper back, rendering him immobile.

The pedestal's manmade, he remembered as he looked at its perfectly square corners just inches above his head. Maybe I have a chance. Was I holding the wand when the ceiling collapsed? He couldn't recall.

When they first broke through the wall into the chamber full of ancient devices, he had commented on the pedestals' precise corners, a dead giveaway that the heavy stands weren't natural.

He and Mark had spent the last two days trying to see if the cache of ancient, complicated devices sitting on pedestals in the remote cavern could help them escape their stone prison. Yesterday they had learned that one of the instruments, a little wand, was a teleportation device. It didn't work on stone, so it didn't remove the huge rock that blocked their escape. But it did move other things, manmade things. If he had it, he might be able to escape from underneath the pedestal that pinned him to the floor of the cave.

He slowly worked his hand down his body along the sandy floor. The wand was nearly two feet long; if it were there he'd find it. It wasn't on his right side but halfway down the left he felt something like a piece of PVC pipe.

That's it!

The other day they'd aimed the wand's beam at the flap of a rucksack. The piece of cloth had disappeared and then reappeared across the room where Mark had directed it. Paul couldn't move the entire pedestal since the wand's beam wasn't wide enough to encompass all of it. But that didn't matter. He only needed was to eliminate the part that lay on his chest.

Since his upper body was on one side of the pedestal and his hands were on the other, he couldn't see what he was doing. He remembered Mark's having used both hands to twist the cylinder in opposite directions. With considerable effort he brought his hands together around the wand and turned it. He could see the gleam of its green beam as the wand activated.

When they first found it, they'd wondered if the wand would transport people. Neither was willing to find out. They did know that the beam would move parts of things, so Paul was careful to keep it away from his body. He carefully pointed it upwards, prayed he had aimed correctly, took a deep breath and pressed a small knob on its side.

Instantly he felt the release of pressure on his body. The section of the pedestal that had confined him was gone. Now he could see an enormous stone that had fallen from the ceiling. Now it was resting a foot above him, supported by the rest of the pedestal – the part he hadn't zapped away. Apparently he'd hit it perfectly; if he'd been off by inches, the stone would have crushed him.

Weak from days with meager rations and running on nothing but adrenalin, he scrambled out and saw Mark's legs extending from a pile of rubble. Paul worked feverishly with his hands to scoop away dirt and rocks. Soon he had freed his friend's body, but Mark was unconscious. Paul felt a weak pulse, so he quickly turned him over, cleared his mouth of some dirt and began CPR. Within seconds the archaeologist coughed, spat more soil and said weakly, "I guess we made it. If this is Heaven it sure is dirty."

GHOST TRAIN

They quickly assessed the situation. There was now a large hole in the ceiling twenty feet above through which shafts of sunlight flooded the cavern. It was tempting but virtually impossible, since they had no way to get up to it.

"Oh my God," Mark said, pointing. "Look at the door! We did it! We can get out!"

When Mark had pulled the trigger of the strange gun-like apparatus, the goal had been to blast away enough of the rock door to allow them to escape. Although the ceiling had collapsed on them, they also got what they wanted. The top of the massive rock had been blown away. Now there was a tight space that looked like it had sufficient clearance for a person to squeeze through.

When they reached the cavern on the other side they'd be able to walk out to the surface, but there was one potential problem. If the man who had left them for dead had posted guards to keep looters away from the crypt, Paul and Mark would be killed the moment they crawled into the room.

Knowing the risk, Paul volunteered to go first. "If you hear anything but an OK from me, fire the gun through the opening. Who knows what it might do to humans? It damned sure blew away a rock wall."

He climbed up and clawed his way through the narrow passage. Mark heard him yell, "No one's here! Come on through!"

———

Two months later

Mark Linebarger left the crypt where he'd been working all morning and called Paul. It was time for their weekly catch-up meeting. "We're making a lot of progress here," he reported with the same exuberance Paul had heard in his voice for weeks.

After extensive study, the archaeologist had become convinced that the artifacts in the crypt belonged to a highly advanced civilization thousands of years old, a civilization which might have been the fabled Atlantis. They

9

had found a series of etched metal plates and Mark was convinced those held the key to everything. But he was stymied. Even when he used the university's powerful, highly advanced computers, the strange markings remained an enigma. Mark was certain that someday they'd break the complex language on the plates. When that happened, they would learn everything about the mysterious crypt and a civilization that hid its technology here.

As he worked from his townhouse in London's West End, Paul listened to the news. He enjoyed Mark's periodic updates from the Guatemalan jungle. The two of them had found strange and amazing objects in the crypt, and Paul was pleased that the archaeologist was now the spokesperson for the ongoing project. Paul shunned publicity for a variety of reasons; for him, simply having been part of the discovery was satisfaction enough. Mark was armed with plenty of funding, both from the university where he worked and from Paul himself. An extended concession from the government allowed him plenty of time to learn more about what the ancients had left behind.

Paco Garcia, the wealthy criminal who'd left them for dead, was located by Guatemalan undercover agents in a condominium in Cabo San Lucas, Mexico. Rather than dealing with the formalities of extradition, the agents chose a simpler method to bring him to justice. They whisked him away one night in a private jet. Now he was in a Guatemala City jail, facing charges of corruption and theft from the government. His attempts to keep the mysteries of Piedras Negras for himself had been foiled.

Paul Silver had moved on, back to a world of finance and armchair adventure. In addition to the fantastic crypt, he had found something in that jungle that he believed would never enter his life again. He had allowed Hailey Knox to get into his heart. Then in an instant it was over, just like the few other times he'd let someone come too close.

He would never, ever again get involved emotionally. He needed no one now. No one at all.

CHAPTER ONE

Bucharest, Romania
Present day

"How the hell long does it take an old man to die, for God's sake?"

"Shut up, Christina. He can hear you, for all you know."

"I've sat here for hours and I'm tired of waiting. I think I can move things along." She grabbed hold of the frail, bruised skeleton lying in the bed and shook him violently. "Die, you old bastard!"

The guard moved toward her but paused when Philippe jerked her back. He hissed, "Stop it, you idiot! It'll happen soon enough on its own. He's got broken bones already! Let him alone! Have a little compassion for once."

"Another hour. That's all I'm going to give it."

"Really, darling? Then what? Do you intend to kill Grandfather?"

Listening closely, the guard remained impassively by the door. He wondered the same thing and he was ready to move if he needed to.

When Philippe saw her cruel smile, he knew she would have killed him for sure. Given where they were, it was impossible to pull off, but she'd have done it if she could. He was certain of that.

The only movement from the old man was his faint breathing; things had been exactly like this since he'd fallen into a coma forty-eight hours ago. The inmate who'd savagely beaten him, a young murderer dying of HIV, had been in the hospital bed next to Nicu's. The convict claimed he attacked because he was bored and thought it sounded like fun. Now Nicu Lepescu was clinging to life.

Milosh Lepescu, the oldest of the grandchildren, stood on the opposite side of the bed from his siblings. He'd observed their bickering but said nothing. These three were the only remaining relatives of the one-hundred-five-year-old man who had birthed their father, Ciprian. The grandchildren were all he had left, and they were impatiently waiting for him to die.

As more time passed, the girl became restless. With a huff, she struck her grandfather's arm roughly and walked to the guard, who was desperately trying to mind his own business.

"Let me out," she demanded. He selected a key from a ring, unlocked the cell door, and she went out into the hallway. The door closed behind her with a metallic slam.

Philippe left the old man's hospital bed and walked to the barred window three feet away. He gazed idly at the ancient cobblestone street running just outside an electrified fence. Soon Christina returned, her breath reeking of cigarettes. She asked Milosh, "Any progress? Is he dead yet?"

He ignored her, leaned close to the frail body and whispered words in Romanian, the only language the old man knew. He'd asked the same question a dozen times over the past two days, but the inert figure never responded.

"Where is it, Grandfather? Where is the book?"

Nicu suddenly opened his eyes wide. Milosh stepped back in shock; he'd never really expected his grandfather to hear him. And maybe the old man hadn't. Maybe this was an involuntary action, simply part of the dying process.

His lips opened and shut vigorously as he twisted his body, thrashing his arms in the air. He was trying to speak, but nothing would come out.

"Grandfather! What is it?" Milosh yelled, the noise bringing Christina and Philippe rushing to the bed. The guard became alert instantly. He removed his walkie-talkie, prepared to call for help if necessary.

Nicu exhaled a guttural whisper none could understand.

"What's he saying?" Christina yelled. She looked down at him. "What are you saying, you decrepit fool?" She reached out to hit him again, but Milosh pulled her arm back roughly.

"Leave him alone," he said, leaning close to his grandfather's face.

"What is it, dear Grandfather?" Milosh whispered soothingly into the old man's ear.

A bony, skeletal hand grabbed Milosh's jacket, pulling him closer with a surprising last burst of strength.

He barely opened his lips and softly uttered a single word - a word spoken so quietly Milosh wasn't sure he heard it correctly.

Apostol.

Then his grip relaxed and his hands fell to his sides. After one hundred and five years and a tumultuous life filled with greed, hatred and malice toward his fellow man, the old Nazi went to claim his reward, whatever that was. Philippe took his wrist and held it for a moment. He felt no sadness, no remorse. He also felt no pulse. Nicu Lepescu was gone.

Though no one voiced it, each of them had the same thought.

How ironic that Grandfather died a prisoner just like the thousands of prisoners he had a hand in killing.

CHAPTER TWO

Two months earlier

"Are you joking? Is this a prank call?"

Mrs. Radu paused, struggling to compose herself. She had dreaded calling the old man's grandchild, but it had to happen. She didn't care so much what happened to Nicu himself except that she didn't want to lose her comfortable job. She was well paid and the work was easy.

"Mr. Lepescu, I assure you I am serious. Your grandfather was arrested for murder yesterday afternoon. He's being held in the Bucharest jail, and you must come immediately!"

Milosh didn't believe it. His grandfather hadn't entered his mind in years. He didn't even know Nicu still lived here in Bucharest. By now the old man must be - what - maybe a hundred?

"I don't believe you. Who are you, and how did you get this number?"

"My name is Ana Radu. I'm his housekeeper. The building superintendent called me yesterday. He told me the police were at Mr. Lepescu's apartment. I wasn't here - Mr. Lepescu gave me the day off. As soon as I heard, I went over to his house, spoke to the officer there, and they told me he killed a drug dealer in the Ferentari. I got your number from Mr. Lepescu's address book. I'm thankful it still works."

"Wait a minute. He killed somebody in the *Ferentari?* In the *ghetto?* This is bullshit. What's a hundred-year-old man doing in the ghetto?"

"He's a hundred and five, Mr. Lepescu," she replied, frustrated that he still didn't believe her but aware how bizarre this must sound. "I have no idea what he was doing there. Adriana took him. She takes him everywhere. I know she's behind this somehow."

"Jesus, lady. This is getting weirder by the minute. Who's Adriana? Never mind. You know what, I've spent just about enough time on this nonsense. Try this on somebody more gullible." He started to hang up; he was out of patience and her story was obviously an attempt to get him to wire money. These scams were going on all over Eastern Europe. They happened to have picked the wrong patsy this time. His grandfather was far, far too old to be hanging around in the most dangerous section of Bucharest.

"Please don't hang up," she pleaded. "Take down this number. It's the police officer's phone number." She also gave him the officer's name. "He can confirm what I've told you. Once you know it's true, please call me back. Someone has to come. I don't know what to do with his things . . ." She began to cry.

Maybe this is true, he thought. *She isn't asking for money. At least not yet.*

"All right. I'll make the call. What's your number?" He hung up and searched the Internet for the number of the main Bucharest police station. He didn't use the number the woman had given him - that could be part of the scam.

The person who answered the phone at the police station transferred him immediately to the officer's line, and within minutes he'd heard the story. His aging grandfather Nicu Lepescu had indeed fired three shots, killing a known drug dealer, Denis Ilie. The murder had happened in a third-floor room of a seedy hotel in the Ferentari. When the police arrived at the scene, Nicu handed over the murder weapon and confessed to the crime.

Milosh rummaged through his desk for the numbers of his siblings, Philippe and Christina. Philippe had lived in

Lucerne the last time Milosh spoke with him, and she had been in Vienna. But that was long ago and both numbers were out of service. He'd try to find them later; now he needed to get to Nicu's house.

Once Mrs. Radu gave him the address it took less than thirty minutes to drive there. Ironic, he thought, that his grandfather lived half an hour away, right here in Bucharest, and he hadn't seen him in maybe fifteen years. There certainly had been no love lost among any of his family.

He and the housekeeper sat at the kitchen table in Nicu's comfortable flat. She sipped tea as he slowly drank a beer. She'd been the daily housekeeper for ten years, she explained, and until Adriana Creed appeared, he had only rarely left the house. He had no friends, no callers, no interaction with anyone else until the gypsy girl showed up. She said that Adriana, a young fortune-teller turned constant companion, had come into the old man's life three years ago.

"She sits with him for hours, they go for walks, she pats his arm . . . It's . . . I hate it!" She began to cry and Milosh began to understand.

"She's taken your place."

"Not really," Mrs. Radu answered quickly. "I was never a 'companion' in that sense of the word. I was always around in the daytime and we would talk. I would attend to his needs and make sure he had everything he wanted. Now she does all that. She's just taken over."

She's jealous.

Through intermittent tears she told him about Adriana, where she lived and how often she came here. They went out a lot, she explained, and her getting the day off yesterday wasn't unusual. Sometimes Adriana took him away for the day and Nicu gave Mrs. Radu time off. She appreciated it, actually.

She said the police had interrogated her for hours. She went home exhausted, returned this morning, searched Nicu's papers and found Milosh's name and number. She'd never met Nicu's grandson, although she'd worked here ten years.

"What do the police say Grandfather did? It all sounds crazy! I wanted to look on the web, but I decided to come here first."

"I agree it's unbelievable, especially if you had seen your grandfather the past few years. He's old - really old - and frail. He gets around, but he can't do much without my help. Well, since Adriana came, it's her help too, I suppose. She went with him to the ghetto, you know. The desk clerk saw them both go upstairs. She never came back down."

"What? The desk clerk saw her, but when the police got there, it was just him - right? The officer didn't tell me anything about another person."

"He told me Nicu said she was there, but she left before he killed that man. The desk clerk heard three gunshots from upstairs. There were only two occupied rooms; he went to the other room first and heard the people inside having sex. That seems to be what that hotel was used for. When he got to the room on the third floor, the door was open. The old man was sitting in a chair next to a body lying on the floor. Apparently the dead man had rented the room earlier. The desk clerk said the girl was nowhere in sight, and he asked the old man - your grandfather - what happened."

"Mr. Lepescu . . ." She began to sob. "He told the clerk to call the police. 'I've killed this man,' he said. How could he have done that? And why? The policeman said the dead man was a drug dealer. Why would Mr. Lepescu go to the ghetto and kill a drug dealer? He wasn't involved in drugs."

"Sometimes people hide it . . ."

"You don't understand. There was no hiding anything. Before that girl came into his life, he didn't leave this place for weeks on end. Whatever he got, I brought to him. He wasn't strong enough to go out on his own. Did she get him hooked on drugs? As much as I dislike her, I can't believe that. It's as bizarre as the murder itself."

Mrs. Radu's immediate concern was what to do about Nicu's everyday affairs. Should she come every day with no one here? Should she start going through his things? Was she going to have a job?

Milosh asked her to sit tight for a few days, perhaps a week, while he tried to contact his siblings. "We're his only relatives, unless you know something I don't," he said.

She confirmed she knew of none either. Milosh's father, Ciprian, had died long ago, and the three grandchildren were the last of the Lepescu line.

He assured her she'd be paid. "I'll call you when we need your help. Grandfather's merely in jail - he's not dead - and chances are he will be released at some point, either because this is all a huge mistake or we will get him out on bail. We still need you. Come once a week, tidy up, and stay in touch if you hear anything."

He went to the police station and spent an hour with the officer who'd interviewed Mrs. Radu yesterday. Given his grandfather's advanced age, Nicu was being held in a hospital ward with other sick inmates. Milosh was told it could be weeks before anyone could visit him.

Adriana Creed hadn't been charged because no one could place her at the scene when the crime occurred. Nicu said she had left down the back stairs and he had acted alone to murder the drug dealer, although he had offered no motive or explanation how he knew Denis Ilie. For now Adriana was considered a person of interest, but no warrant had been issued. The police wanted to question her, but she had disappeared. Since cross-border movements within the EU weren't recorded, he thought it was possible she was no longer in Romania.

Milosh gave the officer his phone number and went home to try to contact his brother and sister. After a couple of hours checking public records on the Internet, he found Christina. Lepescu, it turned out, was a fairly common name in Romania, but not so much so in Austria, where she apparently still lived. Christina Lepescu had applied for a work permit to be a waitress in an upscale restaurant in

Vienna. He called the place and learned when she'd arrive for her shift. When he knew she'd be there, he called back.

She was surprised to hear from Milosh after all these years, and astonished at the news about their grandfather. She asked him what to do, and he said to stay put for now. If anything changed, he'd call her.

Doubtful that she'd know, he asked if she had any idea how to contact Philippe.

"Our criminal brother?" she'd responded. "I have a cell number somewhere. It's so old that it may not work." She found the number and gave it to him, explaining that the last time she spoke with Philippe he was in hiding, having been fired from his high-paying job as an investment manager for a wealthy man. "He was looking for the name of a lawyer he'd used once before, but I couldn't remember it. I asked him what was going on and he said he was in trouble. I think he stuck his hand in the till once too often." She laughed. "But isn't that just like him!"

Milosh spoke with Philippe. As he had left things with Christina, he told Philippe he'd call when he had news. The Romanian jail system still operated much as it had under the Communists. Inmates charged with capital offenses weren't allowed visitors. Not even an inmate who was 105 years old could see his family.

It was two months before Milosh spoke with his siblings again. The superintendent of the prison had called him early that morning.

"Your grandfather was beaten by another inmate last night," the man had advised. "He's in a coma and they've moved him to a private hospital cell. You may visit but you should come quickly. He's in bad shape, not expected to live."

CHAPTER THREE

The three sat in a bar a few streets over from the prison where their grandfather had died two hours ago. When the assistant warden had asked them who was going to pick up the body, none had an answer. He pulled out a list of morticians the institution kept for just this situation, and Milosh picked the first one. A barrage of paperwork followed; then they had to wait an hour for the prison doctor to examine Nicu's body and officially declare him deceased.

Milosh and Philippe ordered wine, but in typical fashion Christina ordered champagne and declared, "It's time for a toast!"

"Why are you so cruel?" Milosh asked her. "What did he ever do to you?"

"He was a damned Nazi. He let thousands die . . ."

"And exactly why are you suddenly such a bleeding heart? You *care* about something other than yourself? I've never seen this side of you."

"You don't know anything about me! I haven't laid eyes on either of you in years. You, Milosh - from what you've told me the past couple of days, I figure you're as broke as I am, so you're happy he's dead. As far as the Nazi thing, you're right. Who cares? It's like ancient history. It's something I read about in school, like it never really happened. And Grandfather himself? I never knew him. I heard the stories about prison time for war crimes like we all did, but he wasn't a real grandfather to any of us. He didn't give a shit about us or our father. Now he's gone. Good riddance, I say. Let's find his stuff and divide it up."

Philippe smiled. "What a touching memoir. Remind me to have you give the eulogy at my funeral."

"I can only hope it's soon, my dear brother. I know you love me as much as Grandfather did."

While they sparred, Milosh sat quiet and withdrawn.

"You're a barrel of laughs today," Christina hissed at him. "Speaking of Grandfather, I wanted to say something. You killed him, Milosh."

"Are you crazy?" he shouted - his usual calm demeanor gone. A few customers turned their heads to look.

He lowered his voice. "I killed him? What the hell are you talking about, you crazy bitch?"

"Ooh! A little on edge, are we? Do you have something to hide? What did you whisper to him there at the end? Those words that got him so agitated, he died! You did a great job moving things along by the way, but I want to know what you said. And what he said back. When he grabbed your coat, I saw him whisper something to you."

For what seemed like forever, Milosh stared at her in silence. He knew exactly what the old man had said. He had whispered the word *Apostol*. But what did it mean?

Philippe leaned in close and spoke softly. "*Do* you have something to hide? She asked you a simple question." His words became harsh. "Tell us what he said. Do it now."

He'd intended to keep this to himself until he could find out what the word meant, but Milosh had never been able to stand up to his younger brother.

"If you must know, I asked him where the book was. He said a word. Maybe he was trying to answer me or maybe he was delirious. He said something like *apostle*. Are you satisfied now that you've learned such an important secret?"

"I don't believe you."

22

"Christina, I don't give a shit. What you think, who you are, what you're all about - none of it means anything at all to me. I could care less about you or Philippe. We're in this boat together, trying to figure out Grandfather's assets. We already know he had accounts and property. We need to work in harmony just long enough to see what and where our inheritances are. Then both of you can go straight to hell. And say hello to Grandfather when you get there."

Philippe believed Milosh. He knew his grandfather hadn't said *apostle*. The word was *Apostol*.

CHAPTER FOUR

After Nicu died, his housekeeper told the grandchildren about Adriana. .The old man was 105, but in her heart Mrs. Radu firmly believed the girl was doing something sexually with Nicu. She simply was too reserved and old-school to discuss it. Instead she talked about the daily visits, the hours behind the locked bedroom door, and how Adriana had called the old man "darling."

"I don't know what the girl was doing to . . . I mean *with* him," she concluded with a snort. She'd said more than she intended to.

Christina laughed hysterically. "Do you think she was getting Grandfather off? Seriously? He was a hundred and five goddamn years old, for God's sake. An erection would have killed him. I don't know what the hell she was doing, but I want to see the will. Her name had better not be in it. That's all I have to say."

The housekeeper turned red, embarrassed at Christina's words and disgusted that these three seemed interested only in what they were going to inherit.

The grandchildren went to work. They scoured the apartment, looking for anything that could help them determine what his estate looked like. None of them had contacted him for fifteen years or more, so they had no idea about his financial situation. Did he have a will? Debts? Assets? They hoped to find written records.

As they searched through his papers, they also looked for a legendary book. When they were teenagers, their mother had disclosed a dark family secret, a rumor that their paternal grandfather was an extremely wealthy man. Somehow during World War II the high-ranking Nazi had managed to amass vast assets that he had hidden away. He went to prison for twenty years for the crimes he'd committed, but he never told where the fortune was hidden. There was a diary, their mother whispered, that would reveal everything. No one had ever seen it, but if it existed, it would literally hold the key to hidden treasure.

"Where is it, Grandfather? Where is the book?" Although the others didn't know it, those were the questions Milosh had whispered to his grandfather a dozen times in the days before his death. And at the end he had answered.

Apostol.

Although finding the diary would have been ideal, none of them really believed such an important book, if it even existed, would just be sitting around in Nicu's house. And it wasn't, although Christina found a box full of his papers in the closet. There were bank documents, some keys, his last will and testament, and various keepsakes, including his commission as an SS officer in the Army of the Third Reich. She pawed through things, found a simple two-page will and scanned it. Then she tossed it to Milosh.

"It's just us. Now we have to find out what the old bastard had."

Nicu's will couldn't have been simpler. Everything went to the three of them in equal portions. There was no provision for Mrs. Radu and none for Adriana Creed. And there was no mention of a diary.

Milosh and Christina cleaned out drawers and closets. They offered many of his things to Mrs. Radu, who made a feeble attempt to appear grateful for the handouts while inside she seethed with rage. She had been the old man's helpmate for a decade, yet he left her nothing. Now his grandchildren were offering her his castoffs - the things they didn't want.

GHOST TRAIN

He truly was a bastard, the housekeeper thought to herself. He'd left everything to his grandchildren, none of whom she'd ever laid eyes on in the ten years she'd worked here.

Philippe was the only one of the three who had a financial background. They handed him the box of documents; he sat at the kitchen table and began to sort things out while the others emptied the attic. Nicu's bank statements were all from the National Bank of Romania's branch just two blocks from where he sat. They were mailed quarterly; the most recent indicated a balance of well over two million Romanian lei, around six hundred thousand US dollars. He hadn't touched the principal for thirty years; there were quarterly interest deposits plus a deposit each month from Waddell's, an international real estate firm with offices in Bucharest. He wondered about that but soon figured it out.

The statements revealed that occasionally a small amount would be moved into a checking account, which had a current balance of a few thousand lei. He asked Mrs. Radu about it, and she said that was the household account. She could sign checks and used it to pay Nicu's utility and household bills. Every time the account got low, money appeared from some place she didn't know about. From the statements Philippe learned that there was an automatic sweep from the savings account every time the household account needed replenishing.

There were yellowed papers dating back to the 1950s, savings account statements from banks in Germany. These may have long since been closed, Philippe told his siblings as they looked over the documents. He set them aside to investigate later.

One surprising thing Philippe found in his grandfather's box was a deed. He called the housekeeper over and asked if she had ever paid rent or a mortgage payment. She said she hadn't, and he informed his siblings that their grandfather owned not only the flat in which they were sitting, but the entire seven-story building. And it appeared to be debt-free.

"There's a monthly deposit into his savings account from Waddell's," Philippe told the others. "It's significant - over ten thousand US dollars a month."

"Waddell's - isn't that a real estate company? Why are they paying him?"

"Give them a call, Milosh," Philippe replied. "I imagine you'll find they're managing this property for Grandfather, and that money is rental income." Ten minutes later Philippe's hunch had been proven correct. Per Nicu's instructions, the firm deposited net rental income after repairs and expenses, but no statements were mailed. The agent promised to email the past twelve months of statements so they could see where things stood.

It was impossible not to think of the family secret - the rumor that Nicu had accumulated staggering wealth at some point. The deed made it seem possible. He'd never worked after his release from prison and lived modestly, yet he never lacked for anything. Without mentioning the rumor, they asked Mrs. Radu if she had any idea how he existed without working. She shook her head. It was a mystery to her too.

Philippe pulled two keys out of the box and glanced at Milosh and Christina. Both were busy with other things. These were unmistakably safety deposit box keys from two different banks. One was imprinted with the name of Nicu's bank a few blocks away. The other was unmarked. It was taped to an index card with the word *Stadt* written on it.

As he examined them, Christina looked over at him. "What have you found?"

He smoothly slipped the card into his pocket without her seeing it. "Looks like Grandfather had a safety deposit box at his bank."

Christina whooped. "Give me the key! I'm going to the bank right now!"

"We'll all go," Milosh replied. "I suppose we'll need to take Grandfather's will."

An hour later all the formalities had been dealt with and they stood in the bank's vault, a steel box sitting in front of them.

Christina squealed, "I can't wait any longer!" She grabbed the hasp that held the lid closed, but Milosh knocked her hand away.

"Dammit, stop! I know nobody cared about Grandfather but can't we at least pretend to have some sense of decorum?"

She stepped back with a flourish, waved her hand and said, "By all means. After you. Open the lid."

The box was empty.

Christina was livid. "Shit! What the hell . . ."

Philippe had said nothing until now. "All we have to do is look at the bank's record. Just like they did with us today, they will have a list of every person who accessed this box. Learning who was here may explain why there's nothing in it."

The bank officer with whom they'd dealt earlier was only too happy to accommodate them. Nicu Lepescu had been a valued client of the bank for decades, he assured them. The huge sums he kept on deposit all those years had improved his standing as a customer, the grandchildren thought to themselves.

"Let's see," the man said as he thumbed through the same large ledger they'd signed themselves a half hour ago. The leather-bound book was reminiscent of banking fifty years ago, with row after row of inked entries and signatures.

"Ah, here it is," he responded at last. "The last time the box was accessed was nearly two months ago. November 17, to be precise. That was when Mr. Lepescu and . . . Miss Creed - Adriana Creed - came."

The three looked at each other in surprise. *November 17?*

Milosh asked, "They were here together on November 17th? Are you certain that was the day? What time was it?"

He glanced at the ledger and ran his finger down to the entry line. "They signed in at 10:15 a.m. on November 17. Is there a problem?"

Milosh looked at his siblings, giving his head a quick shake - a sign to be silent. "No. Keep going."

The banker scanned the entries. "Twice before that she came alone."

"How could she have accessed the box without our grandfather?"

Oh, these meetings, the banker thought to himself. If he'd done one, he'd done a hundred where the heirs suddenly show up to find out where the spoils are hidden. With a smile he replied, "I knew that would be your next question. Let me look." He turned to a computer on his desk, entered a few keystrokes and said, "Early in November Mr. Lepescu came into the bank with Miss Creed. They sat here in my office, exactly where you're sitting now. He added her to his safe deposit access card that day. She came back the next day alone, then again a few days after that. Two weeks later Mr. Lepescu and Miss Creed came together."

"Did she take anything away the times when she was here by herself? Are there cameras?"

"We don't keep records of what people take from their own boxes. And of course there are cameras. There are cameras everywhere, but not in the particular room where you examined the box today. Our customers expect privacy when they are handling their property. We of course have video that would show her departure from the vault itself. That footage would reveal anything she carried out with her. However, we cannot show them to you, Miss Lepescu. Your grandfather authorized her to access the contents of his safety deposit box. She therefore had the right to do whatever she wished with whatever was inside. The bank will absolutely respect her legal rights in that regard."

"So I presume you can't tell me if my grandfather took anything on the last visit here. It wouldn't make sense she came twice, then again with him, to see an empty box."

"I can't tell you if they took anything out of the box. They did effect another transaction with me that day. Since your grandfather was obviously still alive at that point, his assets were his, to do with as he wished. Your rights to information and property only began upon his death. Perhaps your grandfather's records will reveal a transaction with our institution on that day."

He closed the ledger and said, "Is there anything else I may do for you?"

Now they stood on the sidewalk outside the bank. Milosh asked the question that burned in his mind.

"You heard him say Grandfather and Adriana Creed accessed his safety deposit box on November 17. I wonder what they were doing at the bank on the morning of the very day he killed a man in the ghetto?"

"We need to find that bitch," Christina replied tersely.

Milosh agreed. "But no one's seen her since Grandfather died. She's gone."

Philippe snorted. "Then let's find her. I suppose that'll be my job, as always." His brother and sister glared at him. It was always like this when they got together. Thank God it hadn't happened often in the past few years.

One of the three knew exactly what had happened that day Adriana Creed came to the bank with their grandfather, but volunteered nothing.

CHAPTER FIVE

By the middle of 1941 the railroads were doing a brisk business in Germany and the countries it occupied. Hitler controlled much of Europe as country after country joined the Axis forces, either willingly or by force.

The gas chambers were first fired up at Auschwitz in September 1941, and soon thereafter concentration camps throughout Nazi Europe had a steady inflow of prisoners. Trains filled with human cargo rumbled through towns day and night, the anguished cries of Jews torn from their families mixing with the *click-click* of wheels moving down the line. As the hated Nazis marched into one country after another, they slaughtered thousands of "undesirables" on the spot, but many more were herded into cattle cars, prodded and beaten like the bovines the cars previously carried. These prisoners were headed for one camp or another. The rail business was booming, thanks to the atrocities of Hitler's government.

By 1944 high-speed trains with dozens of boxcars thundered through towns and villages day and night. These weren't the death trains; whatever these carried, it wasn't people. The massive boxcar doors had imposing locks, and each carriage was marked with huge swastikas. In contrast to the trains carrying humans, these were much more heavily guarded. Every other car had armed soldiers clinging to its side. The townspeople wondered what cargo these trains transported; whatever it was, it must be valuable indeed.

Adolf Hitler envisioned an expansive, beautiful gallery - the Fuhrermuseum - in his home town of Linz, Austria. It would be his gift to the Master Race he was creating. Most museums relied upon donations and gifts from wealthy benefactors to build their collections. Hitler's would accumulate masterpieces much more expeditiously. The Fuhrermuseum was going to display the epitome of everything - the *Mona Lisa*, Michelangelo's *David*, masterpieces from Renoir, Rubens, Picasso, Matisse and the like. It made no difference that each of these priceless works already had a home. They would be "appropriated" by Reichsmarschall Hermann Göring to hang in the Fuhrer's new gallery.

Hitler had appointed Göring to supervise the largest art theft in history. When German soldiers captured new territory, the Reichsmarschall's troops came in behind, looting museums and private homes of wealthy Jews and so-called enemies of the state, who were sent off to camps. The value and sheer numbers of what they stole was staggering, and it created a major logistical problem for the Reich. At the time of the looting, Hitler's museum hadn't yet been started - it was supposed to begin in 1945 and be finished by 1950. In the meantime, Göring scrambled to find places to store both gold bars and museum pieces.

Some of the finest were placed in the bunker beneath Nazi headquarters - the Chancellery buildings in Berlin - where the Fuhrer himself could enjoy them. Others were hung in the fairy-tale Neuschwanstein Castle in Bavaria and in Hitler's hunting lodge in Austria. As Hitler's fears became reality - as Allied troops recaptured city after city - he quickly ordered the stolen treasures to be moved again - hopefully to a place safe from enemy bombs and from those who would repatriate them.

Some tunnels were employed as hiding places, but Hermann Göring primarily chose mines - the Altaussee salt mines being the biggest. By early 1944 the works were moving by rail across occupied Europe. Things became frantic because Hitler was running out of time. Germany was losing, and as the war wound down, Hitler's trusted lieutenant scrambled to hide the art in occupied countries such as Poland, Romania and Yugoslavia.

In 1945 Allied soldiers captured cities, unaware some were very close to where the booty was hidden. Hitler had issued an order called the "Nero Decree," requiring the mines and tunnels to be destroyed if Allied troops got too near. If he couldn't have the artwork, neither could the rest of the world.

Once the Allies were just a few miles from the Altaussee and Heilbronn mines, an Austrian official ordered them to be blown up. Unwilling to bear the loss of the objects, Hitler countermanded his own decree, but the Austrian ignored the reversal and ordered the destruction to proceed. Fortunately, local residents charged with the task refused to detonate the huge bombs that were primed and ready.

In other places across the occupied countries, the Nero Decree was followed to the letter. Priceless works, even paintings by Picasso and Renoir, were lost forever as retreating German soldiers destroyed mines and put individual pieces to the torch. Thanks to the rescue efforts of a special force of Allied soldiers called "Monuments Men," thousands of paintings and sculptures - plus millions of dollars in gold - had survived.

Unfortunately for the Fuhrer and fortuitously for everyone else on earth, the Allies put a stop to Hitler's plans for a museum - and everything else he wanted - by winning the war.

CHAPTER SIX

A sharply dressed man sat in the law offices that handled Nicu Lepescu's affairs. The solicitor with whom he was meeting was businesslike and professional, as a young man on the rise in a large law firm should be. The lawyer listened politely as the stranger explained what he wanted. The visitor's request was so unusual that at first he wasn't sure he understood it.

Once the man finished, the lawyer asked for clarification. "I'd like to repeat what I heard you say, to be sure I'm following your request. You're asking me to speak with my client Nicu Lepescu, whom you say is a distant relative of yours, convince him to have his fortune told, and bring a certain gypsy fortune-teller to his apartment. Then I depart, leaving her there with him. Am I understanding your request?"

"It is absolutely correct," the man replied.

The lawyer snapped, "Then I absolutely refuse, sir! If you want Mr. Lepescu to hire a fortune-teller, talk to him yourself. For all I know, you could be asking me to allow a robber - perhaps even a murderer - into his flat. This is an outrageous request!"

"I can't talk to him myself. We have been estranged for many years. He believes I am dead, and I want the fortune-teller to give him information about me. I hope and pray this action may solve our long-standing differences. A third party might accomplish what I cannot. He believes in prognostication, as all we gypsies do. A fortune-teller could help me reconnect with the only remaining family member in my life."

The man pulled a cashier's check from his pocket and handed it to the solicitor, who glanced at it, turned away then looked again. It was made payable to him personally, not to the law firm. And it was for twenty thousand Romanian lei - almost five thousand dollars.

"What is this?" he stammered as a wave of euphoria flooded his mind. He was overwhelmed with loan and car payments and his rent. He struggled to make ends meet while putting up a facade of success for his friends to see. He worked seventy or eighty hours a week, but his income never quite covered his expenses. His debts were killing him; accepting this simple job could put him back on the right course.

The man sat patiently as he watched the young solicitor work through his thought process. Then the visitor spoke quietly.

"I'm hiring you, not your law firm. I don't want you to have to explain my request to a panel of your superiors, who would immediately dismiss it as absurd. In fact, it isn't unusual at all." He produced a one-paragraph letter from a law firm in Zurich. "Here is a letter of reference from my personal attorney. He can vouch for my character and my integrity. There's no need to be concerned. All you need do is meet with Mr. Lepescu, convince him that getting his fortune told is a good idea, and bring the girl to see him. A pretty simple job for twenty thousand lei, don't you think?"

Fifteen minutes later the lawyer sat alone in his office. The man had been well dressed, he spoke intelligently, and he was sophisticated. He'd explained exactly how he wanted the entire situation to work, and he'd given the solicitor a week to get it accomplished.

All that remained was to check the reference. As the lawyer placed the call, he held his breath, praying this would work. The attorney in Zurich had confirmed the man had been a client for decades. He was a wealthy individual who was forthright and trustworthy in every respect.

GHOST TRAIN

The young lawyer called his client and accepted the job. Gushing with excitement at his sudden good fortune, he overlooked the fact that the Swiss lawyer and the new client had virtually identical voices.

CHAPTER SEVEN

Until three years ago Adriana Creed had made ends meet, but nothing more. She was thirty years old and made a decent living as a fortune-teller. A gypsy in Bucharest, Romania, she had a steady clientele. Locals and tourists alike sometimes waited in line to have the beautiful Romani caress their palms and whisper their futures. Some months she made enough to buy groceries, pay the rent and feed a habit she struggled to control. Other times, mostly in winter months when freezing cold kept visitors away, she'd go days without a client.

She finally resorted to something she didn't really want to sell, but when it came down to it, the decision was simple. She had something men would pay dearly for - her body. She carefully selected the clients who'd be offered these services. When a handsome man came in to have his palm read, she'd hold his hand and tell his fortune. She'd end by saying that an interlude with a young gypsy was in his future. Her other hand would slip under the table, lightly caressing between his legs. More often than not, they ended up in Adriana's back room, where a twin bed with clean, fresh linens awaited. She made a hundred dollars, sometimes more, for a half hour of pretending, and she felt no remorse at all. Did she enjoy it herself? Occasionally, she admitted, but she really never gave it much thought. Even though she only sold her body to those men she thought looked interesting, it usually wasn't satisfying. Only her addiction gave her a release, but sleeping with these men paid the bills.

Adriana's life changed forever that morning when a young man walked into her shop. He was her age, dressed impeccably in a suit, tie and starched white shirt, and she immediately sized him up as someone who had plenty of money. As it turned out, his reason for coming wasn't to enjoy either of her skills - her crystal ball or the delights she provided in the back bedroom.

He explained that he was a lawyer whose aging client was eager to know about the future. He said he walked this street to his office, so he'd passed her storefront every weekday for months. He'd seen the beautiful gypsy and he had randomly chosen her when his client demanded to have his fortune told. He offered her three times the money she'd have accepted to accompany him on a home visit to see his client. The man was smooth, glib and professional. She'd never met a lawyer, but this is what she assumed one would be like.

And she bought his story without hesitation. After all, it was so close to the truth that it seemed perfectly logical.

A cab dropped them outside a seven-story apartment building on the fringe of the city center. They took an elevator to the fourth floor, and a housekeeper let them in. Adriana glanced around the living room - the apartment was spacious, airy and immaculate. The housekeeper stood in the kitchen, glancing warily at Adriana as the lawyer ushered her into a bedroom.

Heavy curtains were drawn tight, and it took her eyes a moment to become accustomed to the room's half-light. It was a dramatic contrast to the sunshine beaming through the windows in the front room. There was a double bed a few feet away. An old man lay there, his head propped up with pillows.

"Open the drapes," the man commanded in a clear, strong voice. The lawyer pulled the drawstrings, and suddenly the room was filled with light. Adriana looked around - it was like taking a step back in time. She saw an antique writing desk, an overstuffed chair and ottoman in the corner, and a massive armoire. Two shadow boxes hung on one wall, their faded glass masking what appeared to be war medals. A duvet covered the bed's occupant up to his chest.

The old man pointed to a chair next to his bed. "You're beautiful, child," he said to her. "Sit here. Are you Romani?"

"Yes, sir," she replied as she sat. "I am a gypsy."

"I am a gypsy as well. But I am old. Can you tell me what lies ahead?"

"Of course."

"Very well. Leave us." He gave the young solicitor a dismissive wave, and the man left the room, closing the door behind him and leaving Adriana alone with her client.

CHAPTER EIGHT

Thirty minutes after she had entered the old man's bedroom, Adriana Creed emerged with a broad smile.

"Nicu asked for you," she told the lawyer.

They're already on a first-name basis? the young man thought as he went into the bedroom.

Adriana popped her head into the kitchen and said brightly, "Goodbye, Mrs. Radu. I'm sure we'll be seeing more of each other!"

He told her my name? The housekeeper frowned as she watched the impetuous young girl exit the apartment. Mrs. Radu had taken care of Nicu Lepescu for the past seven years. Other than the night nurse who was on call in case Nicu wasn't well, she was his sole permanent provider. Most of the time Nicu was ambulatory. He shuffled and hobbled, but then again he was really old. Nicu was doing pretty well for a man who'd lived over a hundred years. He resisted her attempts to hold his arm when she accompanied him to the market. He knocked her hand away when she tried to help him rise from his chair. He wanted to be self-sufficient. That wouldn't last much longer, but for now there was nothing she could do to dissuade him from trying to do everything himself.

When she was first hired, Mrs. Radu had been shocked by the shadow boxes hanging on Nicu's bedroom wall. Few Romanians would have the nerve to display such medals - decorations he'd been awarded for his service during the war. Every one of them contained the small swastika of Adolf Hitler's Nazi regime and one - the one she hated the most - commended him as an SS officer. A Jew killer.

The story was that Nicu would have been executed except the War Crimes Tribunal couldn't directly connect him to the deaths of over three hundred thousand Jews while he served as an officer at Auschwitz. If that weren't enough, there were thousands more - the prisoners whom SS commander Lepescu saw in cattle cars as they passed through Bucharest North train station. The court handed down twenty years without parole.

Unrepentant and unashamed, he quietly served his time, was released and then proudly hung his Nazi medals on his bedroom wall. The housekeeper was repulsed when she first saw them, but she hardly noticed them now. Nicu never spoke of the war, he treated her well and paid her a handsome salary. She forced down her initial feelings - the repulsion of working for a former SS storm trooper. He'd sent his own countrymen to their deaths and even today still proudly displayed the medals Hitler awarded him for doing it.

The young lawyer came out of the old man's bedroom, walked into the kitchen and said to her, "The girl made quite an impression on Mr. Lepescu. It seems he wants to see her again."

"Hmmpf," the matronly housekeeper snuffled.

In the three years since her first visit, Adriana had become a fixture in the old man's house. At first he asked her to come once a week. They would spend an hour or more behind the closed door of his bedroom. Mrs. Radu often tiptoed over, putting her ear to the door. Sometimes she heard muffled laughs and conversation too faint to understand. Usually she heard nothing at all.

One day she'd had enough. She wanted to know what was going on, so she fixed a cup of tea, walked to his bedroom door, knocked one time and opened it. "I made you some tea . . ."

The bedcovers were pulled down and the old man lay naked atop the sheets. The girl was sitting on the bed beside him, her hand on his chest. They both looked up in surprise and Adriana pulled her hand away.

"Don't ever come in here without knocking again!" he yelled. Startled, Mrs. Radu dropped the teacup. It hit the floor with a crash, tea flying everywhere. She shut the door and got a towel from the kitchen. As she knelt to clean the spill, she heard the click of the bedroom door lock. A few times after that the housekeeper would quietly turn the knob when the girl was inside, just to see. She found what she'd expected - now they locked the door every time they were together in the bedroom.

Before long the gypsy fortune-teller was with Nicu every day. They often walked to lunch at a nearby restaurant, and she took him for strolls in the neighborhood park. *That's what I used to do*, Mrs. Radu angrily thought to herself. It incensed the housekeeper that the saucy girl was taking her place with Mr. Lepescu.

She reminded herself time and again this was not her affair. Whatever Adriana was doing didn't matter as long as she wasn't hurting him. He was obviously happy with her visits, whatever they amounted to. But curiosity eventually got the best of her once again. One day after Adriana left, the old man came in and sat at the kitchen table.

Mrs. Radu tried to sound casual. "The gypsy girl seems to be here more and more these days. Is she giving you a lot of information about your future?"

"She does far more than that," he replied with a raspy, mischievous laugh.

"What exactly does that mean?" she snapped before thinking.

His voice hardened. "Why are you asking, Mrs. Radu? Exactly what business is it of yours what I do with Adriana?"

She apologized for her impertinence, he went back to his bedroom without a word, and nothing was ever said again. From then on, Adriana opened the front door every day with a key he had given her. She would breeze into the flat; now and then she'd put wine and cheese on the kitchen table and instruct Mrs. Radu to put them in the icebox. The housekeeper complied, but her surly response and glaring eyes made it clear how she felt about the gypsy girl's issuing orders.

One day Mrs. Radu heard Adriana open the bedroom door and say brightly, "Good morning, darling!" Then the door was closed as usual and they spent an hour or more together.

That was when she became convinced the girl was up to no good.

CHAPTER NINE

The Bad Man had been locked away for a long time. His services hadn't been needed since Roberto Maas died in that wonderful fire in London. What a clever nickname he'd invented for the part of him hidden deep inside his brain, the Bad Man thought. Until the past year or so, he would appear now and then, taking over the man's personality completely. When that happened, he did clever, naughty, bad things to people he didn't like.

They call people like us schizophrenic, he thought to himself. *That's bullshit. I'm as sane as he is. We just live in the same person's mind. I hate him, he hates me. But when he needs me, I make him beg. Then I make him let me out to play. He hasn't done that in a long time. Maybe soon. Maybe I can play with the girl.*

Today his other personality - the good one - sat with Adriana Creed in a coffee shop in Bucharest's old town. While they caught up on things, the Bad Man began having sensual thoughts about Adriana. As she had matured, she'd become strikingly beautiful - even more so than in those days they spent together at the university. She'd been a mere child then, innocent about love and sex. Today, he fantasized, she would know so much more. Not only could this intoxicating woman bring him to heights of ecstasy, he could do the same for her.

Just to make things interesting, he mused, right at the summit of their passion - just as they climaxed - maybe he'd kill her.

No! Stop it now! Stop thinking like that!

Damn. That was his alter ego talking - the good person shushing him up once again, always concerned that the Bad Man would come out when he shouldn't.

Quit worrying so much, the Bad Man whispered as he crept far back into the man's psyche, slithering into the tiny closet where he lived. The Bad Man hated his other personality - the one that was as normal as any man on earth. That one slammed the door shut in his head, locking out the Bad Man. He continued the easy conversation with his old lover from university days.

I've never embarrassed you by coming out when I shouldn't, the Bad Man snarled to himself. *Maybe that'll change if you don't leave me alone!*

CHAPTER TEN

After all these years, they were as comfortable as if they'd parted only yesterday.

As he had walked in, he saw her across the room, her striking beauty only enhanced by the passage of time. She stood to greet him and her familiar, breezy kiss made him smile. Thoughts of the exciting, passionate nights during the two years they had lived together flooded her mind as he sat. She had been only seventeen and he was nearly twenty back then, much older and wiser.

The years helped her gloss over the bad parts - the times when he wanted to dominate and control her every move, the times when he became so angry he hit her, the times he mocked her and called her names. When he had done those things, she told herself it was her own fault. He knew best and she was just a girl. She should obey him. All men were like that - savage sometimes and gentle other times, she convinced herself. After all, he was her white knight, her rescuer and prince.

"*Mon chéri*, it's been ages and you look just the same," she breathed, squeezing his hand. He looked terrific: handsome and impeccably dressed. She'd found him irresistible back then and now - what, he must be thirty-five now! - he still had what it took to captivate her.

Mon chéri. It's been a long time since a woman called me darling. "How long has it been - seven years?

You're absolutely stunning, you know. Some things never change!"

"You flatter me!" She flushed and stammered. She hadn't expected him to affect her like this. "What brings you back to Bucharest? When I never heard from you, I presumed you'd moved on to greater things. Aren't you a big-city banker now?"

"Something like that," he dodged smoothly. "But look at you, Apostol! You look wonderful. Did you finish school?" He knew the answer already. He knew everything about her.

She laughed when he called her Apostol. It was her middle name and had become his nickname for her. He watched as she tossed her hair the way he'd loved back then. "Hardly! Once you graduated, I quit. I guess school wasn't for me. I'm a gypsy - you are too, I know - but I think there's more rebel in me. Maybe an education would have helped me become rich and famous like you, but telling fortunes is an easy way to make a living, and for now it suits me perfectly."

From a private investigator he had learned she did more than tell fortunes in that shop down the street. The fact that she'd become a prostitute - although that was a word she'd never use herself, it was a fact - was immaterial. He needed her in a different way, although he couldn't suppress a wave of lust as he imagined how she'd be today compared to the child he'd loved long ago.

Oh, so now it's not just me. Now you want to screw her too! The Bad Man was always around, just out of sight, waiting for an opportunity to come out.

Go away! This isn't about that!

"You're deep in thought all of a sudden," she commented, watching his face as he secretly battled with the Bad Man. "Have I lost you so soon?"

"Of course not. You know you'll never lose me."

"Ha! So tell me what you're doing here. Why *did* you come back?"

He'd rehearsed this scenario so many times that the answer flowed smoothly.

"There's something I need, darling. I have a job for you, something you're uniquely qualified to accomplish. I want to hire you to find some information for me from your friend Nicu Lepescu." He explained why he couldn't do this himself and it made sense to her. Nicu would never have helped this man. But she could help him.

A half hour later his explanation was complete and she knew exactly what she had to do. She had no idea why, but he wanted her to get some specific information from a man she was already close to. He wanted to know where Nicu Lepescu kept his diary. She told him how simple this would be, since Nicu confided everything to her. Her old lover told her to take things slowly to keep the old man from getting suspicious. Taking her time was fine with Adriana. It was to her benefit to stretch things out since she'd be paid a thousand US dollars every month until the job was done. That money would come in very handy indeed.

Excellent! I'll be seeing a lot more of you, the Bad Man squealed with delight as his alter ego said, "Here's the first installment." He handed her an envelope filled with hundred-dollar bills, kissed her cheek lightly and left.

CHAPTER ELEVEN

After Nicu's funeral, Adriana sat in her living room, reflecting that she felt no sadness over the loss of a man who'd supported her for the past three years. At first her visits had been strictly professional - he had chosen her, a fortune-teller, to be his de facto priest. She told him what he wanted to hear. Yes, you're going to heaven. Yes, you're forgiven for your sins. No, you won't burn in hell for eternity. He'd seemed preoccupied with death and the afterlife, and as a fortune-teller, her made-up comments gave him assurance.

After she'd been coming about a year, she arrived to find him weeping. She asked him what was wrong, and he said he had to confess his sins before he died.

"I know no priests. I have no church. Will you hear my confession?"

How crazy is this? The girl who'd never darkened the door of a church felt strange in the role of priest. "Of course, Nicu. Anything you want."

She took his hand and he began to talk. By the time they took a break, he'd been confessing non-stop for almost an hour. It seemed as though he had every sin catalogued in his mind, just waiting for this moment. And there were plenty of sins to talk about. As soon as he began talking, his tears had stopped. There was no more sadness. He enumerated his sins matter-of-factly, without remorse or concern, as if he were simply telling his life story. The

Jews whose plight he ignored, the gold and artwork the Reich stole, and his unwavering support for the Nazi Party were astounding revelations. On the outside he appeared to be a crusty old grandfather, kindly but gruff, and now she knew exactly what he really was. Just beneath the surface was a monster whose hatred of those different from him would never change. He hadn't just sent his fellow humans to the death chamber - he thought it was well deserved. He'd *enjoyed* it. He was still glad to have had a part in it. This confession was simply a chronicle of his life, not a repentant plea for forgiveness.

A half-hour later Nicu was finished confessing. He hadn't told her everything but he'd covered the biggest missteps of his life. The gold and the jewelry remained his secrets.

Exhausted, the faithless Adriana didn't know exactly what was supposed to happen next, but she presumed he didn't know either. She made up words that sounded reasonable to her.

"Your sins are forgiven. You are a child of Christ."

She didn't believe either of those statements was remotely true.

My God, she thought as she brought him juice afterwards. *This man is the devil incarnate. I don't know if there's a hell, but if there is, Nicu Lepescu's going to see it the second he dies.*

———

She and the old man became closer and closer. Now she was both his confidante and his companion. He enjoyed her company and she tolerated it because the benefits got better and better. She had no idea where he had accumulated wealth, but he was unquestionably financially secure. He often gave her jewelry and cash, bought her anything she wanted, and he had once told her to get a nicer apartment. In return she held his hand as he lay in bed, caressed his brow when he napped fitfully, and made him comfortable. There was nothing sexual about the relationship, although Mrs. Radu would never believe it.

Adriana laughed to herself as she thought of the day the housekeeper had barged in on the pretense of bringing him tea.

Nicu had been naked that day, as he was almost every day when Adriana rubbed lotion on his tired, sagging skin. It wasn't enjoyable to her, but it was part of a day's work and it made him feel better. When the housekeeper saw her rubbing his chest, there was no telling what she thought was going to happen next, Nicu had told her with a laugh.

From then on Nicu asked her to lock the door when they were in the bedroom, as if he delighted in making Mrs. Radu wonder what they were up to. In truth there was nothing that even *could* have happened, and he asked for nothing more than her soothing body massages.

He asked about her past and she told him the truth. She'd lied about it so much she had to concentrate to keep from throwing in things that weren't true. She owed him the truth. He had helped her more than anyone else ever had. So she told him what she herself had been told.

There was no mistaking her gypsy genes, so she knew that part was true. The story was that a dashing gypsy boy and an Italian exchange student had carried out a mad affair. They were both seventeen, and when the girl turned up pregnant, the boy did what every gypsy would do - he disappeared.

Embarrassed to have their pregnant daughter at home in Italy, her mother came to Bucharest and stayed until the baby was born. Adriana's young mother insisted on naming her, so she became Adriana Apostol, her last name being that of her gypsy father. Days later she was handed over to an orphanage, and when she was six months old, she was adopted by Simon and Carol Creed from Bristol, England. Romanian babies were often adopted by Westerners in those days and she was just another of many. She was now Adriana Apostol Creed.

Sadly, the adoption didn't work out. The Creeds divorced and Carol brought Adriana back to Bucharest, paying an enormous cancellation penalty to abandon the baby. After that setback, the year-old child finally got a lucky break. A Romanian family with no money but lots of love wanted a child. The orphanage had been paid twice for Adriana - once when the Creeds adopted her and again when the wife brought her back. The older she became, the more difficult it would be to adopt her out. Everyone wanted cuddly babies and the last thing the orphanage needed was a toddler. The orphanage gave Adriana to the Romanian couple.

Her new parents were a laborer and his wife, a hardworking woman who took in wash. They slaved day and night but could never afford anything but the basics. There was never a penny left over, never a birthday present, never a gift at Christmas. There was love but literally nothing more.

She hated her new last name - Denu. She wanted the name on her amended birth certificate, the one the orphanage gave her new adoptive parents. She was Adriana Apostol Creed. From the time she was eight she was using that name, and her parents didn't object.

"Apostol." Nicu had rolled the name off his tongue. "A beautiful name. I like it. From now on, that's your nickname."

As a teenager Adriana supplemented the family's meager income by working after school as a fortune-teller. She was strikingly attractive - worldly, dark and sultry even at fourteen - and most people assumed she was older. She knew how to entice men to pay more than they intended. When the beautiful girl stroked their hands softly as she whispered their fortunes in a sexy tone, the men gave her big tips. It was completely aboveboard, but there was plenty of innuendo. She had the charms men wanted more of, and soon her income was as much as her father's.

At sixteen she left school to work full time. A year later her parents perished in a fiery car crash, the victims of a drunk driver going the wrong way on a divided highway at night. She mourned, she grieved, she cried, and then she carried on.

GHOST TRAIN

Buoyed by a small life insurance policy her father had been given by his employer, Adriana enrolled at the local university. It lasted awhile, but education simply wasn't important to her. The only thing about her collegiate experience that interested her was the gypsy lover she'd met. They were young, crazy, passionate and intensely sexual partners. Three years older than Adriana, he was a driven individual who craved success. He spoke often of how he intended to break out of Romania and become a wealthy banker in the West.

They talked of his father's death years ago at the hands of the police, which fostered his deep hatred for the government. He was often a part of protest rallies - he even threw rocks now and then - but he managed to avoid arrest. Despite his efforts to get Adriana involved in his political beliefs, she never joined him. She simply didn't care about such things.

At the end of her second year in university, her lover graduated and that magical experience was over. He moved away to seek a career, and Adriana quit school, expecting to never hear from him again. She opened a shop in Bucharest city center, lived behind it in two comfortable rooms, and went back to her old job as a fortune-teller.

She wrapped up her life story without telling Nicu that five years ago she'd begun selling her body along with her prognostication skills. He didn't need to know that; besides, she was *his* companion now. She had left that life behind. She was well set, thanks to Nicu.

As good as things were for her financially, they soon became even rosier. One day recently when they were out for one of their frequent lunches, he suggested, "Let's go by my bank. There's something I want to do." They met with a vice president, and Nicu added her name to his safety deposit box access card. The officer excused himself for a moment and then returned with a key for Adriana.

As they walked home Nicu explained, "There are things in there that will be good for you to have once I'm gone. My only heirs are three worthless grandchildren whom I haven't seen in years. There's plenty for them - I have put aside a decent sum for a rainy day and my house is paid for. I bequeath to you everything that's in the box. Along with other things, there are two books. Take everything whenever you want - just make sure it's cleaned out before I die so my heirs don't grab what's left. You're not mentioned in my will, and since they have no idea what I own, they'll never miss anything. What's in the box is all yours, but you must promise this - never, ever tell anyone that the things in the box came from me. Don't tie anything back to me or they'll take it away from you."

She hoped he didn't notice her involuntary shudder. Whatever was in there must have been something from the war. His words scared her, but more than that she was curious.

He added, "Keep the two books together. They're important, but we're finished talking about them. Don't mention them again to me. I'm absolved of my sins. You heard my confession."

Adriana struggled not to dwell on what might be in the box, but she quickly assured herself it was normal to wonder what he'd considered important enough to lock away in a bank vault. It was only natural human instinct to be curious. Anyone would want to know.

She stood impatiently on the sidewalk outside the bank before opening time the next morning. She'd brought along a cloth shopping bag, just in case. *Nicu told me I could take everything whenever I wanted.* Maybe today there would be something to take. Soon she was in the vault with the same bank officer they'd dealt with yesterday. He inserted his key, directed her to do the same, and he pulled out a metal container the size of a small microwave. He struggled and huffed as he carried it to an adjacent private room.

"It's very heavy," he wheezed, slamming it onto a table. "Call the guard when you're finished and let him replace it for you."

Once he had gone, Adriana lifted the lid and looked inside. First she saw the two books Nicu had mentioned. One was a thick leather-bound volume with a bold swastika on the cover, and the other was a worn copy of Adolf Hitler's manifesto *Mein Kampf.* She set them aside then drew a deep breath as she stared at what else there was.

Oh my God! Oh my God! She needed a fix. Her heart was racing as her mind struggled to comprehend why he'd done this.

Three-fourths of the way to its top the box contained neatly stacked gold bars, each carrying the imprints *Reichsbank* and *1 kilo.* She recognized the name of the bank; it had been closed by the Allied forces after World War II. Before that it was owned and operated by the National Socialist Party. The Reichsbank was Adolf Hitler's bank, the bank of the Nazis.

Adriana removed enough bars to see to the bottom. She counted twenty-three in all. She had no idea what they were worth, but she was certain the old man had just given her a secure future.

She dropped one bar and the books into her bag, closed the box and called the guard.

———

When she got home she tossed the bag on the table and went to her kitchen to prepare things. Once everything was ready she sat on the couch, sucked the liquid into a syringe, crossed her leg on the opposite knee and inserted the needle into the skin between her toes. This was the second time today and the heavenly rush was instantaneous. She frequently told herself she hated heroin, but she didn't stop. When she was doing this - when she was shooting up - she loved it. It made her calm, happy, at peace with the world.

There's really nothing wrong with it, she mused idly, reassuring herself the drug hadn't become her master. A few times in the past she'd tried to prove she wasn't an addict. Those times were always in winter, when there were no customers for either of her services - caressing a client's palm or something else of his. When the brutal snows came and the sidewalks were icy, people stayed indoors. They didn't come to visit the sultry gypsy. Without money she couldn't buy heroin, so she'd make a decision to stop using.

The outcome was always the same. She would lie in bed in utter misery, racked with fever and stomach pain, then suddenly she'd get relief. Her comfort didn't come from beating her addiction. In fact, it was just the opposite. Just as things got as bad as she could handle, she'd hear a wonderful sound - the tinkle of the tiny bell on her front door. A customer! Desperately hoping it was a man - most of her patrons were, thank God - she would quickly fix her hair, let him in, seat him at the table in the front room, tell his fortune and excite him until he paid her for sex. In the summer she could pick and choose her clients for the back room. In the bleak gray winter she took whoever came through the door. He could have been the Hunchback of Notre Dame - at this point all she wanted was money. Fast. And somehow it always came through just in time.

The fortune-teller's own fortunes had turned remarkably better on the day she met Nicu Lepescu. The old man gave her money from the very start - payment for her prognostications at first, then gifts "to help you get along," he'd said. She wore the beautiful things he gave her until the day she had heard his confession. Once she understood, she was overwhelmed with guilt. Whose jewelry had this been? Was this bracelet ripped from a proud woman's arm just before she was ushered into the gas chamber? Adriana never asked; she simply stopped wearing the jewelry.

He lavished so much on her that she'd have done anything for him - whatever his aging mind could come up with - but all he wanted was companionship. *He genuinely likes me,* she thought. *All I need do is take care of him and pretend to like him in return.* Seeing him every day as a grandfather merely wanting someone to talk to, she found it impossible to believe he could have done those things he told her about. But who in his right mind would fabricate such a horror story about himself? She just kept her mouth shut, smiled and laughed with him, and made him comfortable.

Now she held a gold bar in her hand, the first one she'd ever touched. She was overcome with conflict. This time Nicu hadn't just given her a Jewish lady's bracelet. He'd given her a boxful of gold bars. Exciting thoughts of how much money there might be flooded her mind as she pushed back the inevitability of what the gold represented. Everyone had heard the horrific stories of how the Nazis accumulated gold.

She went to bed, replacing the negative thoughts with plans, hopes and dreams. If this was the key to her future, she would accept the good luck her friend had bestowed upon her.

The next morning Adriana left early. She had to be at Nicu's at ten, but there was one thing she had to know. She found a different bank with a teller window offering gold for sale. She took the bar from her pocket and asked, "How much can I get for this?"

The young clerk looked at the name on the bar. _Reichsbank_. She saw him raise his eyebrows in surprise, and then he said, "Give me just a moment, please." He took the bar and turned to a table behind him. She watched as he weighed it and examined it closely, then called an older man over - a supervisor, she presumed. They had a brief, quiet conversation.

The supervisor brought the bar to her and said, "This bar's quite old. We don't see many . . . uh, wartime bars anymore." He hadn't used the word _Nazi._ "If I may ask, where did you get it?"

"I'm sorry, I'm in a bit of a hurry. No time to chat. May I just find out its value?"

He made a computer entry and said, "At today's exchange rate, one hundred fifty-one thousand five hundred fifty-nine Romanian lei."

She stood shell-shocked, mouth agape.

"In dollars . . .?" she managed to gasp.

His fingers flew as he calculated the conversion.

"Thirty-seven thousand four hundred US dollars."

She couldn't talk. She was dizzy and needed to go outside in the fresh air. She nodded at the supervisor, put the bar back in her pocket and left. In a daze she walked back to her store, the visit to Nicu put aside for the moment.

Her mind raced with crazy thoughts.

There are twenty-three bars.

That's -

She was so frazzled she couldn't do the math in her head. Once she was home, she made the calculation, looked at the answer a dozen times, then sank into a chair, at last understanding what the old man had done for her. He'd done it all. He'd given her a new life.

Eight hundred and sixty thousand dollars.

CHAPTER TWELVE

"Where are you? He's asking for you." The housekeeper's words were short and clipped, so full of hatred her feelings couldn't be mistaken.

"I'm . . . I'm not well," Adriana replied, her hand shaking so hard she could barely hold the receiver. "I'll come later this afternoon."

"Don't come if you're contagious. Don't make him even sicker than he already is."

"I won't. I'm not contagious. I just have -"

Mrs. Radu interrupted sharply. "I could care less what you have. I could care less if you ever come back here. But he wants you. So that's that. Do it." She hung up abruptly.

An hour later, fortified by her old friend the needle, Adriana walked into Nicu's flat, said nothing to the housekeeper, and went straight into the bedroom. She locked the door behind her as usual, and two hours later they emerged. He was dressed for an outing.

"See you later!" He waved breezily to Mrs. Radu as he closed the front door.

They sipped espressos and studied the menu at a tiny sidewalk café. It was two in the afternoon - he said he'd worked up an appetite waiting for her.

"I was worried this morning. Where were you?" he asked pleasantly.

She told him exactly what she'd done, how she'd learned the value of his gift. "Once I realized what you'd done for me, I had to go home because I thought I would faint. Nicu, are you sure . . ."

He laughed and dismissed her concern with a wave of his hand. "You're the best thing that's happened to this old man in years. You've given me renewed inspiration, a reason to keep on going and a new appreciation for living. There's plenty more for my ungrateful grandchildren to fight over - much more than I've given you, in fact. Please don't give it a thought. You deserve the best, my dear." He paused and took her hand in his. "Thank you for everything you've done."

"All that gold. Where on earth did you get it?"

"Never mind the specifics, girl. The simple answer is I was paid well for the work I did."

"I can never thank you enough." She squeezed his hand, maintaining the charade of warmth and tenderness, making her face beam. Only her eyes could have betrayed how she still felt about this maniacal killer - a man who'd admitted he'd callously sent thousands to the gas chamber. She forced a pleasant expression and he never noticed a thing.

"Just being here with me is enough. I know it's silly, but . . . I love you, Apostol."

She kept her composure through lunch and for the remainder of the afternoon. As she prepared to go home, he asked about the books.

"Do you have them?"

"Yes, but I haven't looked at them."

"Fine. Just remember to keep them together. That copy of *Mein Kampf* is special."

"What's so special about it? Aren't there millions of copies around?"

"Trust me. Guard it until you decide you need it. It will help you someday. Now go on home, my dear, and come see me tomorrow."

Back in her living room, she sat in the dark with the gold bar in her lap. She couldn't suppress the horrors anymore. Last night she'd managed to replace bad thoughts with rosy pictures of her future. Tonight she faced the truths she knew lay within twenty-three gold bars from the Reichsbank.

I'm as bad as he is . . .

No. This isn't about me. He *did these things, not* me. *He somehow got this gold - this tainted Nazi gold. But they're just gold bars. They didn't come from the prisoners.*

She allowed that thought even though she knew better. The gold came from the concentration camps. She'd heard the stories and seen the horrible pictures: barrels overflowing with gold fillings, rings, and coins. Everyone had. It was what the Nazis did.

Suddenly queasy, she ran to the bathroom. Barely making it, she threw up the toilet lid and retched over and over until there was no more left.

Under the covers she pushed the bad thoughts away, willing herself to fall asleep calmly and dream idyllic dreams.

CHAPTER THIRTEEN

It was well after midnight, but Adriana hadn't slept five minutes total. *The dreams! My God, the dreams!* Adolf Hitler himself handed her a gold bar as a grinning Nicu stood next to him. A thousand naked people lined up outside the gas chambers, dropping gold watches and rings into a barrel just before they were ushered inside. The crazy, tormented nightmares wouldn't stop, and every time they ended, she awoke in a drenching sweat.

Finally she gave up trying to sleep and brought the diary to bed. She opened it to the first page. The flowing handwriting was unmistakably Nicu's - she'd seen it often around the flat on one document or another. She lay back on her pillow and read the secret thoughts of a proud man, an officer in the Nazi Party who was on top of his game.

Bucharest, Romania
January 2, 1944
Today is the first at my new post and so I begin a new diary. For two years I have had the pleasure of working under Rudolf Hoess, the commandant of the Birkenau camp at Auschwitz. A storm trooper myself, I was assigned the important duty of building an extension to the existing rail lines to bring prisoners much closer to the gas chambers at Birkenau. This saved much time and was a very efficient way to dispatch individuals whom the Fuhrer considered unnecessary.

After my successful completion of that project, I was handed another. Commandant Hoess himself chose me to repair Krema V, a set of ovens that had broken down and fallen into disrepair. Auschwitz was a busy place and crowded beyond belief. We had to stay on top of things to ensure there was room for incoming prisoners. Within a few short weeks, my crew and I had the crematorium up and running again.

Before Commandant Hoess ended his term at Auschwitz last month, he recommended me for the prestigious position of stationmaster in Bucharest. As I was both a loyal Nazi and a Romanian, he considered me perfectly suited to oversee the movement of troops, prisoners and goods throughout my home country. It is gratifying to serve the Reich and to be recognized by my superior officers.

Heil Hitler!

Last week I returned home from Poland. I moved into a new flat near the city center, more in keeping with my new position and salary, and today I am officially the commander of Bucuresti Gara de Nord - the Bucharest North railway station.

I have been assigned something else - a top-secret mission - one I trust will enrich the Reich and my own standing even more. For understanding I turn to my Fuhrer's famous book. It will guide me.

89889 88380 89448 86244 04801 67018 80094 04004 89889 57216

93980 25765 77294 04439 06798 87312 89889 76631 24697 80499 39651 35637 00793 78767 18288

99725 81971 08675 28565 95453 94789 70222 70481 22820 39246

89889 17479 55268 15343 89889 96116 04800 04439 91585 79835 15084 09338 45333 04439 42450 53795 46319 68749 89889 03334 44587 47387 65545 11070 74494 31106

61272 23888 36042 73022 88639 68345 04800 20020 21088 17883 27497 98657 85176

GHOST TRAIN

89889 57404 08934 89889 11879 18952 24292
08270 56336 12138 71290 40719 32433 10407 49927
31365 40314 60204 04439 26428 01861
89889 04439 70886 95048 04800 86908 20424

———

The odd numbers continued on to the bottom of this page. The next four pages had nothing but numbers as well.

All of this is so strange, she thought as she wondered what they could mean. *Nicu had told her to keep the books together. Was Mein Kampf the book Hitler referred to - the one he called famous? It must be, but what did it have to do with the diary? And what did all the numbers mean??*

As the clock chimed twice, she read on, skimming pages and randomly selecting entries. Almost every page had a number sequence or two. She found one that had a lot and read the written entry that preceded the numerals.

March 29, 1944

Two dozen trains a day arrive and depart my station. Many simply pass through, carrying troops or loaded with prisoners. The latter cry for mercy, but they have nothing to cry about now. They are on their way to the camps. Plenty of time for crying there!

Our station is critical to the war effort. It is the largest in the country and is the place where most Romanian troops board trains to go to the Eastern Front. Things are busy; there are hundreds of people milling around all day and all night, seeing off sons heading to the front to fight for Nazi Germany. How proud I am of these brave young men.

Now and then trains of a different type come into Bucharest. I have advance notice of their impending arrival, and preparations are made according to the rules set in place by Reichsmarschall Göring. They are guided to special tracks adjacent to the main building but away from prying eyes. There is a heavily secured room, easily accessible for loading and unloading the boxcars. That room is guarded round the clock by an elite team led by Lieutenant Schlosser. He is an SS officer like myself, and we have become good friends.

89889 14052 41564 05912 39428 12321 20202 69999 47164 42228 30479 65727 59982 03776 45837 93093

04439 96961 19393 25543 53977 95230 98029 16189 35156 25138 81749 11916 47973 86685

23665 12725 43948 48494 01293

89889 53314 70663 71731 68527 78140 49300 35819 49705 08048 33019 31547 62522 69595 74935

58913 06980 04439 21934 91362 56518 61050 00571 55450 64254 90957 10848 51177 77072

52505 26206 78544 21529 19134 73204 37551 71067 43960 51841

89889 52246 73867 62118 97366 91621 35415 77476 24734 09521 02044 24474 57182 85616 26870

03112 21270 66795 56777 13389 89889 79612 18325 28747 44364 24070 84953 02303 03371

86005 91346 75324 89889 52634 38344

07773 72929 77460 16982 71861 80665 07369 27259 67588 93482 68915 42617 04439 37940

35544 89614 53962 04439 60370 68252 18050 68656 90278 78528

13777 89889 51825 93887 41144 25931 18454 40885 73592 02028 43280 19523 37681

89889 73188 29799 33408 96023 34735 45158 60775 40481 01365 18714 19782 16577 26190 70792

89889 97755 56098 81069 79597 10573 17645 22986 06964 55030 84274 04439 39412 89889 09100 48621

03501 12305 39008 32340 99227 25122 73997 74256 26595 43021 67184 21254 59043 19118 65452

99891 49689 04439 21918

10169 89889 13114 56907 25527 46226 57571 . . .

Following this page were six more containing nothing but numerals arranged in five-digit sequences like the ones on this page.

Glancing at other dates, she observed that the numbers showed up often in the middle of a line of text. They must be some kind of code, a way for him to keep a word or phrase secret in an otherwise innocent sentence. What had caused him to go to all that effort? What was he hiding?

She reread the passage he'd written about how the prisoners cried for mercy. In the callous way he described them, he could have been talking about sheep. But these were human beings. What a monster Nicu was! A proud, evil Nazi monster! She wept for the millions who had been slaughtered in the Holocaust by demons like Nicu Lepescu.

Finally feeling sleepy but wanting just a little more, Adriana turned to the end of the journal and read the last two entries.

August 20, 1944

I fear the Reich has little time left. Rumor has it the Red Army is advancing and is less than fifty miles away. If they capture Bucharest, things will be finished for the Nazis in Romania. Times are bad and people are desperate. Even members of the SS such as I get only sketchy reports from the battlefront. What I do hear is alarming. I now believe that Germany cannot win, although I dare not discuss my thoughts with anyone. In these dark days, criticizing the Reich is treason and grounds for execution, so my concerns will be recorded only here in my secret journal.

Today we realize the fruits of our labors. It is bittersweet - I am proud of my contribution. Sadly, my project is being rushed into use because the war is almost over for Hitler and the Fatherland.

For six months I supervised the project while my subordinates kept the Jews hard at work. We lost many, but there were thousands more at Auschwitz to replace them. The tunnel will at last be put to use today. It isn't entirely finished, but I was ordered to stop. We must move now,

Reichsmarschall Göring told me. Yesterday the prisoners threw open the massive doors into the main tunnel under 27843.47747.08012.47747.92001/48286. The Jews built a switch at a nearby rail line, brought the tracks here, and installed three hundred meters inside the tunnel itself. Even though this was my project, I was never told the purpose, but lately I have begun to understand what is going to happen.

In recent weeks rumors have been circulating everywhere. There is talk of a mysterious train - a ghost train. For weeks people have been talking about more than a dozen train cars crammed with the very best spoils from conquered cities across Europe. The rumor is that the train carries Old Masters worth millions of marks. And gold too - more gold than one can imagine. These rumormongers asked me about the secret train. I am stationmaster, and I should know, they said. They are right. I should know. I told these men nothing. I have an important position and I know an important secret. Lieutenant Schlosser and I spoke of it just yesterday.

Our secure storage room at Bucharest North Station is full to the brim. Trains have arrived for weeks, loaded with everything imaginable, including tons of gold. All of that cargo has been offloaded and stored here at the express order of Reichsmarschall Göring. No one knows why.

I think the men who are spreading rumors of a train filled with treasure are wrong. My theory is that it will arrive empty. Everything in our storerooms - every item Lieutenant Schlosser and his troops are guarding - will be put on that train and taken away to a secret place. Perhaps it will be my secret place! How wonderful it would be if my project ended up being the place where the future of Nazi Germany was hidden!

Five pages of numbers followed that entry.

August 21, 1944
At last! Last night I learned the secret! After too many drinks at the club, my commander confided that Die

GHOST TRAIN

Geisterbahn - the Ghost Train - will come today. It will arrive empty, just as I predicted. Our troops will load the cargo from our storage facility at the station and then the train will proceed to
27843.47747.08012.47747.92001/48286.

I am beaming with pride. When Reichsmarschall Göring picked me to supervise the project at 27843.47747.08012.47747.92001/48286, I knew it was going to be important. Until this moment I had no idea how important it would prove to be. I hadn't heard of Operation Geist then, of course. It's top secret. Only a handful of officials know about it. I am one of those privileged ones, but even I am not privy to everything.

Dozens of special trains have come through Bucharest North Station in the nine months that I've been in charge. Lieutenant Schlosser and I have supervised more than a hundred transfers. Our secure storage area has held thousands of boxes and crates, most thinly disguising the gold and priceless objects that they contained. Even today the secure area is filled to the brim. For what reason? Now I know!

Until now the treasures were always sent to Poland or Germany or Austria. I am well pleased that I contributed to the war effort in this important way. A project that I personally oversaw, here in my homeland, will be the salvation for the Reich. I only wish it could have been sooner. The Allies are dangerously close. I hope they do not arrive today. The Ghost Train must make its journey safely. This is the last hope for a Fourth Reich, which, God willing, will someday rise from the ashes of the Third. May the riches on this train be the foundation of a new Nazi regime. Heil Hitler! Heil mein Fuhrer!

As she closed the diary, she reflected on how often he wrote about gold bars. They must have been a part of the stationmaster's daily existence. They were offloaded, stored and shipped onwards every few days. Had Nicu gotten the twenty-three bars by stealing from the shipments? His diary said the storage room was heavily guarded by special troops. Taking such a chance would have been an enormous risk; the Nazis would have killed him if they caught him stealing, but there was so much being transported from place to place, maybe they didn't even count it. But no, it must be something else. She couldn't believe even he could do that. As much as she detested what he stood for, she couldn't believe the old man would have stolen from the Reich he apparently loved so much.

She picked up the other book - *Mein Kampf* - and turned to the flyleaf, where Nicu had written his name and the words *This is my most important book.*

Nicu had told her the book was critical. He hadn't even mentioned his diary, which she'd have thought he'd consider more important than Hitler's manifesto. *He must have been one dedicated Nazi,* she thought to herself. He considered the Fuhrer's book the most important one of all. Crazy.

She put the diary on her nightstand and closed her eyes, hoping tonight's sleep wouldn't haunt her like the others had.

CHAPTER FOURTEEN

Awaking drenched in sweat once again, she opened the drapes wide and let the morning sunshine stream in. It was a warm, welcome feeling after another night of terrifying nightmares. There were packs of jackals circling sheep, moving closer and closer, then tearing them apart with their teeth. Once the sheep were dead, the predators moved on. They weren't hunting for food. They were killing for sport, their jowls glistening with the blood that dripped from their grotesque, smiling mouths.

One of the jackals had a vicious, evil face. A human face. *His* face. After that particular dream she'd screamed and clawed at her bedclothes until somehow she awoke. Afraid to sleep again, she lay panting until she knew it was morning.

After a shower and some coffee, Adriana felt better. A fix helped too, after which she walked to Nicu's bank with her rolling travel bag. This morning she rationalized the entire situation. She had to stop killing herself over Nicu's sins. She had no fault in any of this. She had lucked into an incredible situation, befriending an old man who had no one else to bestow his gifts upon. None of this was her doing, and no one could blame her for accepting his largesse.

Half an hour later she was at home with ten gold bars, nine of which she'd just gotten from the bank. She left the other thirteen in the lockbox for another time. The sheer weight was one issue, but safety was another. She would certainly be robbed if people knew what she had. She added the two old books to the suitcase and stuck it in her closet behind boxes of last season's clothes.

She took that first gold bar back to the bank where she'd received the valuation yesterday, handed it over to the same clerk and said, "I'd like to sell this bar."

"Of course," he replied, clearly remembering both the beautiful woman and the Nazi bar. "May I have your identity card, please?"

She stuttered, "Wh-Why? Why do you need my identity card?"

"The law says we must record all transactions of this value, Miss. The government doesn't want to lose any tax opportunity, you know," he joked.

She was shocked. She hadn't considered this possibility.

"I've left my card . . ." It was a stupid excuse since it was against the law for Romanians to be without their cards, but it was all she could think of. "I'll get it and come back." She glanced at the security camera over the door, wondering if they were recording her visit. Would they call the authorities? That made her nervous, but there was nothing she could do.

She couldn't give them her ID card. She couldn't explain to the government how she suddenly had gold - a lot of it - without involving Nicu. The government was in the middle of everyone's lives in Romania; she would be interrogated, perhaps even jailed, until she revealed where the bars came from. She had to find another way.

She walked for thirty minutes, making several turns and backtracks in case someone was following her. She felt silly doing it, like she was a spy or something. But then again, what if someone *had* followed? The government was everywhere; maybe the bank clerk called the police when she left. Once she felt certain no one was following, she went home. As she turned on the light in her back room, the bright red swastika on Nicu's diary blazed like the devil's eyes.

She had to call Philippe. She'd had the book too long to wait any longer. She received money from him every month, and her job was to find out where Nicu kept his diary. They both had known it would take time; she couldn't ask Nicu about a diary she supposedly didn't know existed. At last he had mentioned it, and now she had it in her hands.

This is the book Philippe wants. Adriana glanced through it once more, still puzzled by the odd numbers interspersed here and there like a type of code. She set it aside and made the call.

Philippe was very happy to hear she'd found the journal. Within a half hour she'd turned the book over to a courier and it was on the way to Philippe. She hadn't mentioned the other book, *Mein Kampf*, and she tossed it back in the rolling bag with the gold. Maybe at some point she'd find out what was so important about it.

Her thoughts turned back to the problem at hand. How could she sell the gold anonymously?

I should ask Nicu what to do. That would be best, but she was afraid he'd think her greedy and ungrateful for already figuring out how to get rid of his gold. Truthfully, she *was* greedy and ungrateful. Regardless, she needed another answer. Who else besides Nicu might help her circumvent the authorities?

Of course! Denis. Why didn't I think of him earlier?
Denis was her dealer.

Adriana spent the day with Nicu as usual. They visited, ate a lunch Mrs. Radu prepared, and watched TV afterwards. At four she told him she needed to leave early to run some errands.

"I'm not surprised," he replied evenly. "You've been preoccupied all afternoon. You may have been here with me, but your mind was miles away."

"That's not true," she lied with a playful pat on his arm. "You're all I think about . . ."

"Go on home, girl. Do what you have to do. I'll see you tomorrow."

Thirty minutes later she sat in the cavernous Bucharest North train station, ironically the same building Nicu Lepescu had controlled in 1944. She watched Denis maneuvering through the crowd of people hurrying to catch homebound trains. He was in his twenties, tall, thin and dark like most Romanian men. He was handsome, always fashionably dressed, and carried a bag - his man purse, she laughingly dubbed it. The bag was where he kept the products he sold his customers.

"What's up, A?" he asked as he gave her a peck on the cheek and sat next to her. "Why the urgent call? You saw me just last week. Are you needing more already?"

She laughed. "For once it's not that. I need some help. Take a look at this." She opened a bag in her lap and let him look inside. The gold bar lay in the bottom.

He gave a low whistle as he examined it. "Reichsbank? As in Hitler? Wow! What'd you do - kill a Nazi?"

She ignored him. "I want to convert this into cash, and I can't do it without providing my identity card. I was hoping you had another idea."

Keeping it in the sack hidden from the masses of pedestrians around them, he looked it over. "One kilo. Any idea what it's worth? Maybe a hundred thousand?"

"Try a hundred and fifty. Nearly forty thousand in US dollars."

"You know you'll take a haircut if you deal with me. I'm taking all the risk . . ."

"I know that, Denis. Believe me, if I could walk into the bank and get full value for it, I wouldn't be sitting here right now. But I am. I don't know what else to do."

"I guess you don't want to let me borrow it overnight," he said. "I know we're good friends and all . . ."

"Not that good." She laughed. "I'll keep the bar for now."

He told her what he'd do. Presuming the bar was solid gold, which Adriana knew wasn't an issue, he'd take it off her hands. "I'll give you half its value," he said.

"Half? Are you crazy? You're taking the risk, but God, Denis. You'd be getting nearly twenty thousand dollars for each bar . . ."

He perked up instantly. His voice was eager, less cordial. "Each bar? There are more?"

Damn. She wished she hadn't said that. She didn't know Denis at all. He appeared to be a nice guy, but after all, he was a heroin dealer. He could be a robber, a murderer, whatever. She shrugged off a nervous shiver.

"There are more. In a safety deposit box."

"And you want me to cash them all in for you?"

"Yes, but not for fifty percent . . ."

"Oh, girl, it'll be even more than that now. Do you know the risk in converting hundreds of thousands of dollars of gold into cash? Now it's sixty percent."

She was becoming really nervous. She'd made a serious mistake. Suddenly a drug dealer with whom she'd had a business relationship knew she had gold - lots of gold - and he was going to take most of it for himself.

I should never have done this! I should have talked to Nicu!

"I'm . . . I think I'm not going to do anything right now," she said, stumbling on the words.

This time his eyes were steely, his voice hard. He took hold of her arm, squeezing so tightly it hurt. "Yeah, go shop it around, bitch. Seriously? You don't have any choice. I don't know how you got a bunch of gold, but I'm in, regardless. I'm taking the bar. I'll get it appraised and meet you here tomorrow night at eight." He grabbed the sack and walked away.

She cried all the way home.

What have I done?
What if Denis kills me?
Should I tell Nicu?

CHAPTER FIFTEEN

Adriana sat on the side of Nicu's bed, sobbing as the old man held her hands in his.

"I've made a huge mistake, darling," she confessed.

"Tell me, girl. Let me help you."

She explained what she'd done. He already knew she'd taken the gold bar to the bank and learned its value - she told him that a couple of days ago. Now she'd gotten an outsider involved - a man she'd known from childhood, she said. She said nothing about his being her heroin dealer. Nicu didn't know she was a user - no one did except Denis. She was always careful - she never injected in places people could see. She went for veins in her ankles, her feet, the back of her legs - places people wouldn't notice even when she was naked. No one wanted his fortune told - or his sexual desires gratified - by a heroin addict.

"I'm afraid, Nicu. He wants sixty percent . . ."

For the first time in their years together the old man was harsh. He dropped her hands and said, "You foolish girl. I wasn't surprised when you took a bar to the bank and learned what it was worth. But I thought there was more to you than greed. Now it seems what you want to do is sell my gold. That's your prerogative, of course. I told you it's yours, to do with whatever you wish. I'm an old fool. I thought somehow you might feel about me like I feel about you. How ridiculous is that?" He laughed bitterly. "Now I see a different side of Adriana Creed. And that's fine. We all have more than one side to ourselves, don't we?"

"I care about you, Nicu . . ."

Ignoring her, he resignedly sat on the side of the bed and put on his slippers. "There was a time I could have taken care of this for you. Now I'm too old. The friends whose help I could have enlisted are all dead. This is going to be up to you." He walked to the closet, rummaged around inside for a moment and came out carrying something. He brought it to the bed and handed it to her.

It was a beautifully inlaid wooden box with a hinged lid.

"What is this?" she asked.

"Open it."

She lifted the top and saw a pistol nested in faded satin. There were two carvings - the initials N.L. on its stock and a swastika on the barrel.

"Where did you get it?"

He took it out and cradled it lovingly in his hands. With a cold laugh he said, "It's my Dragon Luger from the war. I hid it from the Russians and I've kept it cleaned and oiled, ready for anything, all these years."

She recoiled in shock. He had changed suddenly. His savage laugh, his cold eyes, his inhuman expression - everything laid him bare before her. She already knew what Nicu Lepescu had been, but until now she had seen him as a kindly old man. She looked into his face and saw the jackal from her dream.

"You're giving me this to protect myself?"

"Not at all, my dear. I'm giving you this because you're going to kill him."

CHAPTER SIXTEEN

Adriana and Denis sat on the same bench where they'd met last night. She hadn't brought the Luger. In the first place, she'd never held a gun in her life. In the second place, shooting someone in a crowded train station would be unbelievably foolish. There had to be another way.

She'd really screwed things up. Even though Nicu gave her sole possession of whatever was in the safety deposit box, she hated that she appeared to be nothing more than a greedy leech, out for what she could take from him. In reality, that wasn't far off the mark. She couldn't bring herself to have feelings for the monster who had become a decrepit shell of his former self. But she had played a role and played it well. She had acted as his friend and his companion. That relationship was most likely gone now, and she'd leave it at that. Every woman for herself.

"What did you find out about the bar?"

Denis held up a sack. "You were right. It's worth around thirty-six thousand dollars. I'm going to give you fifteen thousand each for the bars you have. How many are there?"

"There are four in all," she said without looking him in the eye. She could lie with the best - after all, she pretended to love the sex she had with one client after another - but this was different. This was her future and she didn't intend to let Denis rip it from her. She'd give up a little to keep hold of the rest.

"We split fifty-fifty. That's it. Take it or leave it. I have other places I can go . . ."

Denis grabbed her arm roughly. "You're in no position to bargain, my friend, and no, you have no place else to go. I have one of your bars already" - he held up the sack - "and I'm certain you're lying about having just three more. You're going to bring me all of them. I will decide the split and you'll do what I say. Otherwise I'll hunt you down and take everything. Do you want some of the money or none of it? Don't be stupid! Noon tomorrow. The Eagle Pensione Hotel in Ferentari. If you're not there, you're a dead woman. You can't escape me. Do you understand?"

She nodded, hanging her head dejectedly in what she hoped appeared to be desperation. It had become clear what she had to do. She had no choice, no other place to turn. She hailed a taxi and went directly to Nicu's flat.

———

She sat in her usual place on the side of the bed next to him. He lay propped on pillows, listening as she finished telling him what had happened.

"I offered you the gun," he said quietly.

"I can't do it, darling. I've never even held a gun before."

He patted her leg gently. "I know that. I knew it yesterday when I showed you the pistol. I saw your face. It's likely we won't need it in the first place. It will be our insurance policy, to make sure this friend of yours does what we ask."

"What do you mean? Are you going too?"

"Of course. I have nothing to lose, my dear. As much as I wanted to be angry at you yesterday, I can't. You mean everything to me. Consider this a little last-minute adventure for a man who's lived a long, long time. Now we have work to do. We only have until noon tomorrow to get several things accomplished."

He went to his closet, pulled out a dusty old suit hanging in the back, and reached into the inside jacket pocket. He removed a black credit card and a small piece of paper with an address in Linz, Austria. The card was completely blank except for the familiar metallic strip on its back. He handed the items to her and said, "Keep these safe. They're the keys to your future. The only thing else you need are six numbers. Memorize them now and never, never ever forget them." He recited them to her and made her repeat them back over and over until he was certain she knew them by heart.

Then he explained exactly what the black card was and how to use it.

He began by saying, "Please don't castigate me for what I was. You've done things you regret - everyone has - and so have I. I confessed my sins to you. All my sins were long ago, and I paid my debt to society for my misdeeds."

Misdeeds. Her mind wandered as he spoke. She thought about Jews in cattle cars, screaming for mercy. *Misdeeds.*

He explained that after the war there had been a concerted effort by the Allies in particular and the world in general to right the wrongs perpetrated by Nazi Germany. "You're far too young to understand what it was really all about," he told her with a smile. She forced a smile back, a false smile that belied her disgust at what she knew it *had* been about. Death by extermination. Grisly experiments. Man's inhumanity to man.

She focused on his words.

"As the war came to a brutal end for our beloved Germany, those of us at certain levels were given the opportunity to have a future. If we had assets - any kind of assets, regardless of their type, value or location - there would be help for us. Some people had art, some had hard metals instead of the now-worthless wartime currency, and others had diamonds. It didn't matter anymore where they came from. An ultra secret private investment firm was established in 1946. In a tongue-in-cheek move the founders headquartered it in Linz, Hitler's home town, right under the noses of the Allies. Very soon thereafter it had hundreds of millions on deposit and its huge vaults held objects that would never be on public display again.

Chalices, crucifixes, priceless art that once belonged to the church or perhaps prominent citizens - all of those things were now property of certain Nazis. Those Nazis entrusted the goods to the bank for safekeeping.

"Who owns that firm? I have no idea, nor does it matter. I'm sure many of the initial depositors are dead by now. Some were executed for war crimes. Some made deposits and never returned for one reason or another. The firm itself must be wealthy beyond imagination. It has operations all over the world, and you may use that black card to access the account from every major city on the planet. Everything is completely secret and totally secure. I've been paid interest on my holdings for all these years, and my account is as impregnable as it was the day I opened it. Whoever holds the card - that card in your hand - has total control over it."

He explained that although it wasn't a credit card - it couldn't be used to purchase goods or services - it could be used to withdraw cash from ATMs worldwide while not producing any traceable transaction receipt. The bearer remained anonymous thanks to a maze of encrypted movements between the ATM and the firm where Nicu's assets were deposited.

He told her they were going to his bank tomorrow at ten a.m. to sell the remaining thirteen bars of gold in Nicu's safety deposit box. The proceeds would end up in this account, he continued, waving the black card in front of her. The other ten bars would be no problem either. He instructed her to take them to the address on the card, the place in Linz, Austria, where they would do whatever she needed with no governmental or regulatory involvement.

As she listened, her earlier revulsion at his "misdeeds" disappeared. When he explained what the black card represented, she forgave him. In an odd twist of fate this monster had become her savior. It was that simple, and she *must* forgive his past. She had to get over it. Especially now.

The more he talked, the more euphoric she became. She didn't need a heroin dealer named Denis anymore. She would never have to work again. Like always it seemed, once again Nicu had solved her problems.

That day, for the first time since she'd met him, her warm, tender attention toward Nicu Lepescu became real. She cried sincere tears of affection for the old Nazi who was willing to do anything to help her. Despite what he had once been, no one else had ever cared about her like this. Whatever happened was in the past. The black card proved the lengths to which he'd go to help her. She kissed him lovingly - not the peck on the cheek she always gave him. This was a real kiss - a lover's kiss. She'd never done that before; it surprised both of them and he hugged her tightly for a minute or more.

"I'll never be able to thank you enough, Nicu."

"It's nothing, Apostol." He laughed, using her nickname. "Just a little token of my affection. I told you I love you already!" He held her a moment longer. Somehow they both were aware that one way or another, things were different now. Everything in their lives was about to change forever.

"I love you too. I will always love you. No matter what happens." She'd never uttered those words to him before, but they were sincere now.

Adriana let herself into his apartment at nine since they were going to the bank in an hour.

"Good morning, Mrs. Radu!"

Silence. Not even her usual snippy greeting. Then she heard Nicu say from the bedroom, "I gave her the day off. Come help me finish getting dressed. I'll get your gold cashed in; then we'll deal with your friend the swindler."

The banker accompanied them to the vault, where Nicu removed the last thirteen gold bars. He asked the banker to convert them into US dollars and advised where to wire the proceeds. He signed several documents and they left. Next up was their appointment with Denis.

Bucharest's Ferentari ghetto was considered one of the most dangerous places in Europe. Tourists were warned there was no protection for them there. Thieves, murderers and drug-crazed lunatics haunted these twisted streets. Even the police dared venture into the ghetto only during daylight hours. After dark it was a threatening maze of danger where anything could happen. The awful things done at night would still be waiting for the cops in the morning, they rationalized as they patrolled along the fringes.

Their cab driver refused to go into the Ferentari, so they had to walk the last few blocks. Vagrants loitered everywhere and several wolf-whistled at Adriana. Nicu kept his hand wrapped around the Luger in his pocket. Just before twelve they entered the dark, fetid entrance to the Eagle Pensione Hotel. Aged furniture sat in a decrepit lobby that hadn't been painted in twenty years. The place reeked of cigarette smoke. Marijuana too. The latter wafted from behind the ancient counter that was the front desk.

The desk clerk stood and watched them cross the lobby. He wore a ragged Def Leppard T-shirt and he needed a shave and a bath. As he took another drag from a joint, he gave Adriana a leer. He watched her and the old man walk to the elevator. She had to be a whore - no decent woman would come in here - but she had class. She didn't look like the ghetto girls. He wondered idly if her unbelievably old client would be able to perform. Who knew? Who cared? Maybe he just liked to watch her. It made no difference to the clerk. He was happy they hadn't stopped by the desk for a key. That wasn't unusual and it meant less work for him. Lots of the whores rented rooms by the week. Without another thought he went back to a flickering black-and-white TV on the counter, where Lucy and Ricky were arguing in Romanian.

The ancient elevator was slow and creaked loudly as it carried them to the third floor. They got out and looked around. They didn't hear a sound. Nicu walked to the far end of the hall, opened a door marked "Stairs" and pointed at them.

"Remember these, just in case. This is the back exit."

She knocked on the door of room 304.

"It's open."

She went first. The drug dealer sat on a seedy couch behind a coffee table. He glanced up in surprise as Nicu came in behind her and closed the door.

"What the hell is this? Who's the old fossil?"

"Mind your manners." Nicu spoke quietly as he took a seat across the table. "I'm here to move things along. I'm her . . . her adviser, you might say."

"Her adviser? Shit," Denis muttered. "All right, whatever. Give me the bars."

As always, Nicu's voice was shaky. "Not yet. I want to hear your offer. And I want to see the gold bar she gave you."

"Who gives a shit what you want?"

Adriana said, "Show it to him, Denis. I've asked him to help me, and he wants to be sure you still have it."

Denis pulled the bar from under the table and tossed it over. "See that name on the bar? Reichsbank? I'll bet you know something about that, don't you, old man? You're plenty old enough to have known our beloved Fuhrer," he said mockingly. "Did you goose-step around the square -"

"Shut your mouth, you little prick!" Nicu's words were suddenly firm, strong and harsh. There was an evil tone to them that made Adriana cringe. The words caught Denis by surprise. He hesitated, then decided to let it go.

"Like I told her, I sell the bars and she gets fifteen thousand each. Nobody asks questions, nobody wants to know where this Nazi gold has been all these years. You understand? If Adriana could take them to the bank, she wouldn't be talking to me, now would she?"

Nicu spoke softly.

"What? Speak up, for God's sake!" Denis was becoming impatient, irritated. This old man wasn't a part of this transaction and she'd been stupid to bring him here.

"I said you're not offering a fair price."

"Fuck you. Do I care what you think? She'll take what I offer or . . ."

"Or what?"

"Shut up!" Denis yelled. Then he glanced over and drew back in alarm as he saw a Luger pistol in the old man's hand.

"What the hell are you doing? Are you crazy?"

Nicu held the gun steady, aiming it directly at Denis, and he spoke quietly once again.

"I may be an old fossil, but I'm certainly not crazy. Adriana will pass on your offer. Take the bar, Adriana. We don't need to deal with this amateur."

Suddenly Denis lunged across the table. He was in midair when three shots rang out. His body fell on Nicu like a sack of flour, blood spurting everywhere. With a heave Nicu pushed Denis to the floor. His body lay still.

"Holy Mother of God!" Adriana yelled. "You've killed him!"

"It was the only way, my dear," he said with a rueful smile. "It was inevitable and it was what I came to do. You should be grateful. I've solved a problem for you. You must leave quickly. After our visit to the bank today, you're set for life. I'm an old man, as he said . . ."

They heard the creaking of the elevator. He handed her the gold bar and said, "Get out! Hurry! Take the back stairs. Destroy your cell phone so they can't track you, and buy another one later. Go to Linz quickly, but be careful to avoid the authorities. Use the black card! Now go! Disappear!"

In the distance they could hear the two-tone sirens of police cars. Gunshots apparently brought the authorities into the ghetto when other crimes wouldn't. They'd be here in moments. She stuck the gold bar in her coat pocket, kissed Nicu's cheek and ran away. She would never see him again.

CHAPTER SEVENTEEN

Adriana ran through the squalid streets of the Ferentari ghetto, glad she'd paid attention when they walked in a half hour ago. As she waited for the traffic light to change, a filthy, toothless man came up behind her and squeezed her buttocks roughly. She drew back in fright and ran directly into oncoming traffic, dodging angry drivers but getting away. Then it happened again. One of the addicts she passed on a stoop began to chase her. She was terrified - she knew better than to be a woman dressed in nice clothing, alone in the Ferentari. She ran and ran, hoping she was still going the right way.

After three blocks she popped out onto a broad avenue with tall trees, free from the ghetto and her pursuer at last. She hailed a cab, went to her store and had him wait. She was inside less than five minutes. First she used a hammer to destroy her cell phone. The pieces went in the trash. She pulled the rolling suitcase from its hiding place and tossed her credit cards, passport and a wad of euros she kept hidden behind the toilet into it. She quickly gathered some toiletries and a clean set of underwear. She was leaving with little more than the clothes she was wearing - plus a fortune in gold - but there wasn't time to spare for anything else. Except one thing, the most important thing of all. She pulled her drug paraphernalia and five small vials of liquid from her nightstand drawer and put everything in her suitcase. She couldn't leave without the essentials.

The vials would get her through until she was situated somewhere. She preferred the old-fashioned way: spoon, lighter, citric acid and water to create liquid heroin for the syringe. It was potent and more satisfying. Liquid O was a new thing, very popular with people who didn't want to inject heroin. It was sold in eyedropper vials and inhaled. It was therefore easy to conceal and didn't attract attention like drug paraphernalia did. When you wanted a quick fix - like she needed right this moment - it was perfect. She had a long night ahead of her, and Liquid O would have to do until she could get the real thing.

She hadn't given much thought to her departure from Romania except for Nicu's admonition that it should happen quickly and simply. She had the taxi drop her at the station, where she looked at the massive departures board and picked the next train leaving to any destination to the west. She paid cash for a private sleeper berth on the overnight train to Budapest and sat for an hour gripping her suitcase, struggling to stop the alarming thoughts in her head. After the murder, how quickly had the desk clerk told the police about her? Were the authorities looking for her even now? What if they'd found her fingerprints at the hotel? What if she were caught with ten kilo bars of gold? How would she explain herself?

The train pulled out of the massive station on time, beginning its sixteen-hour journey. Passengers were reminded that shortly after midnight, they must present themselves and their documents to officials at the border. So much for seamless border crossings in EU member countries. These Eastern European ones couldn't get past the need to keep track of everybody. Adriana didn't care - she just wanted to get out of Romania as quietly as possible, away from authorities who might be looking for an accomplice to a murder.

It would have been nice to eat dinner in the comfort of the dining car, but she couldn't leave the suitcase. She opted for privacy, buying a sandwich and a split of wine from the trolley and eating in her tiny room. She popped the first vial of Liquid O and inhaled it deeply, savoring the warmth and comfort she immediately felt. She put the bag next to her bed, covered herself and dozed a little until she felt the train begin to slow, then come to a full stop. An announcement in Hungarian and Romanian ordered all passengers to show their papers. This was the most terrifying moment of all. If they were looking for her, it would be all over in moments.

She heard boots outside, then a knock. She opened the door to two soldiers with automatic rifles slung over their shoulders. They gave her passport a quick glance, nodded at her and left. She held her breath for twenty minutes until the train lurched, then started moving again. Within minutes Adriana was sound asleep for the first time since Nicu Lepescu had killed her drug dealer. She felt safe. She had gotten out of her home country and she was in Hungary.

She awoke to the announcement that the train was thirty minutes out of Budapest's Kaleti Station. She was surprised to see sunlight pouring through the windows. She'd slept well and felt good. She pulled her rolling bag down the hall to the bathroom, freshened up and had a quick coffee in her room.

According to the board at the station, the next train to Linz departed in two hours. She bought a first-class ticket and walked out to the busy street. At a shop nearby she bought an outfit, put it on in the dressing room, then had breakfast at a brasserie. She bought a prepaid cell phone at a kiosk in the station and used it to call Nicu's apartment, hoping Mrs. Radu would be there and could tell Adriana what had happened to Nicu. No one answered then or the two other times she tried that day.

In the afternoon after an uneventful train ride, a decent lunch and another quick passport check at the Austrian border, her train chugged into the Linz station on time.

Adriana was bone-tired - she'd have loved a couple of hours in a real bed - but she had a mission. She could sleep later. She looked at the paper Nicu had given her and showed the address to a policeman. He pointed to a nearby street and held up two fingers - two blocks. She confirmed she was going down the right street then began to look for number 153. As she stood at the door, she realized it certainly wasn't what she had expected. From Nicu's conversation she thought it was a bank. In fact, this was the banking district - from where she stood she could see at least a dozen. Her building was sandwiched in among them, but it bore no name.

I guess that isn't such a surprise. What did I expect - a big sign that says Bank of the Nazis?

It was an inconspicuous stone structure with gold numbers "153" above the door. She looked for a buzzer, but there wasn't one. She noticed a simple card reader on one side of the entryway and remembered Nicu's instructions. She pulled out the black card, inserted it in the slot, and the door swung open silently.

She entered, rolling her suitcase behind her, pushed open another door and found herself in what appeared to be a small ATM lobby. There were several machines, each in its own three-sided privacy booth. A chair sat in front of each machine. No one else was in the room and she noticed several cameras above her near the ceiling. Unsure exactly what to do, she chose a booth, took a seat and inserted the card in the machine.

"Welcome. Please choose from the selection below." The words appeared on the screen in Romanian, followed by a list of choices.

She found it interesting that the card had triggered the words in Nicu's native language. Another visitor, she presumed, would have seen the welcome greeting in his own language. Very sophisticated, but once Nicu had explained exactly what this was all about, she expected nothing less. It was a bank of sorts, but unlike any other she'd encountered.

She perused the list and selected the first choice. *Confirm account balance.*

She was prompted to enter the six numbers Nicu had required her to memorize.

Although nothing about Nicu Lepescu should have surprised her, the next screen that appeared certainly did. She'd calculated the value of the thirteen gold bars Nicu had converted into cash and deposited into his account here. After fees and whatever, she expected the account to contain around $450,000.

USD1,496,388

This amount does not include accrued interest since the beginning of the last quarter.

Adriana began to hyperventilate. *What the hell?* Once again Nicu had done something remarkable for her. When he converted the thirteen gold bars into cash, he'd put the funds here, but his account had already held over a million dollars. Now that money was hers too.

Once again she cried. She hadn't heard anything since she left Bucharest, but she was certain he'd been arrested. He didn't need the assets now - both of them had known that even before he killed Denis - but she was still amazed at the sheer volume of what he'd accumulated. Where it came from, he never said. She knew his background. He'd been big in the Reich regime - an SS storm trooper, a concentration camp official and a stationmaster in Bucharest. Those were important positions, but they didn't make one wealthy. After the war he'd been convicted of his crimes and spent twenty years in prison. When he was released, he never worked again. Yet somehow he now had millions of dollars of assets.

Deep inside, Adriana knew how. She just didn't know *exactly* how. And she chose not to think about it anymore. She couldn't do anything more for the Jews. She didn't care about the Nazis from whom Nicu had probably stolen the gold. She had to let it go. This was *her* life now.

She went back to the previous screen, chose the line *speak with a representative* and received an immediate response.

A representative will be with you shortly.

Without a sound, a young man entered the room and motioned for her to follow him. They walked down a short hallway past closed doors - she was reminded of a funeral parlor, it was so quiet - then he opened one and stood back so she could enter. He closed the door softly behind her.

An impeccably dressed man in his fifties pulled out a chair, seated her and said, "May I have your card, please?"

The man inserted the black card into his computer and looked at the screen. Then he asked her to enter her numeric password on a keypad in front of her. When she was finished, he checked the screen again.

"Thank you. Everything is in order. How may I help you?"

Nicu had told her what to say. "I have ten one-kilo bars of gold. I would like to convert them into US dollars and deposit the funds into this account." She pulled the bars from her suitcase and put them on his desk.

He picked up one bar and examined it closely. Unlike the clerk at the bank in Romania, the word *Reichsbank* didn't faze him. His fingers flew over the keyboard. Within seconds the same young man from earlier entered, put the bars in a briefcase and left.

The transaction took less than five minutes and involved no signatures, no identification and no names. The older man appeared to neither know nor care who she was, and he never told her how much money she was getting. Nicu had assured her as long as she had the card and the password, everything would work perfectly. He'd also told her to trust these people without hesitation. And as usual, he was right. Everything couldn't have gone better.

The man returned the black card to her. "Is there anything else?"

"Where may I access my account in other cities?"

He pulled a business card from his desk and handed it to her. It had one line: www.2f8d8k4h.com

"That website will give you what you need to know."

He stood and ushered her back into the first room she'd entered, turned without a word and went back to his office.

This place is perfect for people who don't like to talk to each other, she thought. While accomplishing a large financial transaction, she and the man had exchanged maybe twenty words total.

Curious about the gold sale, she went back into a booth and checked her balance again. It was larger by $364,750.

The gold had now become cash. That simply and that quickly. Unbelievable.

Thank you, Nicu. Again.

CHAPTER EIGHTEEN

After a long night on the train from Bucharest to Linz, then going straight to the strange building where her black card worked miracles, she was exhausted. She needed to rest. She stopped at an ATM, inserted the black card and punched in her numeric password. Within seconds she had withdrawn five thousand euros.

Now that she had plenty of money, she walked into a Hyatt, the first nice hotel she saw. She strolled through the quiet lobby to the front desk and asked for a room. No, she advised, she didn't have a reservation and she would be paying cash. When she heard that, the clerk called over her supervisor.

"We can, of course, accept cash as long as you present your identity card and passport," the lady assured Adriana. "I assume that will be no problem, Miss . . . uh . . ."

Adriana swallowed hard but said nothing.

The supervisor spoke more harshly this time. "It's the law in the EU. We don't accept guests without identification. Period."

Adriana was spooked. She was afraid the Romanian authorities would trace her. In an attempt to appear unconcerned, she breezily said, "No, thanks," and left, rolling her suitcase behind her. As she walked the sidewalks aimlessly, she knew she had to have a new identity. How the hell would she get that done? She was so tired she couldn't think. She walked away from the main business area into a section of restaurants, storefronts and less expensive hotels. She chose one, walked up a flight of stairs and looked around the lobby. It wasn't the Hyatt, but it certainly wasn't that sleazy hotel in the ghetto either. This was a perfectly acceptable second-class hotel, and she was intent on making this work.

There was no one in the lobby except her and a man behind the desk who was maybe twenty years old. She told him her luggage had been stolen and she had only this rolling bag she'd bought and a little cash she fortunately had hidden in her sock.

"I'm willing to do whatever it takes to get a room, after what I've been through," she said sweetly, laying a hundred-euro note on the counter. "This is for your help in getting me situated."

Since he earned about thirty euros a day, the clerk was instantly motivated. "I'll need your passport before you leave," he told her as the note went smoothly into his pocket. "As long as your bill is paid in full, if you happened to leave without remembering to come by and give it to me, there's not much we can do, is there?" He smiled, took the payment for her room, and handed her a key.

Wishing she had the real thing, Adriana settled for a vial of Liquid O, slept for five hours, went out for an early dinner and a bottle of Gewürztraminer wine, came back, popped another vial and slept until morning. She'd intended to leave Linz today, and maybe it could still happen. First she had something to do. Would it work? She had no idea. Nicu had led her to believe this little black card could solve any problem. Today she'd find out if that was true.

Two hours later she sat at another man's desk in that same anonymous building where she had converted her gold. It was time to see just how many services this strange, secretive firm actually could provide.

As before, she handed over her black card and entered her passcode. The man glanced at his computer screen then back to her.

"Everything is in order. How may I help you?"

GHOST TRAIN

She took a deep breath and said, "I need a new identity."

———

She didn't leave Linz that day, nor the next. Two days and fifty thousand dollars later, Adriana Creed was past history. Now she was Carey. Armed with a Dutch birth certificate and identity card, an EU passport and a credit card, she took the train to Vienna, then a taxi to the airport. A two hour first-class plane ride landed her in her new home, Amsterdam.

Carey Apostol rented a room in a cozy boutique hotel in Old Town, telling the clerk she'd be here a week, maybe two. Without hesitation or fear she handed over her new passport and credit card, and everything went perfectly.

Adriana had chosen the name Carey because it was Western. She hated the Romani names that branded you a gypsy. If she was going to start over, it would be as a Western European. Choosing a last name was easy - she simply used the middle name she'd been given at birth, a name almost no one knew.

Now she was Carey from the Netherlands.

Carey Apostol.

CHAPTER NINETEEN

Almost three weeks after his cremation, Nicu Lepescu's grandchildren sat in the pew along with his housekeeper in Biserica Curtea Veche, the oldest Orthodox church in Bucharest. Although the old man hadn't seen the inside of a church in fifty years, his will provided for a small contribution to the church and instructed that his funeral be held here.

Being gypsies, the Lepescu family cared little about religion. Ciprian, the father of Milosh, Philippe and Christina, had never taken his children to church at all. Today there was no casket. Nicu's body had been cremated, prompting a caustic comment from Christina about how ironic it was that he'd sent so many Jews to the crematoria, and now it was his time to burn.

Since it was an historic site, the old church remained open to tourists during weddings and funerals. Today groups of sightseers dutifully tromped through the back of the ancient building as the service was being held up front. There were only the four mourners, if they could even be called that. According to Mrs. Radu, Nicu had had no friends; he was 105 years old and hadn't exactly been a social person anyway. In truth, what friends there might have been had abandoned him long ago when he went to prison. When he was arrested in 1951, everyone deserted him for fear the authorities would discover they'd been monsters too.

No one else came to pay their respects to the former SS officer - the man who'd made sure the trains of death were packed full and ran on time from Bucharest to the Nazi camps, the man who had smiled and shook his head as Jews, stuffed into steamy boxcars, begged for water. He was the person who could have done something but instead ignored these men, women and children who were heading to hell on earth. Society said Nicu Lepescu had paid the price - he served nearly twenty years at hard labor - but no time in a cell could undo the horrors he had perpetrated on an entire class of people who were his own countrymen.

One individual sat in the last pew of the church, blending with the tour groups that shuffled through a large open area just behind him. He couldn't hear the cleric's eulogy, but he watched the four attendees, an older woman and three people in their thirties, obviously Nicu's grandchildren. The woman was respectful, but the deceased man's relatives were clearly uninterested in the service. It looked as though all they wanted was to get this over with.

The trio sat impassively as the cleric droned words about a man he'd never met, thoughts designed to make the family more comfortable that their loved one was one with Christ as they spoke. The grandchildren knew differently. If Nicu Lepescu was in Heaven today, then nothing in the Bible could be believed. According to the Bible, many men committed sins and Jesus Christ forgave them. But few men had systematically sent other human beings to their deaths without compunction and without a hint of remorse.

Soon organ music filled the sanctuary. As the priest began speaking, a beautiful young woman slipped into a pew on the other side of the aisle a few rows behind the grandchildren. Mrs. Radu saw her come in. Her face a mask of rage, she turned and exploded, "Get out, you whore! You have no place here!"

The woman stared at Mrs. Radu for a moment and then looked away as if she hadn't heard.

"Get out, I say!" She was louder, her demeanor forceful and angry.

The priest stopped talking as Milosh confronted the housekeeper. "Mrs. Radu! What are you doing? Who is she?"

"It's Adriana Creed!" The woman literally spat her name. "Call the police!"

Philippe remained seated as Milosh and Christina leapt to their feet in unison. They looked around the cavernous old church: the pew where Adriana had sat was now empty. They ran to the back of the sanctuary, where a hundred tourists milled about, but she was nowhere in sight.

Christina and Milosh pushed through a group of tourists leaving the church and looked around the courtyard.

Adriana had vanished once again.

As the confused priest waited for the two to return, Mrs. Radu whispered to Philippe, "She should never have been here." He shrugged, saying nothing but thinking, *what hypocrisy for any of us to be here.*

Paul Silver, the man who sat in the back row, wasn't a mourner. He'd come for one reason - to get a look at one of the grandchildren. Once he saw the profile, Paul knew this was the right Philippe Lepescu. He slipped out of the pew, his mission accomplished.

Seeing a burst of activity toward the front, he sat back down to watch. *Who's the attractive girl?* he wondered as she took a seat across the aisle and behind the family. The woman who was sitting with the grandchildren had glanced back at her, then turned and yelled at the girl to get out. The cleric paused as two of the grandchildren stepped into the aisle. Paul watched the girl race to the back of the church, quickly lost amidst throngs of tourists exiting the building. Within a moment the funeral continued, but Paul was gone too. The only one of Nicu's grandchildren who'd ever known Paul didn't see him. He wouldn't have recognized Paul if he had. Paul had spent a fortune changing his appearance since the days when Philippe had been his partner.

Soon the cleric began intoning a closing prayer. Mrs. Radu bowed her head in reverence. Milosh, Philippe and Christina Lepescu stared straight ahead, eyes wide open, as their grandfather was fervently prayed into his eternal home.

May the Lord God bless and keep you . . .

"Rot in hell," Christina muttered as the three left their grandfather's funeral service.

CHAPTER TWENTY

A few weeks after Nicu's death, the Lepescu grandchildren sat around a table at La Bonne Bouche, a cozy bistro in Bucharest's historic old town. They spoke about Adriana and how she'd simply vanished. The storefront where she'd worked and the living quarters behind it were locked tight. That day at the funeral when Mrs. Radu shouted at her was the last contact they'd had. And that hadn't been contact at all. Even though Milosh and his sister ran after her, they didn't see the girl run across the street outside. Neither had gotten a look at her face, so they wouldn't know her if she walked in right now. Philippe was a different story. He knew her well, but his siblings knew nothing about that part of Adriana's past.

The oldest of the three, Milosh had taken responsibility to dispose of Nicu's local assets, since he was the only one who lived in Bucharest. The three had agreed to periodic meetings and today's was the first of those. Christina had come from Vienna and Philippe from Lucerne for an update.

Milosh was thirty-eight. He played piano at bars here and there in Bucharest while he dreamed of performing with the symphony. He had sufficient desire but not enough drive or ambition to get it done. Financially he'd gotten by, but only barely. Nicu Lepescu's death couldn't have come at a better time. He was broke and tired of working.

It was the same for Christina. She aspired to be an actress and had attended university, but she never seemed to get the breaks that would land her an acting role. Once she turned thirty, she had effectively given up trying. Now she waited tables at one of Vienna's nicest restaurants. Like Milosh she survived, but she wanted more. Nicu's death made life easier for her too. With this inheritance the pressure of bills, rent and daily expenses would be over.

Philippe could use the money too, but he was far better off than his siblings, thanks to his criminal activities. He still lived in Lucerne, where he'd once run a vast investment company owned by Roberto Maas. Maas was a shadowy figure with a past - a man you wanted on your side. Philippe had come into Maas's life poor, but now he had significant assets. As they became good friends, Roberto had entrusted his associate with more and more responsibility, at last giving him passwords, transfer information, and allowing him full access to everything. As Roberto grew to appreciate Philippe's friendship, he had made him a partner in a variety of investments that reaped tremendous rewards for both of them.

Philippe repaid his employer's trust and generosity with fraud and deceit. Cocky and confident that he wouldn't be discovered, he began to embezzle money. A mistake revealed his crimes and Roberto fired his former friend and partner. Fearful for his life but at the same time seething with hatred for his former boss, Philippe disappeared. Despite his being the criminal, he blamed Roberto for making it easy. Rejected, he vowed to extract revenge on his former benefactor.

When Roberto Maas died in a mysterious fire in London, Philippe came out of hiding and resumed the good life in Lucerne with his four hundred thousand stolen dollars. He was free from the man he had gone into hiding to avoid.

His brother and sister were aware that Philippe was a thief. He'd been that way his entire life, always choosing to cheat and steal rather than use his wits, education and charm to earn a living. They didn't know exactly what he'd done in Lucerne, but they saw that he went from working-class comfortable, to being in hiding, to being suddenly wealthy, all in a matter of months.

Philippe had used his university degree and banking background to run Roberto's huge financial conglomerate, and ultimately he had sole oversight over more than a hundred million dollars. Thanks to his crimes he was suddenly unemployed, but he was also very well off. Although they didn't know specifics, both Milosh and Christina assumed he'd done something illegal because they knew what he was. He was a liar, a thief, a crook, and this time he had stolen four hundred thousand dollars from a man who had trusted him as a friend and partner.

Despite knowing what he was, his siblings were in a dilemma. He was the only one of them with any financial acumen whatsoever. As much as they wished it were different, they needed Philippe to untangle Nicu Lepescu's affairs. So they gritted their teeth and worked with him while vowing to keep him under a tight rein.

At today's lunch Milosh explained where things stood. In the two months since Nicu's death he had arranged for the furniture to be hauled out of the flat, and with Philippe's help, he'd put the seven-story building on the market. It was close to the city center - a desirable part of town - and the estate agent believed it would bring four million lei, almost a million dollars.

Nicu's savings account had been closed. The proceeds, nearly two hundred thousand dollars apiece, had been distributed to them. At last Milosh and Christina had money. Philippe got his portion too. When it was added to what he'd stolen from his partner, he was doing just fine.

Christina asked, "What about Adriana? Have you learned anything about what she took out of his safety deposit box?"

Milosh shook his head. "No. Since she left there's been nothing. She hasn't paid utilities or rent. In a couple of weeks the landlord will break into her place and remove everything. He promised to call me if there's anything I should see."

"Keep me informed," Philippe ordered. "Of the three of us, I'm the only one who's got the balls to make her return what's ours."

"What you mean is you're the only one who's an asshole," the usually reserved Milosh replied flatly.

Christina snickered. "I can't agree more. But Philippe's right. He's a villain, but he's *our* villain." She turned to Philippe. "I'm not interested in your balls, brother dear. I'm interested in your larcenous mind. I have no doubt you can force Adriana to hand over whatever she took from the box. I'm just afraid once she does, Milosh and I will never see our share."

He shrugged. "You'll get what you deserve."

"I don't want what you think I *deserve*. I want one third, which reminds me of something. Remember the box in Grandfather's closet? It had the deed, his papers, all that. I rifled through it and found the will. But something keeps bothering me. Weren't there *two* safety deposit keys? You had the box, Philippe. We handed it over to you and you went through it. Weren't there two?"

"I don't know what you're talking about," he replied smoothly. "I only saw the one."

CHAPTER TWENTY-ONE

In the office of a vice president of Stadt Privatbank in Vienna Philippe waited as the banker thumbed through Nicu's will, flipping pages to locate the section he wanted.

At last he stopped. "May I see your identification card?"

He tossed his card across a massive desk completely devoid of paperwork except for what Philippe had handed over when the meeting began.

"Swiss? I expected . . ."

"Romanian? Like my grandfather? I'm Romanian by birth, but I lived in Switzerland for several years."

"Lived? And now?"

"With all due respect," Philippe replied curtly, "why are you asking all these questions?" He held up the index card with the word "Stadt" written on it. "This key is for a safety deposit box in this bank - am I correct?"

As if he hadn't heard, the banker replied, "Mr. Lepescu, if you had an account with Stadt Privatbank, you would appreciate the lengths to which we go in order to protect our clients. Let me have a few more minutes and perhaps we can get on with your request." He walked out of his office.

That day he and his siblings had gone through Nicu's belongings, Philippe had surreptitiously slipped the key in his pocket. When he was alone that evening he did a quick web search and found one "Stadt" - the Stadt

Privatbank in Vienna. He made a call, learned what he must bring with him, and made an appointment. A week later he sat here in the bank officer's sumptuous, overstated office.

"All right then," the man said at last. "The will shows there are three heirs, all grandchildren of Nicu Lepescu. You are one of those three. Am I correct?" He leaned back and arched his fingers together.

Restraining himself from a sharp retort, Philippe said, "You are correct."

"Where are your siblings, then?"

"I am the family's representative. They sent me . . ."

"Excellent. May I see the power of attorney giving you that authority?"

Philippe had had enough. "What the hell do you think you're doing?" he shouted. "I've flown here from Bucharest, given you everything you requested, and I have a safety deposit box key. I demand access to my grandfather's box."

"I haven't yet confirmed there is in fact a box," the banker said with a smile. "We have rules here, Mr. Lepescu. Rules designed to address the privacy of our clients. I'm merely protecting . . ."

"You're protecting nothing at this point but your own ass! Who's your supervisor? Bring him here!"

"Sir, if you'll calm down, I think we can accomplish your goal without further incident. Excuse me again for a moment."

While the man was out, Philippe walked around his office, looking at university degrees and pictures of dignitaries hung on the wall. Shortly, the banker returned with a slip of paper.

"Here's what I am authorized to tell you. I can confirm that your grandfather does have a safe deposit box in this bank." He looked at the paper. "No one has accessed it since the week it was rented. That was in 1946."

"Who's been paying the fee all these years?"

"In those days the bank had a provision for perpetual leasing. The person who rented the box -

114

presumably your grandfather - paid nearly ten thousand marks for that privilege."

Philippe waved dismissively. "All right then. Let's get on with it. I want to see the box."

The banker replied sharply, "I see you have the same motives as so many other heirs I've dealt with. You want to know what's in the box. You are waiting for the Christmas present, so to speak. Very well, Mr. Lepescu. Here is what's going to happen. Ordinarily I would allow you private access to the box, but you have not provided permission from the other heirs for you to inspect it alone.

"I will therefore accompany you to the vault, open the box and give you privacy while you look. You may see what's there, even though you may remove nothing. If you bring me a power of attorney signed by your siblings, then you may have full rights to the box."

That was sufficient for Philippe. That was all he wanted.

Two hours later he sat at the airport, waiting to board his flight back to Bucharest. He had remained calm in front of the banker although what he saw in the safety deposit box made his heart flutter. He was still stunned.

The box had been larger than he expected. And it was crammed full. It was stuffed to the top with one-kilo Reichsbank gold bars. There had been no way to count them with the banker standing ten feet away. There were far more than a hundred. There could be twice that many.

Millions and millions of dollars of gold.

Damn, Grandfather. Where the hell did you get all that?

Philippe faced a challenge. He had to get Milosh and Christina to sign a power of attorney without knowing why they were doing it. Milosh would be easy, but Christina - she would be the problem. Regardless, he'd get it done. He didn't intend to split this treasure with anyone.

CHAPTER TWENTY-TWO

The Lepescu grandchildren were at the law firm that had represented Nicu. Philippe had called them here, saying there was paperwork to sign. Since they didn't trust him, he intended to avoid the issue by having an attorney explain what was needed.

"Mr. Philippe has told me there are possible bank accounts in Germany," the young lawyer began. "There may be other assets as well; I have looked through my firm's records and it appears that we set up a trust for Mr. Nicu a few years ago. I don't know the status of that, and without a power of attorney from the two of you, I'm unable to provide Philippe information about it."

Always wary, Christina said, "Why don't we look into his affairs together, the three of us? Why does it have to be only you, my dear cunning brother?" She smiled wickedly at the lawyer. "We have a lot of history with our brother, you must understand. He's not everything you might think. And some of the things he *is* might surprise you."

Philippe replied flippantly. "With all respect, Christina, this is business. This isn't really your forte - it's a little different than making sure your customer gets the sandwich he ordered. I'm the only one of us who has the background to understand this. And I'm following the direction of our attorney." He gestured to the other side of the desk. "Tell her why you suggested me to handle this, Mr. Lawyer. Use small words so she can understand."

"It's both cumbersome and expensive for three people to travel around Europe, searching for assets that may not exist," he explained. "Mr. Philippe is willing to spend his time . . ."

Christina had had enough. "Oh *really?* Philippe, you're such a generous man. You're willing to spend your time looking for assets that might or might not ever be revealed to your two uninformed siblings. This is bullshit. I'm not signing anything. I don't trust you, and I can only imagine what you're already up to."

She whirled around to the attorney, who sat impassively on the other side of his desk. "How are you involved in all this? What has he promised *you* to ensure we capitulate to what he wants?"

"Now wait just a moment," the solicitor blurted with a nervous hiccup. "I don't know what you're talking about."

Milosh hadn't said a word since they arrived. "Christina, lighten up," he ordered. "Give Philippe a chance to figure this all out. He's right - he's the only one of us who ought to be handling the financial side. He helped me liquidate Grandfather's savings account, and I'm going to have him review the real estate papers when we sell the building. Everything will be fine."

Christina stood and walked to the door. "You're an idiot, Milosh. You've always been simple, lazy and worthless. In a way you're worse than he is. He's always manipulated you, and today he's doing it again. If you want to trust him, then go right ahead. But you two will be doing it without me. It's two against one, Philippe, and as dumb as you think I am, I know one thing. Your cozy little lawyer can't give you a power of attorney unless my signature's on it. So you're fucked. I'll be watching you, Philippe. If I catch you cheating me, you're going back to prison."

Philippe's face turned bright red. He was livid. "I've never been in prison . . ."

"If you haven't, you damn well should have been. Save the crap for Milosh. He's always been your puppet, so he'll believe anything you say. I'm out of here." She slammed the door behind her.

Unaccustomed to seeing conflict in his own office, the lawyer nervously shuffled papers around on his desk. Then he said, "I suppose you won't need the power of attorney now, since Miss Lepescu refuses to sign it."

"Give us five minutes," Philippe told the solicitor.

"You can use the conference room . . ."

"I said give us five minutes! Get out! Shut the door behind you!" The terrified lawyer left his own office and sat in the anteroom with his assistant until the door opened and Philippe ordered him back.

When they were seated, Philippe said, "We'll execute the power of attorney now."

"But we must have Miss Lepescu sign . . ."

"It's all good. She dropped by while you were out of the room." Philippe pointed at the document. There was a scrawl on the line above Christina's printed name.

The solicitor gulped. Over the last few weeks he'd become totally under Philippe's control, but the lawyer was promised everything would stay solely between the two of them. Now a third person was here, seeing and hearing everything. He wasn't sure what to do next, but he was determined to save his reputation.

"With all due respect, Mr. Philippe, the signatures must be notarized . . ."

Philippe smiled cruelly. This little shrimp would do whatever he was told. Philippe signed his name and pushed the paper and pen to his brother. "Sign it," he said to Milosh, who did what he was told.

Philippe tossed the paper across the desk and said to the lawyer, "You're a notary. Look at the document. All three signatures are there. Now notarize it like a good boy and earn your money."

CHAPTER TWENTY-THREE

The Bad Man was furious. When people didn't do what he demanded, he went into a rage. Today had been one of those days. That lawyer was lucky. Sometimes people got hurt when they crossed him. Once in a while, it was a lot worse than that. In those instances, people really, really paid for what they had done. Permanently.

Those were the truly satisfying times, the ones when he got to come out and play. That was when all those months spent hiding deep inside the man's brain were rewarded. Very soon he'd play again.

———

Milosh was ashamed at what had happened in the solicitor's office. He felt used, dirty. As usual, Philippe had forced him to do something he didn't want to do, just as he had done with the attorney. Philippe was three years younger than Milosh, but even as children, his little brother held a power over him. Philippe had a natural ability to twist weak people until they did his bidding. It had never worked on Christina. She was the youngest, but she was strong-willed and she had never succumbed to his manipulations. Milosh ended up doing Philippe's dirty work. It had always been that way. Even today Milosh hadn't had the guts to stand up for what was right.

They stood on the sidewalk outside the young lawyer's office. Milosh simpered, "What are you going to do with that power of attorney? Have you found something else of Grandfather's?"

Philippe patted Milosh on the back condescendingly and said, "Just leave the details up to me, big brother. I've always taken care of things. You're the worrier, but everything's under control now. One bit of advice: I wouldn't mention any of this to Christina. I have a feeling she would think *you're* the bad guy in all this."

He hailed a taxi to the airport. As he glanced at Milosh standing there dejectedly, Philippe thought he looked exactly like Winnie the Pooh's gloomy friend Eeyore.

Where it had been uncertain, Philippe's future was now secure. His old partner Roberto Maas had given Philippe a partnership interest in a variety of investments, but all of those had quickly been undone when Philippe got caught embezzling. In Philippe's twisted mind, by canceling their partnership, Roberto had cheated Philippe out of what was rightfully his, out of what Roberto had given him. Roberto must pay, and he had. Philippe had made certain of that on a satisfying night in London when he'd started the fire.

Up to now his only asset was a few hundred thousand dollars. That wouldn't last long, given Philippe's intention to work as little and play as much as possible.

By noon the next day Philippe had emptied Nicu's safety deposit box at the Stadt Privatbank in Vienna. At the exchange rate for that day, his net worth increased by $6,182,677. That was enough to last a lifetime.

On top of the world, he had no idea how soon his fortunes would change.

CHAPTER TWENTY-FOUR

Paul Silver was a collector of rare and unique things that only he ever enjoyed. Given his past, no one else could ever know about them. There were men who still combed the world looking for him, and his well-known penchant for antiquities could betray him.

Years ago, long before he used the name Paul Silver, he had formed a shell corporation to buy a flat in Knightsbridge. Only steps from the famous Harrods department store, it was nestled on a quiet street he'd come to love. He'd displayed some of his collection there, spending hours admiring their beauty. Roberto was disappointed that he had to leave that place behind on the day he died. He couldn't risk keeping the flat or its contents. Even one unique object he kept from those days could tie Roberto and Paul Silver together, identifying both as one person. As far as his enemies would learn, Roberto had perished in a fire. Paul intended to keep it that way.

Thanks to shrewd planning years ago, his wealth remained intact. Paul Silver was the newest incarnation of the young Ukrainian boy who'd long ago killed a man, then systematically blackmailed a hundred Russian oligarchs. In total they paid over a hundred million dollars, and the boy incurred the eternal hatred of every one of them. Killers had stalked him constantly until that night when Roberto Maas died in a fire in St Mary Axe Street. Now he was free - he'd been transformed into a new person. Now his entire life had been rebuilt and his papers confirmed he was an American citizen.

Today he had a different home in London, one of five he maintained worldwide. The three-story Victorian townhouse he owned in Cadogan Square had been substantially altered to accommodate Paul's collecting habits. When he had decided to buy another home in London, he engaged one estate agent after another to show him potential properties. Nothing worked until the afternoon one lady walked him through a townhouse built in 1879 by an earl who was a member of the House of Lords. The place had just come on the market, and she thought it would go fast in this popular area of the West End.

Twenty minutes later Paul had nixed this one as well. Before they left, the agent said, "You may not be interested, but I want you to know that this house holds a secret."

"Really? And what would that be?"

"Come with me." She smiled slyly, hoping her picky client would find this interesting. She took him down a dark hallway on the top floor that ran the length of the house. Ornately carved wooden panels ran along both sides. The agent walked slowly, stooping to examine one panel after another until she found the one she was looking for. She knelt and pressed a barely visible notch near the bottom. The panel slid noiselessly aside to reveal a narrow stairway covered in dust.

"Rumor has it that the earl and his wife hid a mentally ill child up in the attic for years. They were embarrassed to have anyone know they had birthed a defective baby, so the boy was locked up like an animal until he died a decade later. Do you want to see it, or shall we go?"

"By all means, I want to see it."

His interest had surprised her. She'd shown Paul ten homes so far, and other agents had shown him many more. He didn't seem interested in anything; he appeared to be looking for some specific feature that he wouldn't reveal.

"I'll know when I find the right place," he had said, and at this moment he was more excited than he'd been the entire time since she'd met him.

The properties she'd shown the American were all listed at five million dollars or more, and she pre-qualified him to avoid wasting her time. A Cayman Islands bank's letter of reference attested to his ability to finance virtually any purchase he wanted, so she was willing to continue showing him houses until something struck his fancy. Even if it took a year, the commission on such a sale would be worth the wait.

The agent went first, cautioning Paul to watch his step on the steep risers. At the top of the narrow stairway she opened a door, a drawn-out creak revealing how long it had been since someone had come up here.

The attic was huge - it ran the entire length and width of the house. It was invisible from the street because it was behind a mansard roof with what looked to be dummy dormer windows. In fact, they were real but covered in so much dirt that very little light came through.

A bedroom suite was at one end of the room, and stuffing from a mattress was strewn everywhere. There were a few old dusty books on the floor, their covers partially chewed by the same rodents that likely had torn up the mattress. Some old boxes and a trunk sat in a dark corner.

"I realize it would take a lot of work to make this space anything you could use -"

Paul interrupted her. "I'll take it."

"I'm sorry, what did you say?"

"I said I'll take it."

She was astonished. This had never happened in her career. He'll *take it?* What did that mean? Clients usually feigned indifference even if they were interested. This one rather matter-of-factly said he'd take it.

"I . . . Uh, would you like me then to prepare an offer?"

"No. I'll pay the asking price. It will be all cash. Draw up the papers." And that was that.

He'd brought in a crew of workmen from France that he'd used before and trusted implicitly to discreetly remodel the attic into what he wanted. He could have used a contractor in London, but people tended to talk, and he wanted no one locally to know what was going on in the Cadogan Square townhouse.

Today the attic was bright and airy with a high ceiling that made it appear even more spacious. Light paint on the walls, new flooring and display cabinets built into a long wall had made it exactly what Paul wanted. The stairway was so narrow that everything had to be assembled in the attic itself - cases, shelving, long tables and workbenches had been dismantled, lugged upstairs and put back together. The room ended up part museum and part research center. Bookshelves were crammed full of reference material, and at one end of the room he had built a complete laboratory. Scientific instruments and machines rested on shelves, ready for whatever Paul Silver's next project required.

———

Last summer, front-page headlines had blared reports about a newly discovered Nazi gold train. There had been many trains in the later years of World War II that were filled with treasures - unique paintings, sculptures and relics stolen by the Reich from churches, synagogues, homes and offices of prominent collectors. As the Nazis rounded up Jews and shipped them off to camps, Hitler's handpicked men came in behind them, moving more than five million pieces of art and millions of dollars in gold to hiding places in Germany and occupied countries. A movie had even been made chronicling the adventures of the Allied soldiers who recovered the stolen artifacts.

The latest news centered on a long-forgotten tunnel in Poland. Ground-penetrating radar revealed what appeared to be a long train with cannons mounted on it, sitting inside the tunnel. The entrance had been sealed, the track removed, and many of the prisoners who built the tunnel later died under the Nazis. In the years since 1945, the train's location was lost and the story morphed into a local legend.

An old man who claimed to have been there when the train was hidden came forward at last. Near the town of Wroclaw, Poland, his story went, a ten-car train was driven into a mountain tunnel built expressly for this purpose. It contained looted gold, priceless artwork and gems, and it was still there today. The man's attorney was negotiating with Polish authorities, the article continued. He wanted a percentage of the recovery in exchange for revealing the train's exact location.

A true adventurer, Paul was fascinated by this sort of thing. He'd searched for the bones of King Arthur in London, the artifacts of an ancient civilization in Guatemala and been on a dozen other quests to find one-of-a-kind objects. The thrill of the search was as exciting as whatever he ended up finding.

Not everything in Paul Silver's twisted, labyrinthine life had turned out well. There had been losses along the way too. His father had sold him like a draft horse. Later the trusted friend who was his partner betrayed him. Paul had vowed never to allow anyone inside his heart and mind like that again . . . but it happened. Deep in the rain forests of Guatemala he fell in love, if that was what it had been, with a young anthropologist. She'd left him too, and he closed the door to his heart that day. The day he lost Hailey he promised himself never to open it again. Friends weren't necessary. All they did was cause pain, anguish and confusion. He needed none of those. He was perfect on his own, trusting only one person - himself.

Occasionally Paul used his vast wealth to accomplish the impossible. Everyone had a price. Some people were easily swayed so that a simple payoff worked. Others had noble aspirations for one cause or another. An incredibly generous donation from a wealthy stranger's foundation usually greased the wheels and made things happen.

After the story of the Nazi gold train surfaced, Paul visited the Ministry of the Interior in Berlin. The news report put the train in Poland, of course, but Berlin was the place to start. Paul wasn't really that interested in the particular train that had already made headlines. He believed if there was one train that had escaped detection for seventy years, there might be another.

A letter of introduction from a prominent banker in Munich got Paul an appointment with Franz Deutsch, Germany's Minister of the Interior. Since he kept substantial funds on deposit and was a valued customer, the president of the bank was only too happy to write a letter to his friend the minister.

Paul explained to the minister that the news of a gold train in Poland had piqued his interest. He had come here because he was considering a sizable donation to fund the search for similar stolen artifacts. "If there was one train hidden away in a mountain, why couldn't there be more? I'm hoping you can guide me to a proper non-profit organization where a donation could assist the recovery efforts."

Herr Deutsch assured him that would not be a problem, and he seemed genuinely grateful for Paul's generosity.

"Am I chasing rainbows? Do you think it's possible there could be other missing trains?" Paul asked.

"Of course," the official replied, happy to share his opinions with his new benefactor. "I think it's unlikely we will find anything more here in Germany because of how thoroughly the Allied troops scoured for assets when the war ended. In my opinion, one would be more likely to find still-hidden assets in the occupied countries."

Deutsch launched into a history lesson, which Paul enjoyed immensely. He'd heard some of it before, but most was new information.

"By the summer of 1942 the execution of Jews at Auschwitz was in full operation. As far as our research has shown, almost all the trains that the Nazis ran in those early years of the war carried humans. The Reich thundered across Europe, scooping up one country after another. Hitler's pact with Mussolini and the Fascists brought southern Europe into the Axis. By 1943 the Nazis were stealing gold, art, sculptures and anything else they could grab. Heavily guarded trains moved throughout the occupied countries, most destined for places in one town or another where the loot could be stashed. The Allies found a lot, as everyone knows, but more was destroyed as the Germans retreated. And if you want my personal opinion, there's more that hasn't been found.

"Hermann Göring was Hitler's handpicked man to supervise the 'acquisition,' as they put it, of artifacts from the occupation. Outright theft is the correct term for what Göring did," he spat venomously. He stopped talking for a moment to compose himself.

"I apologize, Herr Silver, that I cannot hide my feelings about the Nazi atrocities that were committed. Perhaps you have similar feelings. Are you Jewish, by chance?"

Paul hesitated. He was Ukrainian by birth and wasn't Jewish at all. Paul Silver wasn't even his name - it was simply one he'd chosen when it was time to switch from his last pseudonym. He wasn't sure whether it would help his case now to say he was a Jew or not.

Noting his silence, the minister said, "I'm afraid I've overstepped my bounds. I apologize. To explain, I am a Jew myself. My parents were among the last to be gassed at Auschwitz in October, 1944, three short months before the Soviets liberated the camp. It makes no difference to me if you are Jewish too; I was simply establishing whether you and I had similar interests in this matter."

"No offense taken," Paul responded with a warm smile, smoothly fabricating a story to fit the situation. "The reason I hesitated is that I'm an orphan. I never knew my parents and I was raised in Switzerland. Am I Jewish? I never really thought about it. I have no idea if the surname Silver was my parents' or if it was tacked onto me at the orphanage."

"Ah, I see. Millions of us became orphans too - myself included - when Hitler's men exterminated our parents and grandparents. What the Nazis did disgusts me more than I can ever express." He stopped, clearly overwhelmed with emotion even after all these years, took a deep breath and said, "Enough digression. Now I'm going to give you some information very few people know. Do you know what the Fuhrerbunker is?"

"Hitler's bomb shelter? I've read about it."

"Then you know it was built to be the most secure place in wartime Germany. The walls, floors and ceilings were solid concrete eight inches thick. It was a lavish air-raid shelter for prominent Nazis. Hitler and his mistress, Eva Braun, retreated there when the Allies swept into Germany and ended the war. Undoubtedly you know both committed suicide in the Fuhrerbunker."

"And it was all destroyed in 1959. Correct?"

Franz Deutsch smiled like a child with a secret. "Not exactly." He explained that a good deal of the bunker had indeed been destroyed at one time or another in the years following the war.

"The place was so well built even explosives couldn't fully destroy it. There's a lot left - a meandering maze of hallways and perhaps a hundred rooms. When the Allies destroyed part of the bunker, they found secrets. Some of the walls are false - there are hiding places everywhere. Hitler had much to hide, and some historians think the bunker still holds secrets. I can tell you this - I agree with them. It's just waiting for someone to investigate. No one's been inside for years."

"But the part where Hitler and his cronies had their quarters was destroyed, correct?"

"East Berliners weren't particularly forthcoming in those days, but if they can be believed, with the help of the Soviets they removed everything Hitler had gathered down there in his bunker - furniture, artwork and vast numbers of books, for instance. Anything the Reich had stolen was presumably returned to its owners and the rest ended up in boxes, now stored in the basement of the German Historical Museum. Were the Communists completely honest about what they took and what they did with it? You be the judge," he concluded with a cynical laugh.

"Mr. Silver, I'm willing to help you because you've offered to help me with a project that's very dear to my heart. I believe the Nazis stole far more from my people than has been recovered. If I may change the subject, could I hear your thoughts about what you are willing to contribute to help us continue searching?"

Paul spoke for fifteen minutes about the charitable work of a Swiss trust he'd become involved with several years ago. In reality it was his, lock, stock and barrel, but no one would ever be able to tie the trust to him. He explained that the trust funded archaeological projects and he occasionally suggested suitable avenues for grants. A contribution had recently helped him gain a concession to excavate at Piedras Negras, Guatemala, and he had made a significant find there, he told the minister.

"Perhaps we can do the same here," he said, wrapping up his presentation. "I'd like to ask them for a million dollars, with more later if needed. Would that be enough to help a renewed search for missing valuables?"

It certainly would, the minister said enthusiastically. Whatever Paul's involvement might be, Deutsch believed Paul had the power to influence the trust's donations. He told Paul about a non-profit that had been established in Munich for repatriation of stolen property from Jews and other displaced persons in occupied countries.

"I can think of no organization more highly respected or well run than this one. They will be good stewards of the trust's donation and use it well, I promise you."

"One more thing, Minister, if I may. I'd like to visit the Historical Museum. Are there items from the war that aren't on public display that I might be able to see? I'm thinking specifically about the logs of wartime train movements."

Herr Deutsch jotted a quick note on a letterhead, signed it and handed it over. "Hans Steffen is director of the museum. You'll find him a cordial man, full of information and willing to help in any way he can. Given your particular interest in the Nazi trains, ask him to see the records stored in the basement. I'm told many of them are detailed ledgers of train movements, kept by the stationmasters at major cities in Germany and the occupied countries. This note from me will allow you to see the off-limits storage facility."

Paul agreed to speak to the trustees and contact the minister about their decision. The minister was truly grateful for this American's help, and regardless of the outcome, he had already decided to give this man access to information no one had seen for decades, not even the minister himself. It wasn't for lack of desire, he reflected alone in his office. It simply hadn't been a priority. There was so much work to be done that the tantalizing Fuhrerbunker always got pushed to the back burner.

Maybe this American swashbuckler would find something interesting. The minister certainly hoped so.

———

Thanks to Herr Deutsch's note of introduction, Paul spent the next three days in the basement of the German Historical Museum. Like most others, it was a repository for a hundred thousand items of significance, most of which would never end up on public display. Steffen, the director, was a jovial man in his fifties who gave the introductory letter a quick glance and said with a smile, "The Minister of the Interior is my boss. Have to keep the boss happy, right? Your wish is my command, Herr Silver!"

Paul said he was here to learn more about the trains that had carried stolen things - gold, personal property, masterpieces of art and sculpture, relics taken from churches, and the like. He explained that the Nazi gold train article that made front-page headlines had caught his attention.

"I'm an amateur adventurer." That modest admission really wasn't true, since Paul had been involved with some unique discoveries in recent years. "If there is one gold train, who's to say there isn't another?"

The director said, "I agree. And I suppose you're particularly interested in Die Geisterbahn."

"Die Geisterbahn? The Ghost Train? I've never heard of it."

Steffen continued, "Not many people have. It was so secret that even today no record of it has ever turned up. Would you like to hear the legend?"

"I have all the time in the world for a treasure tale! I'm intrigued already just hearing the name!"

"The story goes like this. Nineteen forty-four was a disastrous year for the Axis powers. It marked the beginning of the end for the Reich. By late summer the Allies were advancing quickly. They had liberated places such as the Crimea, Rome and Cherbourg. They pounded cities in Italy with one bombing mission after another. German forces were retreating and surrendering all across Europe. Prisoners in concentration camps were being liberated. Do you see, Herr Silver? Everything was falling apart at once."

Steffen explained that for over a year trainloads of booty had been moved here and there at Hitler's whim, usually to hide things he wanted to display someday in his Fuhrermuseum. While this was happening, there was something else - a top-secret project called Operation Geist, the Ghost. According to the legend, a secret tunnel was under construction somewhere in occupied Europe. When it was finished, a long train would be driven inside, a train filled with riches beyond one's wildest dreams, to be hidden away until the ascendancy of the Fourth Reich. A new Germany would rise from the ashes of the Third Reich.

The tunnel was finished, a railroad junction was built, and everything was ready for Operation Geist to begin. If Germany faced defeat, Hitler had only to give the order and a train code-named Die Geisterbahn - the Ghost Train - would be loaded and sent to the secret location. The railroad siding would be dismantled, tracks removed, and everything would wait until the time was right.

By August 1944 Allied troops were so close to victory that Hitler ordered the implementation of Operation

Geist. Along with a fortune in gold bars, the Nazis would hide the most important paintings in existence - dozens of Old Masters created by the world's most famous artists. This would be the single most valuable shipment in history, and it would be shipped on a train.

"It was code-named the Ghost Train because it didn't officially exist. Presuming the legend is true, no one has any hint of where it is, even what country it might be in. Not a word about it has ever been found in Nazi records, although in fairness there are still thousands of things stored in the basement of this museum that have never been examined."

Paul commented, "I'm sure you've seen reports recently of a train hidden inside a mountain in Poland. Why couldn't that be the Ghost Train?"

"Here's what I think. The Soviets captured Warsaw in January 1945. The war was all but over for Germany by then, and by May they had surrendered. I think Operation Geist happened earlier, at the latest in summer 1944, and it wasn't in Poland. The Soviets were liberating concentration camps in Poland by then. The Allies could arrive at any moment. I'm ruling out Poland because the Ghost Train could have been seized before it ever got to its destination. I believe it's somewhere else.

"The train also wasn't hidden in Germany or Austria, I believe. Hitler couldn't risk putting it so close. If Germany and Austria surrendered, which was becoming ever more likely, the Allies would leave no stone unturned in the Fatherland. They would have found it. So where is it? I think it's in a more remote location, and it's not in central Europe. Bulgaria and Romania are my top choices. It also wouldn't have been hidden in a country occupied by the Fascists. If Hitler had wanted to put the train there, he would have had to ask his pal Mussolini. This was a top-secret German project, meant to ensure the existence of the Reich and the Reich alone. I can hear Hitler declaring, 'To hell with the Fascists!'"

He paused to take a breath. "Am I boring you to tears?"

Paul shook his head. "Are you joking? You can't stop now! This is getting more and more interesting by the minute." He was impressed by the director's research and the theories made perfect sense. "Please keep going!"

Steffen broke into a huge grin. He was as excited to tell the story as Paul was to hear it. His eyes sparkled with enthusiasm as he continued.

"I created a timeline of Allied victories in 1944. By that summer things were so bleak that Hitler had to realize defeat was imminent. He would have ordered Operation Geist, and Reichsmarschall Göring, the man in charge of handling stolen artwork, would have carried it out.

"Now about the recent news article, that Polish train story you mentioned. It'll take more than an old Nazi's tale to make me believe *that* train exists. He won't tell the government where the train is hidden until they promise him a big cut. He claims to have been there in 1945 and he saw the train himself. I don't believe it. Why did he wait until he's an old man to reveal the secret? Why didn't he go get the train in the sixties or the seventies, when he was young and could have enjoyed his treasure? I'm a total skeptic about the Polish train, but on the other hand, I firmly believe the Ghost Train exists."

He leapt from his chair. "The more I think about this, the more excited I get. Enough talk for now! Ready to begin your adventure? Follow me!"

They took an elevator down two floors to a huge room crammed with rows of floor-to-ceiling shelving. Each row was numbered, and thousands of boxes were arranged neatly on the shelves, each of those carrying an identifying number. It took Steffen only a moment to guide Paul to the correct area.

"All the boxes beginning with 44 and 45-GUT are the ones you'll be interested in, I think. Forty-four is the year 1944. That's when the Nazis started moving plunder to tunnels and caves where the Allies wouldn't find them. GUT stands for *Güterwagen*, or freight car in English. These boxes hold stationmaster logs - the records of train movements throughout the Axis nations. They're very detailed; there will be a train, then a detailed listing of every single car on it and what the cargo was. I looked at a few and found them interesting but ultimately boring as hell, frankly. I hope your search is more intriguing!"

He showed Paul to a table and chair provided for researchers and handed him a business card. "Here's my cell phone number. I'll be upstairs in my office. Just call if you need anything and I'll come right down. Don't keep me wondering, Paul! Let me know if you stumble across something interesting! I won't get any work done today anyway, knowing you're down here searching for treasure!"

From more than a dozen boxes marked with the "GUT" designation, Paul picked the earliest. Inside were five huge ledgers, each containing page after page of handwritten entries. A natural linguist, Paul's fluency in German allowed him to easily read the line items. The cover of the top book in that box bore the name "Hamburg" and the code 44-GUT-058. The first page showed the beginning and ending dates of the book and the stationmaster's name. Each also had a legend explaining abbreviations for the cargo in each car. Although he had prepared himself for what he knew he'd see, it was nevertheless a sobering reflection on those dark days of human history to observe what the trains had carried. Before the war, freight trains in western European countries moved cattle, machinery, automobiles, oil and the like. Now that the war was underway, these Nazi trains transported far different cargoes.

There were two dozen abbreviations. Some were the usual ones for livestock or timber. But there were others. He saw GO for gold. ST stood for *Statuen*, or statues. Paintings were abbreviated GE for *Gemälden*.

Then he saw ones that engulfed him in sadness. JU represented *Juden*, the Jews. PG stood for *politischer Gefangene*, political prisoners. Thousands of human beings became two-letter entries in a stationmaster's ledger book.

Each page represented one train. At the top was a one- or two-line header with the train's name, registration number, origin city and destination city. Below the header were ten, twenty, sometimes fifty lines. Each line was one train car with abbreviations for its cargo.

Paul flipped through a few pages. There were many entries whereby an entire train carried the cargo *Juden*.

Jews. Human cargo was moved from towns all over occupied Europe to camps such as Topovske Supe, Serbia, or Kistarccsa, Hungary, just two of many concentration camps the trains went to. One showed up the most - Oswiecim, a Polish name he recognized immediately. In German it was called Auschwitz, the horrific Nazi extermination camp where so many Jews had perished.

There was a trove of information in these ledgers. Many of the listings indicated the boxcars were filled with artwork and the like. Other trains carried nothing but gold bullion.

On the afternoon of the third day he was still poring through boxes. He had looked through the logs for the station at Sofia, Bulgaria, but he saw nothing that would indicate the Ghost Train might have been hidden there. At last there was only one box left. He pulled it off the shelf and opened it. The first book's cover said "Bucharest." This box would contain the ledgers from occupied Romania.

Something got his attention immediately. Unlike Sofia, Bucharest was one of the few terminals where trains offloaded cargo for storage. He'd seen it in some other books - an entry would record an incoming train loaded with goods. It would arrive and stay for a week. Or perhaps its cargo would be stored, then moved onto a different train. None of these trains carried prisoners - their cargoes were always plunder, the spoils of victory.

Last night one thought had kept Paul awake. If trains offloaded cargo at a station, how did the Nazis ensure the safety of that valuable cargo? Now, as he read entry after entry describing storage in Bucharest, he wondered about it again.

He'd been sitting for two hours and he needed a break, so he took the elevator to Hans Steffen's office. Paul asked how the Nazis protected their gold and artwork.

Steffen explained, "It was fairly simple. During my research, I learned how it worked. Local citizens were terrified of the brutal Nazis who guarded the trains. If people even got close to a boxcar, they'd be shot. Despite the inherent security created by the guards themselves, a few train stations - Berlin, Vienna, Prague, Belgrade and Bucharest, for example - were outfitted with secure, heavily guarded rooms where Nazi plunder was stored short-term. Maybe it would be there for a day - maybe a week. Once instructions were received from Göring, the cargo would be on its way somewhere else.

"The larger things - artwork, statues and the like - often remained in the boxcars. Gold bars were always offloaded into these vaults. The rooms were so well-constructed and so closely monitored that there is no record of a single bar ever being lost."

Understanding it now, Paul returned to the basement. He finished skimming the other books from Bucharest and saw nothing special. As he started to replace the ledgers in their box, he noticed a piece of paper lying in the bottom. Apparently there had been another book, but now there was simply a placeholder where it had once been stored.

44-GUT-1411
January 2, 1944
August 31, 1944
Nicu Lepescu, SS
Stationmaster
Bucharest, Romania
This ledger has been moved to the Fuhrerbunker at the request of Reichsmarschall Göring
August 31, 1944

He studied the piece of paper for several minutes, not fully comprehending what this could mean.

An SS officer named Lepescu had been stationmaster? Could it be possible? Lepescu was a common Romanian surname. Was it simply a coincidence? As he'd done often in the past three days, Paul used his phone to search the web. He entered *Nicu Lepescu, Nazi* and *1944*. The answer confirmed it: Nicu Lepescu was indeed stationmaster from January 2 until the Soviets entered Bucharest on August 31. He also was a Nazi storm trooper, a member of the SS elite, and he had served at Auschwitz under Commandant Rudolf Hoess before being transferred to Romania.

When the Red Army liberated Bucharest, Nicu Lepescu was presumed to be a mere stationmaster. Therefore he was not detained or questioned. In 1951, the Allies learned he had been an official at Auschwitz and was one of Hitler's Nazi storm troopers. He was arrested for war crimes, convicted and spent twenty years in prison.

The article ended with a biography. Paul homed in on a single word.

Ciprian.

Nicu Lepescu had had a son named Ciprian. Was this the same Ciprian Lepescu whose own son had been named Philippe, the man who had been Paul's thieving partner a couple of years ago? He'd have to search public records to find that out. First he must finish his research here. This missing book, the record of Stationmaster Lepescu, suddenly became the one book Paul wanted to find.

CHAPTER TWENTY-FIVE

Paul took the piece of paper to Director Steffen's office. "This was in the bottom of the last box from Romania. Is this book in the archives somewhere?"

Steffen read the words at the bottom. "Hmm. Göring ordered the book sent over to the bunker. Apparently there was something in the ledger he wanted the Fuhrer to see." He sat back in his chair, deep in thought, then said, "To answer your question, there's no way to be sure if it's here. We must ask several more questions ourselves. First, was the book actually taken to the Fuhrerbunker, and if so, was it there when the Allied forces captured Berlin? Why would Reichsmarschall Göring, the man in charge of all train movements, have this particular book sent over for the Fuhrer's personal attention? What made this book different from a hundred others you've already looked through?

"Next we must ask if the Soviets and the East Germans actually removed everything from the Fuhrerbunker before they destroyed part of it in 1951. They were under strict orders to bring everything from the bunker here for permanent archiving. Did they follow those orders? If they didn't, where did some of it go? Were there things accidentally left behind in the Fuhrerbunker, or were things stolen, or were there things so well hidden in the bunker that they were never found? Things that might be there today?"

With a mischievous grin, he paused for a moment to let his words sink in. "Do you see how complicated your simple question really is? Is the book here? I can give you a simple answer, possibly an accurate one. Let's see if it was logged into our inventory." He made several entries on his keyboard.

"According to the inventory of items transferred to this museum from the Fuhrerbunker - and there were over ten thousand, by the way - book 44-GUT-1411 is not here. If we assume the East German records are correct - and that's a big assumption - then that book was not delivered to this museum. Where is it? The bunker? Your guess is as good as mine. So many things of the Nazis simply disappeared at the end of the war. Every Allied soldier wanted a souvenir. Some took little things - medals with swastikas, or pictures of Hitler, or books. Some higher-ranking soldiers took more important things such as papers signed by Der Fuhrer and personal articles of Nazi officials. They weren't supposed to do that, but it was crazy in the occupied countries and everyone was too busy to care.

"Could someone have stolen this book? Perhaps, although I would say not. As you've already seen, the ledgers are bulky and boring, nothing but one handwritten entry after another. If I had to bet, I'd say someone glanced at the book, decided it was worthless and tossed it into the trash. Then again, maybe it's still in the bunker somewhere. Who knows? I'll tell you this - there are things yet to be found in the Fuhrerbunker. I'm certain of that. Indulge me until we are there together in person. Then I'll tell you more legends of Hitler's bunker!"

CHAPTER TWENTY-SIX

A month after their initial meeting, Paul and Herr Deutsch, the Minister of the Interior, were at lunch in Berlin. Paul had delivered his part of the bargain; the Munich non-profit the minister suggested was wealthier by one million dollars, funds that would greatly assist its efforts to recover property stolen during the war. Now Deutsch was ready to give Paul what he wanted - access to the Fuhrerbunker. Although he hadn't specifically said what Paul would be allowed to do, there was a clear inference that nothing would be off-limits.

"I'm not sure what you're going to find when you visit the part of the Fuhrerbunker that wasn't destroyed," Herr Deutsch explained. "Although I haven't been there, I've read reports about it. I firmly believe there are things still hidden there. Given its vast size, there almost has to be. What that could be, only the Nazis knew. I trust you will enjoy looking around. And I will be most interested to hear if you come across anything that might be significant."

That lunch had been two days ago. Today Paul walked down a dimly lit corridor led by Hans Steffen, the museum director who had quickly become his friend. The cool, dank passageway was thirteen feet below a parking lot right in the middle of modern Berlin. Steffen explained that the concrete steps they'd descended and this long, narrow hallway were constructed in the 1970s, years after the partial destruction of the Fuhrerbunker. Electric lights strung along the ceiling cast eerie shadows on the walls.

The director said, "After the Soviets blew up Hitler's quarters, someone in the government decided there should be a proper entryway to the remainder of the shelter, so the East Germans built this."

"What keeps someone from looting the rest of the bunker?"

"It's not a problem. In a moment you'll see why."

They walked a hundred feet and came to a solid iron door as tall and wide as the passage itself. It totally blocked the corridor.

The museum director didn't know exactly who this distinguished guest was, but it didn't matter. The Minister of the Interior himself - Steffen's ultimate boss far up the line - had personally ordered this tour, including a visit to a place no one was allowed to enter. Steffen himself had never gone further than the iron door where they stood. Today that would change, and he was excited that this VIP visitor would finally give Hans the chance to see what he'd only heard tales about.

He explained, "The Russians first tried to eradicate the entire bunker in 1947, but it was so solidly built only a few corridors were damaged. There would be another attempt in 1951. With help from the Russian forces, the East Germans finally cleaned out Hitler's personal quarters in 1959, blew it up, and once again they tried to destroy the rest of the compound. The Fuhrerbunker was so well made and extensive that they gave up, took everything they wanted and installed this massive door. The records from the time indicate there's nothing behind it except worthless items of no value."

He pulled a document from his back pocket, unfolded it several times and spread it in front of Paul. "This was found after the war. Here's what's behind the door."

Paul saw an architect's floor plan of the massive Fuhrerbunker system. Steffen pointed to the bottom corner - there was the date March 1944, a swastika and the signature of Albert Speer, Hitler's master architect. Someone had marked on the plan. There was a black X through the portion of the bunker that was destroyed in 1947, and a series of red Xs marked the area blown up in 1959. The rest of the bunker, a vast area behind the door where they were standing, appeared to be intact.

The plan showed a series of hallways. If laid out straight, they'd have been maybe a mile long. It was a maze of corridors and rooms. Some rooms had tiny notations in faded German, the words so faint they were almost unreadable.

Paul touched the heavy door and its two enormous padlocks. "How often has this been opened?"

"Never. It hasn't been opened since 1959. It requires a ministerial-level authorization to open it. There's been a question for years as to where the keys even are. As you can see, the padlocks are far too large for bolt cutters. If they couldn't be opened, it would require days, maybe weeks with a torch to cut through the thick steel. As far as anyone knows, the keys have been missing for years."

Paul was disappointed. "Really? I thought I was going to get to see it . . ."

The museum director interrupted him with a laugh. "I'm joking. You were sent to me by a minister, correct? Herr Deutsch, the Minister of the Interior himself, told me to show you whatever you wanted to see. He said you were interested in some archival material from the war. So far we haven't accommodated your interest very well, have we? Except for the museum basement, you haven't seen archives. I must correct that immediately. Let's see if there are some here!" He had a sly grin on his face, like a child waiting to open a birthday present.

Steffen reached in his jacket pocket and withdrew a rusty key ring a foot in diameter. It could have been a prop from a production of Macbeth. On it was a huge old key.

"Do you want to see more?" he said with a sparkle in his eye. "I've kept this key safely in my desk for twenty years, just waiting for someone like you to come along!"

He's as excited as I am, Paul thought. "Absolutely!"

"All right then. I've been patient for years, hoping for a time when I could visit this place. I would never be allowed to merely open this door and enter. But *you* - now that's another story! The minister himself told me to extend every courtesy. And I'm pleased to be accompanying you!"

Paul pointed to the iron door. "So what do you think? Do you believe there are things still stored in there?"

"I doubt it, but what I think doesn't matter. Today we both will find out for ourselves! According to the stories, we shouldn't find anything of value. There were many reports from those who were here when this door was built. All of them say the same thing. The Soviets removed everything and imploded the bunker, but they left this part unscathed. They built this door, intending to return some day and finish. One thing or another got in the way, including the fall of the Berlin Wall and the collapse of the Soviet Union. One day you look around and *whoosh* - fifty years have passed since the iron door was last opened. Until today!"

The man inserted the key into the first padlock and tried to turn it. It wouldn't budge.

"Just in case." He grinned, pulling a small can of lubricant from another pocket. He sprayed it liberally inside each lock.

When he tried again, the key turned and the old padlock snapped open. He repeated the process on the second lock with the same result.

"Are you ready to take a step back in time?" he asked his American visitor.

"Ready!"

"Give me a hand." They grasped two handles on the door and began to tug. It moved very slowly, its hinges having sat motionless for fifty-five years, but finally it swung open.

"Now this *is* exciting! Those damned Russians lied, didn't they?" The museum director beamed as he looked down the hallway. "I already see more than I ever expected!"

CHAPTER TWENTY-SEVEN

The corridor continued, but there was no illumination. They could see only a few feet down the hall, and what they saw was a huge mess. There were boxes, papers and books tossed all around. The floor was littered with debris and broken furniture. It was as though someone had been looking for something specific and destroyed everything while trying to find it.

Paul didn't understand the director's sudden exhilaration. "They certainly left this place a wreck. What do you see that you didn't expect?"

"I imagine that will be the first of many." Steffen aimed his light at a painting lying forgotten against a wall, its frame broken and canvas ripped. "Where there's one, I'm hoping there are more!"

He pulled two flashlights from his satchel, passed one to Paul and said, "I feared the lights wouldn't work after all these years. Shall we?" He waved Paul inside and followed behind him.

The corridor was wide and had fifteen-foot ceilings, along which ran pipes and cables. There was a musty smell from decades of neglect, and the side walls were slightly damp. Paul knocked on a wall - it was drywall nailed to studs. Every twenty or thirty feet there was a door, many of which stood open. Paul looked inside the nearest one, shining his light around. It reminded him of his college chemistry lab. It was a classroom - there were chalkboards at the front and a lectern next to a long table fitted with a sink and running water. There were a dozen tables for students, each with its own water supply. Test tubes and pipettes sat in racks, and beakers sat over Bunsen burners in wire holders. Except for a thick layer of dust, the room looked ready for class to resume momentarily.

"How strange," Paul commented. "Why a classroom here?"

"There were a lot of classrooms. Hitler made sure everything was prepared. This bunker was designed to house the leaders of the Reich and their families for months - perhaps even a year - if the Allies bombed Berlin into oblivion. If the Third Reich was defeated, Hitler was ready to launch the Fourth. That's why he hid gold and expensive objects all around. He also intended to see to the children's educations while everyone was living underground."

Paul stooped to pick up the painting. It was roughly two by three feet in size and the canvas had been ripped, perhaps by a knife. He didn't recognize the artist. It was modern art, which meant Hitler considered it degenerate. Paul heard how Nazi forces barged into the artists' homes, ensuring they weren't breaking the law by continuing to paint pictures unsuitable for German citizens to see. Jewish artists were particularly targeted, he recalled, but others had suffered censorship too, including masters such as Vincent Van Gogh.

He turned the painting over and saw something written on the frame. R2109.

He showed it to Hans. "Any idea what this is?"

"Of course. I wouldn't be much of a curator if I didn't. That's a Nazi registration mark. This was the two thousand one hundred ninth painting stolen from the Rothschilds in France in 1941, duly noted by some Nazi soldier at the time. Look how badly this one was treated. This artist obviously wasn't one of Hitler's favorites."

Steffen's excitement was rubbing off on Paul. "Now that you've seen this, are you more optimistic we may find something interesting?"

"As we've discussed, in theory we shouldn't find anything special. At one time there were many paintings in the Fuhrerbunker - Hitler had his favorites brought here, some straight from the walls of museums. Those were undoubtedly removed. But I told you there are over a hundred rooms still extant; this part is unchanged since it was walled up. This section of Berlin was assigned to Russia in the partition. Soviet troops were here regularly from the end of the war until the barricade was constructed. Most likely they took whatever they wanted.

"Seeing this castoff painting excited me because it shows that things really were left behind. One man's trash, as the saying goes, might be another's treasure. I told you I'd give you more stories about the Fuhrerbunker. One lingering rumor is that troops never finished their search down here. It was simply too big, and don't forget the tales of hidden rooms! After the war the Allies were involved in rebuilding Germany, divvying up the former occupied countries and restarting the economies of governments that had been overrun by the Nazis. This place wasn't important enough - and the troops didn't have enough time - for a scouring. That's my opinion. Should we find anything interesting? No. Will we? I've waited years to find out!"

Paul's adrenalin was flowing. He was glad to see the museum director excited over the possibilities. In all his adventures there had been nothing like what might lie down this corridor. He stood at square one of a warren of rooms that might hold treasures of precious metals, lost paintings and sculptures, or perhaps something even more interesting.

He had to stop daydreaming. There was work to do and little time in which to do it. The minister had given him carte blanche to explore the bunker, but nothing lasts forever. As much as Hans was enjoying this, Paul knew the director couldn't stay with him for long. After all, his job was to run the state museum. It also wasn't likely Hans would allow Paul down here unsupervised. Paul had to wisely use the short time he might have.

After that first afternoon, the director had fixed their lighting issue. Now a five-hundred-foot extension cord snaked down the passageway to a portable LED light on a stand. Although that was a huge help, it mainly served to illuminate the incredible mess the departing Soviet soldiers had left in this part of the Fuhrerbunker. The rooms - offices, dormitories for workers, living suites for officers, kitchens and more classrooms - were in significantly more disarray than Steffen had anticipated.

"Why would they turn over bunk beds, pull ovens out and tear chalkboards from the wall? Were they simply out to destroy everything, even the furnishings?"

Paul answered, "I don't think so. I think they were looking for things. You mentioned there have always been rumors of hidden rooms. Maybe that's why they tore off the chalkboards - to see if anything was behind them. Same thing with pulling out an oven - behind there might have been a good place to hide something."

Steffen nodded. "You're probably right. Presuming they didn't find everything, we have a challenge. With as many rooms as we have here, we could be exploring for the next ten years. I have an idea - it may not work at all, but it's worth a try." He pointed at the diagram of the bunker. "This plan wasn't intended for public viewing, and it was probably what the builders used when they built the bunker. If that's correct, even hidden rooms might appear on here because they were part of the original construction. There are lots of closets attached to rooms. Not every room has one, but some rooms do. Let's start there. Using the plan, let's pick a room with closets and see what we find."

The closets in the first three rooms they chose had doors wide open, contents pulled off shelves and thrown everywhere, just like they had seen earlier. So far Hans's theory wasn't working. Far down the corridor they came to another room. This one was an office with four desks, some chairs, bookshelves and filing cabinets. As they had seen before, debris was all over the floor.

Hans looked around for a moment and then consulted his plan. Pointing across the room, he said, "The

150

closet should be right over there." But there was merely a solid wall.

Paul walked along the wall, knocking every few inches. It was solid for a while, but then he heard a hollow sound. He continued pounding up and down as Hans directed his flashlight.

"A stud finder would help," Paul commented.

"Tomorrow we will have one!"

Paul had seen the bare walls behind the destroyed chalkboards, so he knew that every meter there would be a stud. He turned to Hans and asked, "Mr. Director, may I have your permission to kick in this wall?"

Steffen laughed and nodded. "Of course. There's no one stopping you!"

After a quick calculation, Paul raised his foot and gave the wall a solid kick. The drywall gave way, and he did it a few more times until there was a hole large enough to see through.

"We need some tools," he panted.

"Tomorrow we will have those too!" The director aimed his light through the hole. The secret room was two meters square, exactly as the floor plan showed it would be. There were several wooden boxes stacked on the floor and covered by a layer of dust. Like eager playmates they began to rip chunks of the drywall off with their bare hands. Soon they had removed enough to step between the studs.

They both squeezed into the narrow space, neither willing to miss this opportunity. Hans brushed dirt off the top of the nearest box. There were stenciled words and an insignia.

They saw a coat of arms and read the words: *Service chine de Louis Capet et son epouse. Chateau de Versaillles, Juillet 1792. Encadre douze des vingt.*

"Do you read French?" Hans Steffen asked his visitor, his voice quivering slightly.

"I do. And you?"

"Yes. Yes, I do." Hans brushed off a second box and saw almost identical stenciling. He placed his hands on the first box and spoke reverently.

"China service of Louis Capet and his wife. Versailles palace, July 1792. Box twelve of twenty." He pointed to the other box he'd wiped. "That's box fourteen." He counted the boxes quickly. "There are twenty. They're all here." He paused, momentarily speechless. Clearly overwhelmed, he choked back a sob.

"Do you recognize the coat of arms?"

Paul shook his head. "But if I remember my European history, isn't Louis Capet the birth name of the Bourbon monarch Louis XVI, the last king of France? If that's correct, then his wife would be Marie Antoinette."

"You are correct and this is his coat of arms. This china service has been unaccounted for since the end of World War II. Most scholars thought it was destroyed by the Nazis, but now we know better!" His face glowed as he thought of what else might be hidden down these dark hallways. "After waiting my entire life to see this, I think we've done pretty well in our adventure so far." He chuckled.

After spending several more hours fruitlessly searching for another hidden room, they stopped for the day. Every small closet on the floor plan had turned out to be exactly that. There were no more surprises.

They went straight to work the next morning, exploring for hours with no success. So far the tools Hans had brought were getting no use. Just when they were getting discouraged, things looked up. Around one, they found another secret room.

They were in a commercial kitchen with six huge ovens, prep tables, massive dishwashers and row after row of cabinets lined with large tin cans. Most of the labels had come off and dropped to the floor, but some still had theirs. There were green beans, boiled potatoes, tomatoes and the like. The entire place was ready for cooking 1940s-style.

As they'd done fifty times already, they consulted the floor plan. They saw the closet immediately. Its door was ajar and it was filled with what might have been linen tablecloths and napkins. The decades of musty storage had taken a toll on the cloth: everything disintegrated at the touch of a finger.

After a quick look around, Paul said, "Ready for the next room?"

Hans was poring over the floor plan, turning it in one direction then another. "This room has two closets. The second one should be over there where the shelves are."

They threw can after can onto the floor. When the shelves were empty, Paul tried to move them, but they were solidly attached to the wall. Hans tossed him a crowbar and took another for himself. They pried from the sides, and before long the wooden shelf fell forward with a tremendous bang and a huge cloud of dust. Behind the shelf was a bare wall where a door should be. More drywall was ripped away, and soon they found the next cache.

This room was crammed full of boxes. They tore open several - each was packed with brand-new one-thousand-Reichsmark notes from the 1940s.

"There's no telling how much money's here," Paul remarked. "Many millions of Reichsmarks. These are worthless today, aren't they?"

Hans shook his head. "They aren't legal tender anymore, but in this condition collectors would pay a lot for them. You'd drive down the value, of course, if you introduced a million banknotes into the numismatic marketplace at one time. But that's not what should happen to these. While we've been exploring, I've been thinking what should be done here. This part of the Fuhrerbunker needs to become an annex of the German Historical Museum. People need to view the things we've found, exactly as they were discovered."

Paul had been thinking along the same lines, he admitted. And he'd come to respect Hans Steffen more and more as they worked together. The director's excitement at their quest was every bit as high as Paul's own.

"If we don't find anything more than we've already seen, it would make a great museum," he agreed. "Once this is all over, I'm willing to provide the initial funding to make it happen. I'll talk to the minister if that's agreeable to you."

"Oh yes," Steffen bubbled, thinking what a blessing it was that this American had come into his life.

As they moved from room to room, they found more ruined artwork, hundreds of books and a vast array of household goods suitable for a hotel that expected a few hundred guests. That was what the Fuhrerbunker was, after all, and it had been completely outfitted for the arrival of the Nazi elite, who ultimately never checked in.

Paul found everything interesting, but he still held out hope for the one thing he'd started this journey to find - Nicu Lepescu's missing stationmaster ledger.

CHAPTER TWENTY-EIGHT

Last night over dinner Paul had joked, "How much longer are you going to be able to explore with me before the minister makes you go back to your real job?" This was the first time they'd eaten a meal together - a few beers and some good food made the conversation flow easily, and they became even better friends. Paul learned Hans's life story, and Hans in turn heard the background Paul had manufactured for himself.

Paul knew this couldn't last much longer, although neither of them had heard a word from the Minister of the Interior as of yet. Once Hans was pulled off the project, Paul's time here would be finished as well.

"I haven't spoken with Herr Deutsch lately, and I don't intend to call him anytime soon," Hans had laughingly responded. "Maybe he's forgotten I'm not at my desk anymore. What if he's decided he can do without me? Do you need a good museum director, Herr Silver?" That had brought forth a boisterous guffaw from Paul.

By late morning they were examining the sixty-eighth room in the bunker. This was another dormitory full of bunk beds with mattresses torn and sagging from years of neglect. Hans pointed to a door. "There's a bathroom through there and there will be a linen closet in it."

But there wasn't. As they'd discovered twice before, there was no door where one should have been.

Again they broke through drywall to find a hidden room. This one was different. For Paul this one was far more exciting than Louis XVI's china or a roomful of banknotes.

This room was packed full of books.

Hans cleared off a table in the dormitory to hold the volumes they were bringing out. Some were individually wrapped in paper or cloth; others were in boxes. Most were simply sitting on shelves that reminded them of stacks in a library.

Paul was inside, passing books through the narrow space between the stud walls. Like everything else, they were dusty, but they appeared to be without substantial damage. The ones he'd seen so far seemed in remarkably good condition.

After passing out books and boxes for a while, Paul came out to take a look. Most of the works had beautiful bindings, some with lavish illustrations and gold writing in Latin or French. Some appeared very old while others were more recent.

Hans had opened one of the boxes on the table. There were two identically bound books inside. He took one out and examined it closely.

"Do you know what this is?"

Paul looked at the cover. It appeared to be leather and it was undecorated, simple and plain. "No. Do you?"

Hans pointed at the spine, at a certain word.

Gutenberg.

Paul was astounded. "This is one of Gutenberg's Bibles?"

The director nodded and opened the book. Each page had line after line of Latin with lavish illustrations and initials. It was beautiful and in pristine condition.

Pointing to the other book in the box, Paul asked, "Are there two of them? That one looks identical!"

"I know a little about these Bibles because we have one in our museum too," Hans replied. "You'll recall that Gutenberg was the first to print multiple copies of a book using moveable type. You may not know that some of his books were printed on paper - as was the one we have in the museum - but ones like these were printed on vellum. It's much heavier than paper stock. It took two volumes for the entire Bible, with a split after the Psalms. Only four complete vellum sets are known to exist today, although I'd wager at this moment we've just found set number five."

"I'll be damned. Where do you think this one came from?"

"Let's break for lunch. I have a story to tell you about Johannes Gutenberg's Bible."

Paul loved history. Although the Gutenberg Bible wasn't what he was here to find, he was keenly interested in the lesson Hans was about to deliver.

"You asked me where the Bibles we found came from," he began. "We'll have to do considerable examination to be sure, but I'd be surprised if this wasn't the missing copy from Mainz. There was a wonderful Gutenberg Museum there before the war, and it still exists today. That museum owned the finest Gutenberg Bible set on vellum in the world. Mainz was a major trade city, and over the centuries it had built up a substantial Jewish population. In 1942, at the same time the Nazis began systematically rounding up Jewish citizens of Mainz, the Allies began an extensive bombing campaign against the city.

"By late 1942, major buildings in Mainz were being destroyed almost nightly, and a few major Jewish benefactors of the Gutenberg Museum decided to remove the Bibles for safekeeping. According to the story, they were put into a simple box. I think we found that box today. Fascinating!"

Paul couldn't have agreed more. Their food arrived, but he barely nibbled at his meal. He was captivated by the story and urged Hans to keep going while they ate.

"From here the story gets more speculative," Steffen confessed. "Everything I've told you up to now is fact, but where the books went next isn't clear. One account has the benefactors giving the Bibles to the Bishop of Mainz, a known Jewish sympathizer who helped many of them escape from Germany. Another says they were hidden in the lavish basement of a Jewish home. Wherever they went, I think we've just put together the end to the story. Now that we've found the box, I believe the Nazis found the books, someone fortunately understood their significance, and yet another priceless treasure was shipped to the Fuhrerbunker for the personal collection of Adolf Hitler."

"Aren't they among the most valuable books in the world?"

"They certainly are, and the books we found today are the most beautiful and well-preserved examples I've ever seen. The minister will be very pleased to hear about this!"

Paul was eager to return to the bunker. They had spent almost no time in the first hidden rooms; they left the china and currency for others to deal with. This discovery was different. They went through the books carefully, one by one. Paul was on a mission to find the lost record of Nicu Lepescu's tenure as stationmaster.

The rest of the afternoon was a bibliophile's dream. Only the most important things the Nazis stole were good enough to warrant the attention of the Fuhrer. These books were a treasure trove of first editions in French, English, German and Russian. Dostoyevsky, Shakespeare, Bacon, Poe, Dickens, Thoreau - the most important nineteenth-century authors were all represented in beautiful volumes, most of them autographed. These were wonderful old books, lovingly collected by people whose lives had been wrenched from complacency into terror by their government.

Hans and Paul marveled over the things they found, but Paul was beginning to think he was totally on the wrong track. These books were museum-quality items, similar in rarity to the paintings by Picasso and Renoir that had been in the bunker. All this was fascinating, but he was looking for something else. Where would an ordinary, commonplace book - a train ledger - have been stored, and why had it been brought to the Fuhrer's attention in the first place? As they saw more and more wonderful books, he worried that the one he wanted most wasn't here at all.

Given their magnitude, it was impossible to keep these discoveries to themselves. The minister had asked Paul to keep him advised of their progress, and Paul knew he'd be as interested as they were to see the hidden rooms and their contents. At the end of the day he made the call.

First thing next morning Paul and Hans met the minister at the entrance to the Fuhrerbunker. Herr Deutsch was tantalized at what they wanted to show him. Paul had been deliberately evasive, revealing only that they had found some very interesting things in three secret rooms. The minister had rearranged his schedule immediately. This was top priority, and he was giddy with anticipation as Director Steffen opened the two huge padlocks and they stepped inside the tunnel.

An hour later the minister's tour was finished. They had found more than he ever expected, and he had been speechless throughout much of the visit. Outside on the plaza, Herr Deutsch effusively praised Paul and Hans, thanking them for their excellent work and incredible discoveries. Paul asked how much longer Hans could accompany him, and without hesitation the minister agreed to as much time as was necessary to complete the examination. He laughed and slapped the museum director on the back, telling Steffen to make sure his job duties were covered while he was off playing detective and archaeologist.

The minister assigned a contingency of soldiers to guard the bunker around the clock. More militia would come in the next few days to remove the china and books. Those would go to the museum's laboratory for examination and eventual public display. The currency was going to the Bundesbank, the central bank of Germany, where it would be held securely until officials determined its disposition. With a wave, a satisfied Herr Deutsch left as Paul and Hans descended into the bunker to continue their work.

They went back to the books. As he sorted through volume after volume in the dim light, Hans came across a book he instantly recognized. It was a train ledger, identical to dozens stored at his museum. He shined the beam of his torch on the cover. Bucharest. 44-GUT-1411. *The missing book!* He opened the cover and a scrap of paper fluttered out. Hans picked it up and read the words on it.

While Hans worked inside the secret room, Paul was outside cataloging the ones they brought out earlier. He heard Hans say something through the wall, but the words were muffled.

"Sorry, I didn't quite hear you," he shouted.

"I said, I think I've found something you'll want to see. Take a look at this." Hans reached through the wall and handed Paul the note from inside the ledger. As Paul read it, Hans stepped out. He saw Paul's smile. *This is what he's been waiting for,* the director knew.

Paul translated the German words *Mein Führer, hier ist der Hauptbuch für die Geisterbahn.*

My Fuhrer, here is the ledger for the Ghost Train.

At the bottom were two initials: H.G.

Hermann Göring - the man in charge of Hitler's art thefts and supervisor of the train system.

"My friend, here is something special for you." Steffen handed him Nicu Lepescu's stationmaster log.

———

Once he found the book, Paul's time in the Fuhrerbunker had to end. As exciting as the discoveries had been, the bunker was too vast and his time too limited for him to continue here. He had been after one thing, and now he had it. It was time to concentrate on the ledger and leave future exploration to others.

He sat at the same desk in the museum basement where he'd reviewed records a few days earlier. Today's work was far more interesting. At last he had the book that contained something Reichsmarschall Göring wanted to show Hitler himself, a book so important it was hidden away with priceless Gutenberg Bibles. What were its secrets? Where was the Ghost Train? The book lay in front of him on the desk.

44-GUT-1411
January 2, 1944
August 31, 1944
Nicu Lepescu, SS
Stationmaster
Bucharest, Romania

From cover to cover, the setup of this ledger was identical to the others he'd seen. The first page bore a legend with cargo abbreviations, each subsequent page represented one train and every subentry on a page was a car - almost always a boxcar. The only trains that had passenger cars with real seats were troop transports. The soldiers were treated like humans while the prisoners were stuffed into freight cars like animals.

Many of these trains were longer than in other cities, Paul noted. Logistics was one reason for this. Romania was situated far from the concentration camps. Trains would come through one town after another, loading prisoners at each stop. Other freight cars arrived in Bucharest empty but left loaded, sometimes with humans but more often filled with the gold and precious objects that had been stored there.

Paul began by making a few assumptions. First he had to assume the Ghost Train existed; it wasn't simply a rumor. He also figured the entry wouldn't be obvious; it would probably look just like all the others. In fact, Nicu might not even have known there was something different about this train. Third, in order to narrow things down, he'd assume Hans Steffen was right: the ultimate destination of the Ghost Train was a remote place in Bulgaria or Romania. His last assumption was something Hans had also theorized. Hitler would only have ordered Operation Geist when things were grim, no earlier than summer 1944.

He decided to start at the end of the book. He knew from research that two important things happened in the last week of August 1944. After a successful push westward by the Soviets into Romania, on the 23rd the deposed King declared a coup, removing the Axis-aligned dictatorship. King Michael put Romanian troops at the disposal of the Allies, and on August 31 the Soviets entered Bucharest.

Nicu's final entry on August 31 confirmed it. *The Red Army is in the city. I shall remain at my post, awaiting orders from Reichsmarschall Göring.*

To make things easier, Paul created a brief list of dates, trains, origin and destination points, and brief cargo descriptions.

There were no train movements listed for August 31, the day Soviet troops seized Bucharest and the last date shown in the stationmaster ledger. There had been no trains from August 23rd to 30th except troop transports, all heading from the eastern front back to Germany. These were defeated German soldiers returning home. For them, the war was over and they had lost.

King Michael's coup happened on August 23. Before that day train movements were consistent. Three or four trains a day would come and go through Bucharest. Paul took his summarization back to July 1, then stopped. A clear pattern had emerged. During those final weeks before the Axis lost Romania, almost every train that arrived in Bucharest carried gold, artwork, statuary and the like. And every train left Bucharest empty. Valuables were obviously being offloaded and stored at the station in Bucharest in increasing numbers. The sheer volume of crates must have been staggering.

He scanned forward down his abbreviated list, trying to see when this pattern of offloading ended. Seeing something interesting, he turned to the stationmaster log entry for August 21. He wanted to know what Nicu had written.

The particular train of interest was the Pride of Aachen, named for a western city in Germany near the Belgian border. Its number was RE3862 and it had thirteen cars, every one empty upon arrival. It had come from Sofia, Bulgaria, although Paul knew from other entries that Sofia might have been simply the last stop before now but not the actual city of origin.

Hours later this train left Bucharest, each boxcar fully loaded with GO, ST and GE. Gold, statuary and paintings. Its destination was very close. It was going to Sinaia, Romania, only eighty-five miles away.

How odd, Paul thought. He looked back at his other entries; every train was traveling between major cities. All of them except this one. This train's destination was a place he'd never heard of.

He felt prickles on his skin as he searched Wikipedia. Sinaia was a town of only ten thousand people nestled in the mountains of central Romania. People came in the winter to ski, and the best method of transportation was to take the train from Bucharest. The trains ran back and forth only between the capital and the resort town. They went no further.

It seemed an unusual destination for a thirteen-car train filled with gold and artwork. He eagerly scanned his abbreviated listings for the trains between August 21 and 31.

This train never returned.

Paul struggled not to let his mind run wild, but so far everything that should fit, did fit. He ran through the facts as he now knew them.

1. A massive quantity of gold, statuary and paintings was stored at Bucharest North Station during July and early August. It seemed as though the Reich was building up a storehouse of treasure.

2. On August 21 the deposed King was two days from executing a coup that would remove Romania from the Axis. Things were nearly finished for the Reich in general, particularly in Romania.

3. On that day, August 21, the only empty train to arrive here in months, a train with thirteen boxcars, came to Bucharest and left fully loaded with gold, statues and paintings.

4. That train was scheduled to make a short eighty-five-mile trip to the tiny town of Sinaia, a remote place in the mountains best known for its winter sports activities.

5. That train and whatever cargo it carried stayed there. It never came back.

He'd found it. Too many things fit. This was no coincidence. This was the Ghost Train.

He could see the rainbow, but he didn't have enough information to find the pot of gold. Yet.

CHAPTER TWENTY-NINE

Paul had left Nicu's funeral as soon as the girl ran past his pew. At the back of the sanctuary he pushed out the door through a group of Japanese tourists, intent on keeping her in sight. It was a beautiful afternoon and there was considerable pedestrian traffic in this area of shops, sidewalk cafés and museums. Despite the crowds, he dropped in a block behind her. Tailing another person was something he knew how to do well. He stayed close enough to see her but sufficiently far back in case she turned around.

Two streets down from the church, she stopped suddenly and looked back to see if anyone was following. *She's beautiful,* Paul thought as he saw her face for the first time. Wearing a trench coat with a trendy scarf tucked in the belt, she was young, sultry, dark and enticing. Paul slowed to an easy pace and continued walking. She darted into a restaurant and he moved quickly; he had no idea who this woman was or if she knew how to lose a tail. He didn't want to miss her.

A bell jingled when he opened the front door. Just inside, a maître d' greeted him.

"Good afternoon. Table for one?"

Paul glanced around but didn't see her. "The lady who just arrived. Where is she?"

"Oh, are there two in your party? She made a quick trip to the loo. Your table is in the back - she asked for a quiet place." He pointed to a side room hidden from passersby who might glance through the front windows. It was perfect for someone on the run.

There was no time to lose. If there was an exit by the toilets, she could be gone already.

"Where's the loo? I need to use it myself."

As he pointed to a door, it swung open and the girl came out. The maître d' said, "There she is now! Miss . . ."

Paul stopped him. "I'll take it from here. Thanks." He slipped between the tables and took her arm lightly. "Good to see you, darling. Let's go sit down."

The place was packed with customers, none paying them any attention. She looked up as a ruggedly handsome stranger took her arm lightly. She jerked away and exploded, "What the hell do you think you're doing? Let go of me!" Diners turned to look, presuming they were having a spat.

Paul whispered, "Shh. After that episode at the church, I doubt you want to cause another scene here." He steered her to the table and pulled out her chair. As they sat, she began to cry.

"My God, I should never have come back. You're a policeman, right?"

"Far from it. You're safe - no fears. I want some information."

"So exactly who are you?"

"Let's be civilized, shall we? Let's order a glass of wine while we talk. In fact, I'll buy your lunch. I can't imagine anything better than spending time with a beautiful girl who's afraid I'm a policeman! That should make for an interesting discussion!"

He ordered a nice Alsatian white. When it was poured, he held his glass across the table. Since she was stuck with him for now, she clinked it. It could be worse, she decided as they ordered lunch.

He began by explaining a little about himself. He was Paul Silver, an American businessman living in London. He was fortunate enough to have time and resources to indulge his passions - adventure and artifacts.

He's wealthy, she gathered.

"I enjoy discovering things that have been lost or hidden or forgotten. I've been to ancient cities in Central American jungles, I discovered a knight of the Round Table hidden in a crypt in London, and I've done a handful of

166

other things most people would find boring as hell but I find irresistible. I also collect unusual things - not necessarily expensive or priceless items, but rarities that catch my eye. For instance, I own a bracelet worn by Cleopatra, a dagger attributed to William the Conqueror -"

She interrupted him. "Enough for now, Indiana Jones. Presuming your name really is Paul Silver and you're being honest about yourself, you aren't a policeman. Right now that's all I care about. You've told me what you like to do. Now tell me what you were doing at Nicu's funeral. I didn't see you there. And why did you follow me?"

The more they talked, the easier the conversation flowed. There were a lot worse things she could be doing than having lunch with this interesting, good-looking stranger. She just had to be careful.

With a laugh he said, "I'll give you a little more background; then it's your turn." He said he was interested in the Nazi trains that had carried priceless objects across occupied Europe. According to news reports, one of them, hidden for decades, had maybe been located. Ground-penetrating radar had indicated there was a train inside a mountain in Poland.

"In my research I found out Nicu Lepescu was the stationmaster in Bucharest. I presumed he was long since dead. By now he'd have to be over a hundred, but when I first searched, I didn't find an obituary. If he was still alive, I wanted to find him. Bucharest was a huge transport center for the Nazis. Maybe he knew about a trainload of treasure that came through here on its way to a hiding place."

She flinched imperceptibly and he picked up on it. It was subtle, but she had definitely reacted when he mentioned hiding things. She knew something about this.

He continued, smoothly blending fiction and fact as he'd done his entire life. "I came to Bucharest to find out more, learned his funeral was today, and I attended in order to see how much family he had. I had planned to talk to them, to ask if they could help me."

"How did you hear about the funeral?"

"Strictly by chance. When I was ready to come to Bucharest, I tried to find Nicu's address online. I was surprised to see he had recently died and that his funeral was today."

Nicu's obituary had listed his relatives: a deceased son Ciprian and three grandchildren. One of those was a man who was of great interest to Paul. That man was Philippe Lepescu, whose home was shown as Lucerne. From their past association, Paul knew Philippe's father had been named Ciprian. This was no coincidence. Paul decided to go to the funeral, see Philippe in person and confirm it. Then he would settle their unfinished business.

He stopped to take a sip from his wineglass. As he paused, she jumped in with a question.

"Instead of staying to talk to the family, you decided to follow me? That doesn't add up. Your mission was to get information from Nicu's heirs, but you left when you saw me run out of the church. Why?"

He had to make this sound good. He had never intended to talk to the family. He came simply to get a look at Philippe.

"I followed you because of the outburst. I watched it all from the back of the church. The priest stopped the eulogy when that older woman yelled at you. I followed you because maybe you could give me information. The family obviously knows you. At least the woman does. I wondered who you were - maybe a relative? I had no idea, but I took a chance you'd know something about Nicu's background since you attended his funeral.

"Enough about me! I'm here with a beautiful lady and I don't even know your name. Or what you have to do with Nicu. Or why you were so worried I was a policeman!"

Her new identity was so fresh and so expensive she didn't want to reveal it needlessly, so she used her real name. "Mr. Silver, I'll bet you a million dollars I don't know everything about you! As far as who I am, my name is Adriana Creed. I was Nicu's companion for the last three years. I'll tell you why I worry about the police, but first I need to give you background."

"So you were his caregiver?"

"Not exactly. I'm not a nurse, and Nicu already had a housekeeper, that old bitch who yelled at me in the church. She always figured I was out to take his money." She caught herself. "Not that he had much money. I was very young compared to Nicu, and Mrs. Radu thought I was a sponger. But I became his friend. We talked, we did things together, took walks together, went to lunch together. That kind of thing."

Paul asked how they met and became so close. She explained she was a Romani making a living as a fortune-teller. Nicu's lawyer had randomly picked her to tell him about his future. She had liked the spry old man from the beginning and guessed he liked her too. She held back a lot, including his loathsome past and the gold bars he'd given her.

As she continued, his mind wandered. *How could Nicu not have liked her? She's intelligent, attractive, sexy - and she's young enough to be his granddaughter. Any man would have appreciated attention from her. Even a very, very old one.*

"I think my being there made him happy. His appreciation and gratitude made me want to spend even more time with him. He was generous to me - he gave me money, which helped with my rent and living expenses - but our friendship wasn't about that. I would have wanted to help him regardless."

Paul glanced at his watch. Two hours had flown by like minutes. After a delicious lunch and a second bottle of wine, they lingered in the now-empty restaurant, conversing over coffee as easily as two old friends.

"Do you think his grandchildren would help me learn more about Nicu's past?"

She laughed out loud. "Those three? No, they won't help you. They couldn't if they wanted to. They don't know one thing about Nicu. *They* are the leeches. Nicu told me he hadn't seen them in fifteen years. Do you know when they finally came to see him? When he was dying, so they could take whatever he had. That's when I stepped out of the picture. They're vultures. Predators. I've never actually met any of them," she lied. She knew one of them, and she knew him well.

"I knew Mrs. Radu, the housekeeper, of course. I saw her every day. But the grandchildren never came around, not even the oldest one - Milosh - who Nicu said lives right here in Bucharest. They think Nicu has money. And maybe he does, although I can't see how. He hasn't worked in years, since he got out . . ." She stopped abruptly. She'd said too much.

"Got out of where?"

Adriana paused. As the time passed, she was feeling very comfortable with him. Regardless, Paul Silver was a stranger, a man she'd just met. She couldn't afford to tell him everything, so she continued, weaving lies in with the truth.

"Long ago he was in prison for many years. Something about war crimes, I think. He never mentioned anything about his incarceration and I didn't ask. After his release in the early seventies, I presume he had enough assets set aside to live without working. Maybe he made good investments over the years. Who knows? He had enough for himself and gave me a little too. He was a kind man."

Paul thought about what Nicu Lepescu had been. *Maybe there were other reasons he was financially secure after his imprisonment. A lot of Nazi officers helped themselves to things when they could. He was in charge of a major depot along the Nazi train route, a station where gold was stored overnight. There was so much stolen property in those days it would have been impossible to keep an eye on everything.*

"What are you thinking about?" she asked, smiling.

"Just processing everything. You said you stepped aside when he was dying and the grandchildren appeared. Did he die at home?"

He's going to find out anyway. "No. He died in a hospital jail cell."

Paul was confused. "What? The man was over a hundred years old and he was in jail?"

"He killed a drug dealer in the Ferentari ghetto."

"That's crazy. The police would never be able to pin a murder on an old man."

"There wasn't any 'pinning' to it. He did it. He was arrested at the scene, murder weapon in his hand, covered in blood, and with a dead body on the floor next to him. He confessed then and there. I was afraid you were a cop because . . . well, because I was there too.

"I made a rash decision when Nicu shot the guy. Rather than staying around to talk to the police, I decided to move on. I regret that I never saw him again. Two months after he was jailed, another inmate beat him savagely. He was put in a private hospital cell, the family was notified, and that was that. Two days later he was dead."

"Was Nicu an addict? Did he murder his own dealer? And why in hell were *you* there?"

"Let's stop right here, okay? I just met you, under circumstances you must agree are strange. You show up here claiming that you want to know about Nicu's past and you just happen to attend his funeral. You follow me instead of staying with the family, whom you want to talk to. You ask me a lot of questions that are beginning to make me really nervous. I've told you enough. Once I find out exactly what you're doing here and what you want from me, we can go from there. I'm going to the loo. Back in a flash."

The waiter cleared the table and went to retrieve the brandies Paul ordered. When the server walked away, Paul reached for her coat and rummaged through the pockets. He pulled out her passport, a return air ticket to Amsterdam and a key card from the city's downtown Marriott Hotel. Knowing she would return any second, he opened the passport to the photo page and read her name and nationality. He replaced it just as she rounded the corner.

When the server set the brandies down, she grinned, struggling vainly not to like him as much as she already did.

"Are you trying to get me drunk? I hardly know you. Should I be wary?"

"Wary of me? You know better! I'm not a policeman; that should give you comfort. I'm just a guy who likes a little adventure."

Suddenly her countenance turned serious. She took his hand in both of hers and said earnestly, "I have absolutely no idea who you are. I know what you've told me, but is that the truth? Only you know that. I should be cautious. I should be afraid of strangers. But for some reason I feel comfortable with you - maybe it's all the alcohol you've forced upon me! I have always had a difficult time trusting people. It's hard with you too, since you burst into my life just three hours ago." She took a deep breath and continued. "I made a decision in the loo a minute ago. I decided to do something totally out of character. I don't know what it is about you, Paul Silver. I want to get to know you better, whoever you are. So for now let's stop this interrogation."

She lifted her brandy snifter and held it toward him with a smile. "Cheers. I think I'd like a little adventure too, Indiana Jones. How far is your hotel from here?"

CHAPTER THIRTY

Moonbeams glowed through the floor-to-ceiling windows, casting eerie shadows on the bed. He lay quietly next to her, watching her chest softly rise and fall as she slept. Both had been passionate participants in foreplay, then lovemaking, then a thunderous mutual climax worthy of accompaniment by Rachmaninoff.

Neither had had much to say as they left the restaurant, hailed a cab and went to Paul's hotel. No one had asked, no one had answered, no one had hesitated. For different reasons they both ended up in the same place, each needing exactly what he or she got, with no strings attached. She'd ducked her head when they walked through the lobby. He wondered if she was afraid someone would recognize her. Once they were in his room, she had shed her clothes without modesty, watched as he did the same, and they wriggled under the covers. They'd been here since four, and it was nearly nine now.

Paul went to the bathroom, washed his face and brushed his teeth. He was famished and already feeling a little hung over from the afternoon of drinking. He walked back into the bedroom and noticed she was awake. She smiled and gave him a little wave from the bed.

"That was a first," she murmured.

"You're a virgin?"

"Ha! Far from it. What I'm saying is from the minute I met you today I had this overwhelming desire to sleep with you. That's never happened to me before." She'd started to say she'd never had sex so soon after meeting someone, but caught herself. Why lie? Instead she told the truth. She *had* wanted him, beginning the minute they met. Even though she still didn't know what he wanted from her or who he really was, she had gotten what *she* wanted. From the grin on his face, she decided he had too.

In her previous profession she'd frequently had sex only a few minutes after meeting someone, but this was entirely different. This wasn't sex for sale. This was enjoyable, stimulating, deeply involved sex. *This whole thing could go somewhere*, she thought briefly, then dismissed an idea that could get her into trouble. She had a new identity, a new life, and the police were looking for her. As far as she knew, this man could be part of her problem, not part of her solution. This afternoon had simply been what it had been. And it was over.

They ate a late dinner and finished with coffee. They spoke more about him, but not about her. At last he said, "I just realized I don't even know where you live. Do you have a flat nearby?"

She smiled. "Maybe. Are you fishing for an invitation?"

"Maybe. But I'm also interested to know more about you."

"I moved when the grandchildren came in and I wasn't needed anymore."

"You said that earlier. But what you actually said was that you left when he was arrested, not two months later when the grandchildren arrived. You said you left rather than hanging around to be interviewed by the police. Why did that worry you so much?" She picked up the shift in his tone of voice. He was all business now, digging for information. Like a policeman would do.

During dinner, her mind had occasionally drifted, creating sensual scenarios and imagining herself back in bed with him. The sudden shift in his voice and his demeanor wrenched her back into reality, back to danger and caution and fear.

Dammit! She'd let her feelings go wild and she had known better. He was after something, pure and simple. She pulled away from him, moving back in her chair. "Here goes the interrogation again . . ."

"I don't mean it that way. I'm just trying to figure out . . ."

She snapped back at him. "Stop it! What exactly *are* you trying to figure out? Why are you *really* interested in Nicu, and how did you so conveniently drop into my life this morning? All of a sudden I'm thinking our chance encounter was planned all along. I hope you enjoyed our little sojourn in bed. I guess you somehow had that planned too. Congratulations on stringing me along, you bastard. I'm done." She stood and jerked her coat off the chair.

He seized her arm and growled, "We're not finished. Sit down, Carey Apostol from Holland. You haven't had *your* turn to talk."

CHAPTER THIRTY-ONE

He hailed a taxi as they left the restaurant. "Tell him where your place is," he commanded.

"We can't go there. They'll be watching."

"Who? Watching for what? For you? We certainly have a lot to talk about, Adriana. Or is your real name Carey?" He gave the driver the address of his hotel.

She sat in his room and explained her disappearance from Bucharest, stretching the truth but not by much. She admitted she was an addict, although she lied about being in recovery. Her dealer, Denis, had threatened her over money, and Nicu had offered to come to her rescue.

"Denis told me to meet him in the Ferentari, and Nicu said he was coming too. I didn't want him there - he was so old and that place is so dangerous - but he insisted. He said he had nothing to lose at this point. 'I want to talk to him myself,' Nicu said."

When they got there, Nicu pulled a pistol from his jacket, killed Denis and told Adriana to run as far away as possible. "I left Romania that night and went to Austria and Nicu sent me money occasionally. I contacted a friend of Nicu's . . ." She slowed down. She had to make this story believable, to explain how a poor girl could afford a new identity.

Paul observed the subtle shifts in her body language; he knew exactly what she was doing. He'd run enough interrogations to recognize the signs of deceit, but he said nothing.

"Nicu's friend was in Linz. He got me a new passport and EU identity card. He even made a credit card for me."

Interesting. That must have cost a fortune. Also impossible, the way she's explaining it.

"How much money did you pay Nicu's friend? I presume new identities don't come cheap. Especially ones created that quickly, credit card and all."

She paused a moment. "Uh, I gave him four thousand dollars."

Bullshit.

"And this credit card - is it linked to a bank account in your old name or your new one?"

In totally unfamiliar territory, she stumbled. There really wasn't a credit card, of course. She had used the black card Nicu gave her and everything just happened. But she couldn't tell Paul about that.

"It was . . . It was in Carey Apostol's name."

Paul leaned forward and stared into her eyes. "No, it wasn't. You couldn't get a credit card without visiting a bank, spending time, filling out forms. None of this is true."

She exploded. "No, damn you! Most of it's *not* true! I'm *afraid*! Do you get that? I'm afraid of *you*. I'm afraid you're here to kill me. I'm also afraid of the police and going to prison as an accomplice to murder. Nicu *did* kill Denis, but I was there and the desk clerk saw me. Denis was trying to take Nicu's gold . . ." She caught herself. Whimpering, she cowered on the sofa. She knew she was in serious trouble and she couldn't close the door she'd just opened.

He nodded in grim satisfaction. "I knew it. Now we're getting somewhere."

The man she'd gone to bed with, the man who seemed so gentle and trustworthy, was so different now. She saw a deadly side and it alarmed her. She had really made a mistake this time and now she was seriously afraid.

"Please don't kill me! You can have the gold. I'll tell you anything you want to know."

Paul needed to assuage her fears. He'd pushed too hard in his zeal to find out about a hidden Nazi train. He had to find out what gold she was talking about. He had to regain her trust and keep it this time.

This time he spoke in a gentle voice. "Adriana, I'm sorry. I'm not going to kill you, and I don't want the gold. I truly am what I said. I didn't come here looking for you. I think there's a Nazi treasure train - one that came through Bucharest, and Nicu knew about it. I went to the historical museum in Berlin, and I explored Hitler's bunker."

She stopped crying, daubed her eyes with a tissue and whimpered, "Now *you're* lying. The Soviets blew up the Fuhrerbunker. Every schoolchild knows that."

"They blew up some of it a long time ago, but it was too solidly built. There was a lot left, so they built a huge door and walled off the rest. There's much more left than what they destroyed. I've seen it with my own eyes. I've found things the Nazis hid seventy years ago."

Adriana took a deep breath and sighed. "I'm such a fool. Why do I want to believe you so much? How can I know you weren't sent here to kill me?"

"If that were my plan, I could have done it a dozen times already. I followed you from the church because I wanted to know how you fit in with the Lepescus. It'll be easy to find the grandchildren again when I'm ready, but you were a mystery. I didn't know who you were, so I followed you to find out. It's that simple. All I want is help. And I'm willing to help you in return."

She collapsed into his arms. He embraced her quivering body, holding her close.

"I'm so scared. If I hadn't come back for his funeral, I'd be free now."

"You *are* free. You just have to trust me." She raised her face to his and kissed him tenderly. "I do. Why, I don't know, but I do. I'm so tired, Paul. Let's go to bed. Tomorrow I'll tell you everything." Tucked into his bed, wrapped in his arms, she was asleep within minutes.

CHAPTER THIRTY-TWO

As soon as they awoke, she had murmured, "I'm ready to tell you anything you want to know." Now they sat at a rolling room service table, nibbling on breakfast as they talked.

"I'll be more open with you too, Adriana. The things I have to ask may make you uncomfortable, but if we're going to help each other, I need to understand all this. Yesterday you said you went to Linz after your drug dealer was killed. Was that true? And who told you how to get a new identity? That's a risky, complicated thing. Not something your average gypsy fortune-teller would be familiar with." He smiled as he said that last part, and she did too.

She really wanted to tell the truth this time. She admitted Nicu had given her the key to a safety deposit box that contained twenty-three one-kilo gold bars and two old books.

"Nicu gave me one more thing. That credit card I told you about yesterday was real, but it didn't come from the man in Linz. Nicu gave it to me. And it's not really a credit card. It's something else altogether, but I don't know how to explain what it is. I've never seen anything like it before. All I know is that it can do much more than any ordinary card."

Paul heard only part of that. His mind was still on something she'd said earlier.

"You're saying Nicu gave you twenty-three kilo bars? He simply handed you around a million dollars in gold? Why would an old man do that? Wouldn't giving away that much money jeopardize his own future?"

"He *did* give me the bars, and he said he had more assets to leave his grandchildren. I don't know where he got his money, but he wanted me to have everything in that box. Nicu loved me - platonically, of course, but I've no doubt he really did love me. Until I came along, I'm certain he never loved anyone but himself. Regardless of his feelings for me, I could never love him back in the same way. He was a despicable man - a Nazi killer. He had no remorse for sending thousands to their deaths at Auschwitz. One day he asked me to hear his confession, but it was more recounting his life story than a plea for forgiveness. He was proud to have been a Nazi. His war medals still hang on the wall of his bedroom. In a way, eventually I came to love him too because he helped me, but I always hated what he had been and what he had done to his fellow man."

Nicu never revealed where the gold bars came from, she continued. "I'm ashamed. I should care more. I should try to find out if Jews died because of those gold bars. But part of me doesn't want to. I want the financial security Nicu gave me, but I feel dirty. Does any of this make sense?"

He nodded as he poured more coffee. "It does, and don't beat yourself up. This isn't your battle. You don't know the history of those bars. Even if they're stained with blood, nothing you can do will bring a single person back to life. Nicu committed the sins, not you."

They moved back to the bed and lay beside each other, propped on pillows. He squeezed her hand. "Tell me about the other things. Didn't you say you found books too?"

"There were two books. One is an old copy of *Mein Kampf*. I asked Nicu why it was in his safety deposit box and he said something strange. He said it was very important and I should guard it until I needed it. He said it would be helpful someday."

"That *is* odd. Did you look inside it?"

"Briefly. It's not a first edition and it's not signed by Hitler. There are no notes, no underlining or pages turned down - nothing like that. It's just a ragged copy of a very popular book."

"What's the other book?"

She paused for a moment, remembering the evil red swastika on its cover.

"It's his diary. It's a journal from 1944, the year he was stationmaster in Bucharest."

Paul bolted straight up, tossing his coffee and hers all over the bed. Doused with hot liquid, she screamed and then laughed hysterically. As he wiped coffee from her arms, he boomed, "Sorry about that, but this is unbelievable! You have his diary from 1944? Incredible! I have to see that book!"

All of a sudden she stopped laughing. *Shit! Why the hell did I mention the diary? I don't even have it anymore! I should have been ready for this, but he's throwing questions at me so fast I can't keep up.*

"It's not that big a deal," she stammered. "Half of it's unreadable. It's in some kind of numeric code or something."

"Numeric code? Even better. Wonder what was so sensitive he had to encode it? This is amazing! When can I see it?"

She stared silently at the floor. Anything she said seemed only to make things worse.

"I . . . I loaned it to a friend."

He didn't reply for what seemed to her like ages. "Look at me," he commanded at last. "Who did you loan it to? What's your friend's name?" He watched her face closely.

"A friend of mine named . . ." Addled, she hesitated a second too long. "Paul. His name is Paul too, just like yours."

"This friend Paul. Where is he right now?"

She couldn't handle this. By now every answer was simply dropping out of her mouth before she even thought about what sounded logical.

"I don't know. He was going to London for a couple of days, he said. He took the book with him. I think he'll be back on Monday."

"Adriana, this simply doesn't make sense. You're making this up as you go. You say you found a diary in a safety deposit box. The book was so important Nicu kept it locked away for decades, but you loaned it to a friend - a man named Paul, like me - who took it to London. What are you hiding? Where's the book?"

She shook her head and started to cry. *I need time to think.* She hadn't intended to fabricate a story, but she had, and now she was lost. When she was under stress, Adriana relied on her old standby, the friend in the syringe, but she hadn't brought any. This was to have been a day trip - a plane ride down, a funeral and a plane ride back. She should have been back in Amsterdam last night, but instead she'd stayed in Paul's hotel room. Now he was pushing her, questioning her, backing her into a corner, and she was about to break. She began to shiver.

She'd put two vials of Liquid O in her purse yesterday morning just in case. Liquid heroin took away the edge, but it didn't offer the same effect as an injection. She'd used a vial already - she sneaked it yesterday when Paul was in the bathroom. Now she popped the last one, stuck it in her nose and inhaled deeply. Ordinarily she'd have never done this in front of someone else, but at this moment she had no choice. The stress was killing her. The drug calmed her almost immediately.

He watched her, then said quietly, "You need it badly, don't you?"

Adriana screamed, "God, Paul, stop! Stop badgering me! I can't take anymore!"

She needed to get back to Amsterdam quickly, back to her drugs. She couldn't buy heroin here - Nicu had killed her dealer and she didn't know any others. She had heroin in her hotel safe, and she could buy more in the Old Town anytime she wanted. She had to get home before this hit wore off.

She forced herself to calm down and began putting on the only clothes she had, the ones from yesterday. She said, "I don't want to talk about this anymore right now. You're pushing too hard, Paul. Too many questions. You have to give me some space. I'll explain everything later, but right now I'm going back."

He jumped out of bed and held her arms. "Why are you doing this? What are you hiding? There's something in that diary, isn't there?"

"STOP! Stop the questions!" She pulled away, the stress causing her to shake violently.

"You're acting like . . ."

"Like what, Paul? Like a heroin addict? I need a fix, okay? What part of 'I'm an addict' did you not understand? I have to go back to Amsterdam. I'll tell you everything later. Right now you have to let me go."

"I'm going with you."

"No! Leave me alone!"

Adriana stormed out of Paul's hotel room and hailed a cab to the airport. She sat at the departure gate and thought about what had happened. Why had she lied about giving Philippe the diary? Because she was afraid, she realized. She barely knew Paul. What was he doing in her life anyway? She'd be wise to hold a few secrets back. Next week she'd call him. If everything was okay, she'd tell him everything like she promised. Right now she just had to make it back to Holland.

Keeping calm for the next four hours took sheer determination. At last she stood at her hotel room door. Her high had worn off - her hands shook and her heart was beating wildly. She inserted the key card and slammed open the door with a single goal. Stepping just inside the dark room, she dropped her purse and opened the safe. Even though her paraphernalia was right there, she was in no shape to prepare heroin for the syringe. At the moment she wanted to inhale another vial, saving the real thing for when she was calm. She pulled the tiny bottle out, broke the cap and stuck it in her nose. Three deep inhalations and she felt the familiar warmth soaring through her body. Her shaking stopped immediately and she breathed a sigh of relief.

"Feeling better, darling?"

She screamed in surprise as she saw him sitting at the far end of her room. Suddenly she was furious. Her old sweetheart had invaded her personal space and watched her frantically use the drug. Like so many times before with him, she felt vulnerable and scared. A flood of memories flashed in seconds - the bad times, the times he'd hurt her and mocked her, the pleasure he seemed to get from her pain.

"You have no right to be in my room! How the hell did you get in here?"

He rubbed his thumb and fingers together, the universal sign of money. "It wasn't difficult. What was that little bottle you put in your nose? Liquid O, perhaps? Do you have a problem, Apostol?"

He was right - Liquid O was exactly what it had been, the same stuff that kept her from cratering when she fled Romania. The quick fix.

"That's none of your business," she snapped. "How did you find me? Why aren't you in Bucharest?"

"Why so angry, Apostol? I was worried about you. You left Bucharest without even telling me goodbye. It almost seemed like you were trying to hide from me. Partners don't act this way to each other, do they?"

He continued with a sneer. "You're holding out on me. You gave me the diary, but there's something else, isn't there? There's another book. Where is it?"

CHAPTER THIRTY-THREE

Without saying a word, she went into the bathroom, locked the door and stripped naked. She stepped into a steaming shower and ten minutes later came out wearing a hotel robe. Covers pulled back, he lay naked on the bed. His erection signaled what he wanted from her.

"Come here." He spoke softly and patted the bed next to him.

"No, Philippe. I'm not doing that. You had no right to break into my room."

She remembered well the suddenly different, commanding tone in his voice. She'd heard it often enough in the past.

"Come here now. Obey me or -"

"Or what?" she interrupted sharply. "You manipulated me so many times before. I won't allow it anymore."

He held up the black card that was her very lifeblood, the card that accessed all the money she had in the world. "What's this, darling?"

She turned sharply, realizing with a sinking feeling she had forgotten to lock the safe.

"Give it to me," she whimpered. "You don't know how to use it anyway . . ."

"Of course. Anything you say. First, you're going to take off your robe and join me." He patted the bed again and smiled as she did what he commanded.

The Bad Man watched as they made love. *Can I come out for a minute and hit her? Remember how much fun we had back then when you let me hit her?*

As Philippe thrust inside her, he ignored his bad side's pleas. He wanted information from her; hurting her wouldn't accomplish anything this time - except, of course, the intense sexual gratification that domination always provided. That would have to wait for later. He kept going.

Moments later he finished with a series of groans, reached over to the nightstand and handed her the card. She went into the bathroom, returned and began getting dressed as he lay naked on the bed.

"Where are you going? You're not leaving just yet. We have a lot to talk about. That book, for instance. But first tell me about your new name, Carey Apostol."

Of course he knew it - he couldn't have found her otherwise - but it surprised her anyway.

"How'd you find out?"

Philippe laughed sarcastically. "Oh, Adriana, you naive child. Will you never learn? I've had people watching you constantly. I know about the gold bar you tried to sell at the bank. I know the building you visited in Linz. I know everything you've done, everywhere you've been."

She took her time dressing as he continued. It made sense someone could have seen her with the gold bar, but he couldn't possibly know everything. He knew she was at a building in Linz, but he couldn't know what she was there for. Philippe hadn't seen his grandfather in years, and she was certain that Nicu never told his grandson about the people in Linz and the money he deposited there.

"I'm afraid you've been hiding things. That isn't nice, since I've been so generous to you and we were business partners. You were hired to give me information, not to hide it from me. First let's talk about exactly what was in Grandfather's safety deposit box. Was there gold there? Are you a wealthy woman now that you're Carey Apostol? And there was a second book in the box too. I want that book, Adriana."

"No. No more talk. I'm leaving. You hired me to find your grandfather's diary, and I did what you asked. Our 'partnership,' as you call it, is finished. You paid me for Nicu's journal and you got it. Now I never want to see you again. I should never have gotten involved with you this time around. I know what you are - what you've always been. You're a manipulating, controlling demon who enjoyed hurting me. I got away from you a long time ago. This is over . . ."

There was a sharp knock at the door. Philippe slipped into the bathroom and closed the door as she looked through the peephole.

Damn! What was *he* doing here? She couldn't let him in. What if Philippe attacked him - but wait! Paul certainly could take care of himself. Maybe this was exactly the help she needed!

His voice muffled, Philippe called through the bathroom door. "Who's out there?"

Calm now, she answered, "Someone I'd like you to meet."

She opened the door and hugged Paul Silver. "I'm really glad to see you." She gave a head nod and a glance toward the bathroom door.

Surprised at the warm reception, he stepped inside and shut the door. "That's good to hear. I thought maybe you'd be mad." He pointed to the door and gave her a quizzical look as it suddenly opened.

Philippe stepped out, wrapped in a towel. "Do we have company, darling?"

Paul was as stunned as if he'd been slammed into the ground. *Philippe Lepescu! What the hell is* he *doing here?* He slipped his hand into his jacket pocket and gripped his pistol.

"Why don't you introduce me to your friend?" Philippe said as he nonchalantly walked to the bed and dropped his towel. His back was to them as he began to put his clothes on.

He doesn't know me, Paul realized. Sitting at the funeral far away from Philippe had been one thing, but being here a foot away was something else entirely. Paul had done a complete physical makeover after he supposedly died in the London fire. The change was good enough to deceive almost everyone, but if anyone would recognize him now, it would have been his thieving former partner.

There was one thing Paul couldn't change, one thing that would give him away - his voice. Adriana gasped and backed away as Paul took out a Sig Sauer, its suppressor guaranteed to keep the noise level low. Philippe glanced around and saw the stranger holding a gun.

Casually buttoning his slacks, he turned. "Why don't you tell me what's going on, Adriana?"

Paul answered, "I thought I'd killed you, Philippe. I fired two shots point-blank into your body. You outsmarted me that time; then you disappeared. Then you thought you'd killed *me,* didn't you? *You* started the fire in St Mary Axe Street that night."

It was time. Philippe opened the door in his brain wide. The Bad Man leapt out enthusiastically, ready to play.

"Roberto Maas. Is that still your name? I would never have recognized you. It's amazing how you've changed. What in hell are you doing here?"

Paul aimed the pistol. "Speaking of hell, that's your next destination."

"Don't do it!" Adriana screamed. "He has Nicu's diary! If you kill him, you'll never get it!"

Paul hesitated, lowering his weapon slightly. Philippe seized the opportunity. He flew across the room, hitting Paul's arm and sending the pistol skittering into the bathroom. They fell to the floor, struggling in the tight entry area between a closet and the wall.

"Get off him or I'll shoot!" Adriana stood in the bathroom, holding the pistol with both hands, aiming it in their general direction. "Get off him, Philippe!"

Philippe replied with a smirk, "You don't know how to use a gun, darling. And you wouldn't use it on me anyway!" Paul pushed him hard just as Philippe raised his fist to aim a blow. Adriana dropped the pistol, and both men scrambled for it. There was a muffled shot, and Philippe collapsed on top of Paul with a grunt. He was breathing heavily and no longer in a mood to fight. Adriana screamed and screamed.

"Goddamn you!" Philippe moaned softly, doubled up in pain. "You shot me!"

Paul slithered backwards, extricating himself from the dead weight on top of him. There was blood seeping from a wound low in Philippe's side. Depending on the trajectory, it might or might not be enough to kill him. Paul stood and comforted Adriana for a moment, then took the pistol and aimed it at Philippe, who was writhing on the floor.

"Adriana, turn him over and see if there's an exit wound."

"I can't . . ."

"You have to," he said flatly. She knelt and rolled Philippe to one side. They saw a small hole in his back.

"You're in luck," Paul told him. "You're going to live long enough to give me the diary. Just exactly long enough."

"In your dreams," Philippe groaned. "Go ahead and kill me now. It'll save us all some time."

Paul smiled broadly, surprised at how pleasant the feelings of revenge on his old partner were. He'd been an assassin in a past life, and this came back as easily as recalling how to tie your shoes.

"I have plenty of time. Much more than you, actually. And before long you'll tell me where the diary is. You'll beg to tell me. I have a technique that would have made your old Nazi grandfather proud."

————

Adriana sat quietly in her room, waiting for them to return. They'd been gone for a long time. Although the fight and the gunshots had terrified her, Paul had remained totally calm. He was obviously familiar with violence and he knew exactly what he was doing. While she trembled with fear and anxiety, Paul had calmly told her how to bandage Philippe, and then handed him his clothes. He made a couple of whispered phone calls, all the time keeping his pistol trained on Philippe. A few minutes later they walked out, Paul cradling his gun under his jacket and guiding Philippe toward the elevator.

She had halfheartedly offered to come along, but Paul refused. "You don't want to see this," he had said grimly.

What? What do I not want to see? What's he going to do to Philippe?

The moment they were gone, she prepared the syringe. As the cool release of heroin settled her nerves, the conflicts, fears and concerns that had threatened to overwhelm her became merely questions with no answers.

Who *was* Paul Silver? *What* was he? She was baffled; he claimed to be a wealthy investor and adventurer, so why did he carry a pistol with a silencer on it? She'd never even seen one before. Could she trust a man who in seconds had become a totally different person than she thought she knew?

The words between Paul and Philippe also mystified her. A long time ago Paul had pumped two shots into Philippe's body but somehow missed? Philippe then tried to kill Paul? Paul had a way - a technique, he called it - to make Philippe talk that would make the old Nazi proud. What was he going to do? Was Philippe actually the good guy here, and Paul the villain? The more she thought about it, the more perplexing it became.

Maybe I should leave! I can get away and have time to sort all this out. Where can I go? I can't hide. They both found me, even here in a hotel. But I should try.

She was packing her suitcase when she heard a knock.

———

There was a part of Amsterdam full of run-down buildings, shells of former industrial plants that once manufactured farm implements, fabricated steel and built car parts for export to Russia. One of these massive, decaying structures was owned by a Czech company called KATYA 4. As was the case in all of his investments, there was nothing about the building or its owner that could be tied back to Paul Silver. But it was his building, part of a twenty-five-million-dollar portfolio of real estate around the world owned by shell corporations or nominee trusts.

Philippe stood tied to a rusty pole, a part of the support structure for an empty ten-thousand-square-foot former machine shop. Grease and grime covered everything, and cawing crows soared in and out through broken windows fifty feet above.

Philippe had never experienced fear like what he felt now. He knew what Paul was capable of. Paul had been Roberto Maas in the days they worked together in Lucerne. That day when the Russians came in and explained exactly what Roberto had done, he understood how dangerous his sophisticated, wealthy partner really was. The man was a cold-blooded killer. Philippe tried to maintain an expression of nonchalance, but his trembling body gave him away.

Adriana had put gauze and bandages over Philippe's gunshot wounds to stop the bleeding. They weren't potentially fatal; if he died today, it would be simply because Paul took this all the way. He told his prisoner all that as he fiddled with an apparatus on the floor and hooked a pair of cables to it.

"This is a twelve-volt battery with a hand crank," he told Philippe. "I've conducted many interrogations with this setup and it's amazingly effective. The faster you tell me what I want, the less pain you'll experience. Unfortunately, that means less pleasure for me, because my goal here is to make you wish you'd never met me. I promise you this. If you give me what I want without a turn of the crank, I'll let you go. I may break your legs, but I won't kill you. If you don't talk, I will increase the voltage until you scream for me to let you die. But I won't."

He attached the end of one cable to Philippe's right index finger. The other went to a ground pole on the battery. "This is a sample, just to let you know what it feels like." He turned the crank a few times, and Philippe cried out in pain, his finger jerking spasmodically.

"Are you ready to begin?" Paul asked as he undid Philippe's trousers, pulling them and his underwear to the floor.

"Planning on giving me a blow job?" Philippe asked weakly.

"Always the sarcastic one," Paul replied as he picked up the red cable that had been hooked to Philippe's finger. "I know this will pinch a little, but trust me, this is nothing compared to what you're going to feel if you don't cooperate." He snapped the connector onto Philippe's scrotum.

Philippe winced as Paul put his hand on the crank and said, "Shall we begin?"

CHAPTER THIRTY-FOUR

With a battery cable attached to his genital area, Philippe was motivated to answer every question Paul asked. He wasn't anxious to find out what kind of pain there would be if Paul turned the crank, so he sang like the proverbial bird.

He explained how Adriana had been his lover at university and that he had hired her to find out where his grandfather's diary was. The family had always said the diary was important because it held dark secrets. Everyone in the town where they lived knew Nicu had been a Nazi storm trooper and an officer at Auschwitz. They knew he was stationmaster at Bucharest when the death trains came through and that he served twenty years in prison. Philippe's grandfather had been a profound embarrassment to the entire family. Once he was released from prison in 1971, everyone refused to have further contact with him.

Even though the family ostracized him, there was always that tantalizing rumor about Grandfather Nicu's diary. His son Ciprian had said it held secrets about the Nazis and hidden treasure. No one knew for sure if the book even existed, Philippe added.

Once Adriana weaseled her way into Nicu's life, the old man gave her a safety deposit box key and told her the contents were hers. At least that was Adriana's story. Philippe wasn't sure what was going on there, he said. Regardless, she'd found the diary in the box along with an old copy of *Mein Kampf*.

"What else was in the box?"

"I don't know. When we finally saw it, it was empty. For God's sake, take this damned thing off my balls! It hurts like hell!"

Paul unhooked the clamp. "Keep talking and maybe I'll leave it off."

He told Paul that there had been a second safety deposit box key in Nicu's belongings. He bribed a lawyer, forged Christina's signature, and forced Milosh to sign the power of attorney that allowed him access to a hundred and sixty-nine one-kilo gold bars.

The magnanimity of that statement brought Paul to attention. He did a quick calculation. "Six million dollars, two-thirds stolen from your own brother and sister. Nice haul. When you add that heist to the four hundred thousand you embezzled from me, you're a wealthy man. A lying, cheating, stealing, walking dead man, but at least you'll go out knowing you're rich."

"I'm telling you everything!" he pleaded. "Why are you going to kill me if I'm doing what you ask?"

"Maybe just for the satisfaction. You repulse me. You have no conscience, no moral fiber whatsoever. You don't care about a single person except for what they can do for you. But then again, maybe I'll let you live. Maybe I'll just hurt you really badly and let you live."

You just do that. The Bad Man sat in his room in Philippe's head, seething. *You let me live, you stupid bastard, and I'll hurt* YOU! *I won't just hook a cable to your scrotum. I'll cut your balls off and feed them to you while you scream for me to let you die!*

Philippe shushed him. This wasn't a good time to appear aggressive. He needed to get free first.

"Let's go back to the diary. You have it and you've looked at it, right?"

"Yes. Much of it is simply row after row of numbers. It's some kind of code, I figure. Before the first set of numbers appears, there's a line talking about how important the Fuhrer's book is to Grandfather. I think somehow that old copy of *Mein Kampf* that's been in the safety deposit box for years is the key to decoding the diary."

"Where are those two books?"

"Adriana has the Hitler book. I think it may be in her hotel room. I have the diary. I brought it here and put it in a locker at the train station for safekeeping. The key's in my pants pocket."

"And where are the bars of gold you stole?" Paul knelt and reached into the pocket of Philippe's pants still lying gathered around his ankles. Suddenly the bound man lashed out his feet, catching Paul under the chin and knocking him backwards. He lay on the floor for a moment, rubbed his chin and caught his breath, then stood.

Dammit! Why the hell did you do that? That was unintentional - the Bad Man had acted on his own, ignoring the consequence. Philippe couldn't free himself. All he'd done was make things much, much worse. He hadn't wanted to piss off his old partner, but the Bad Man couldn't have cared less.

"That was an intelligent move," Paul said sarcastically. "You kick me when you're tied to the pole." He picked up the cable and roughly attached the connector back onto his prisoner's scrotum.

"Shit!"

"Oh my, does it hurt? You haven't seen anything yet! Wait until you feel this!" He turned the hand crank slowly.

Without emotion Paul watched his prisoner twist about, writhing and screaming. Rotating the crank faster, he said, "I don't think you've told me yet where the gold bars are."

"Stop! Stop and I'll tell you! For God's sake, this is killing me!"

Paul stopped. "Really? I'm finding this very entertaining. You're quite a dancer, you know. You should go into theater."

When the voltage stopped, Philippe's head hung down on his chest. Waste and urine ran down his legs. He took a breath and slurred, "I traded in the gold bars at the bank in Vienna and received unregistered bearer bonds. The total is over six million dollars. They're in the locker with the diary. You can have them . . ."

"I'm touched. How generous of you, offering to give me all that money. Of course I can have them. And I will take you up on your kind offer. And now, as much as I've enjoyed our time together, it's time to bring our little visit to a close. I hope you don't think I mistrust you, but given our history I need to verify what you've told me. It will take me a little while, so here's what I've planned for you until I'm back."

He explained what was going to happen next. Philippe cried and begged for mercy, but Paul merely smiled. He unhooked the clamp briefly, then hooked it back in another place.

Before he left, he gave the crank a couple of turns so his prisoner would experience the pain.

Although there would be no voltage surging through the cable while Paul was gone, the connector was securely clamped around Philippe's left testicle, squeezing it so tightly he screamed for mercy.

But there was no mercy.

CHAPTER THIRTY-FIVE

The locker in Amsterdam's Central train station held exactly what Philippe had said. Paul took out a manila envelope and opened it. Inside were seven bearer bonds that had been issued by Stadt Privatbank of Vienna, Austria. Bearer bonds were a unique asset - they weren't registered to any named individual or company. They were completely private and amazingly simple to convert - whoever presented them for redemption at the bank would receive the proceeds, period. No proof of ownership, no identification, no questions asked. It made things even better that these bonds were denominated in US dollars, the world's primary currency. Six of them were issued for $1,000,000 each, and the seventh was in the amount of $182,677.

He picked up the diary and saw the bright red swastika glistening on its cover. Thumbing through a few pages, he came to the ciphers Philippe had described. Paul already had a good idea what they were. Later he'd try to prove it. He put everything in his valise and took a cab back to the warehouse district. Now it was time to finish things with his old partner.

Still tied to the center post, Philippe had passed out and slipped to the floor, sitting naked in his own waste. His left testicle, the one to which Paul had clamped the connector, was swollen to the size of a golf ball.

———

When Adriana heard the knock, she stopped packing and let Paul in. He glanced at the bed and saw her half-filled suitcase.

"Are you running away again?"

Enraged, she pounded on his chest with her fists. "What I do is none of your business! Where's Philippe - did you kill him? Who *are* you? I felt secure with you and I took a chance trusting you. You're some kind of wealthy adventurer, you said. I just begin believing you, and suddenly I learn that you two once tried to kill each other. Then you pull out a gun with a silencer and shoot him, right here in my hotel room. Thank God no one heard it. I want to know who you are, what you want with me, and exactly what's going on."

"So do I, Adriana. I want to know exactly what's going on too. You see, Philippe told me everything. You weren't Nicu's friend and confidante at all. You're a criminal just like Philippe. You were working for him the whole time, helping him steal from his grandfather and his siblings."

She broke down in tears. "I didn't do that! He only wanted the diary, and Nicu had given it to me by then anyway. I didn't steal from Nicu. He gave me everything in his safety deposit box. His grandchildren didn't know about it, he said. He told me to empty the box soon, before he died, so they wouldn't get it first. All I did was what he wanted. I'm telling you the truth! You have to believe me!"

"How much gold did you take?"

"All there was - twenty-three bars. Nicu gave them to me. I already told you that."

"But understand this. I don't believe you. Philippe stole over a hundred and fifty bars. They were in a safety deposit box, just like you say yours were. Here's what I think really happened. Nicu had only one box. The gold bars you got came from Philippe. They were part of the hoard he stole from his own brother and sister. It makes total sense that he gave you some of the gold. After all, you were his lover and his partner in crime. According to him, you were even screwing his brains out today, just minutes before I knocked on your door. Deny that, Adriana! It happened, didn't it?"

She screamed, "Stop it, Paul! Stop it! Yes, that happened, but it's not like you think. I hate him! I hate him! You're all wrong about this. Please believe me." She embraced him, but he pushed her away roughly.

"Prove it, Adriana. Prove I'm wrong. Give me the other book. I know you have it."

"First him, now you! What the hell is it about that old book? You're as bad as he is!"

She ran to her suitcase, furiously dug to the bottom and pulled out Hitler's manifesto. She threw it across the room and yelled, "Here! Have fun reading how Adolf intended to rule the world. Get out, Paul! Go to hell! I never want to see you again!"

As he walked into the hallway, she slammed the door behind him.

CHAPTER THIRTY-SIX

For the better part of two days Paul had worked on the diary. His original theory had been correct: the numerals were words, encoded using a process called a book cipher. It was a remarkably simple but extremely effective way to encrypt a message. In fact, it was one he had used himself in the days when he worked as an assassin for the CIA. The sender and receiver each had identical books. Words were then encoded using page numbers and word counts in that book. Since both parties had exactly the same edition of the book, the code could easily be decrypted. In Nicu's case, there was no receiver; he was simply encoding things he didn't want people to see. He therefore needed only one book as his decryption key.

As soon as he heard how important Hitler's book had been to Nicu, Paul was sure that *Mein Kampf* would solve the puzzle. Once he got into it, he expected to find that Nicu had encoded certain words using the book as his key. The old man had instructed Adriana to guard the book until she needed it. In its flyleaf he had even written the words, "This is my most important book." The final clue - the icing on the cake - was the sentence Nicu had written in the diary, just before the first numbers appeared.

For understanding I turn to my Fuhrer's famous book. It will guide me.

It wouldn't take long to determine if these numbers constituted a book cipher code. Paul knew exactly where to start. He turned to the end of the book and saw that there were 913 pages. Next he counted the words on a random page, getting a rough idea how many words there were per page. The page he'd counted had 527 words, so he knew that a typical page would have somewhere around that number. Now he was ready to test his theory that this was a book cipher. He looked at the first numeric line, Nicu's entry for January 2, 1944.

89889 88380 89448 86244 04801 67018 80094 04004 89889 57216

If he was correct, these ten sets of numbers actually were a ten-word sentence. The first number was 89889. The first two or three numbers, 89 or 898, would be the page. The last two or three numbers, 889 or 89, pointed to a certain word on that page. Since the book had 913 pages, the first numbers could be either page 89 or page 898. The last number, indicating which word to use, was either 889 or 89. Since an average page had 527 words, Paul knew it had to be 89. He turned to page 898 and counted words. The eighty-ninth word was *das* - in English, *the*. That was the first and also the ninth word of the sentence.

It was a slow process because every word required a different page and a sometimes long word count. That was the beauty of the book cipher. It was impossible to decode without knowing which exact book to use, and it was incredibly simple if you knew. Ten minutes later his theory was confirmed. He had decoded a complete sentence of ten German words. In English there were eleven.

The Reich is building a secret tunnel for the Ghost Train.

He shuddered with anticipation. This was exactly what he'd hoped for. He worked on a few more sets of numbers, every line of which became a complete sentence.

Paul skimmed the book, roughly counting how many numeric sequences there were. There were so many that he knew the decoding project would take days. He flipped back to check the last entries, the ones for August 20 and 21, 1944. He found it interesting that the diary ended on August 21 but the train log from Bucharest

Station continued. Its last entry was ten days later, a day before the Red Army entered Bucharest.

When the Ghost Train left Nicu's station on August 21, the Nazi's mission was obviously complete. He'd have confirmed it arrived in Sinaia, Paul knew, but presumably there was nothing more to write in the diary. He knew his beloved Reich was going down in defeat. He must have chosen to end his journal on a success, not the looming failure he could see coming.

As he read Nicu's last two entries, he noticed something intriguing. Both days talked of Operation Geist, the Ghost, and the last notation said that the Ghost Train was coming to Bucharest that very day. From what little Paul had seen in the journal so far, all earlier references to the Ghost Train had been encrypted. Now when things were almost over, there was no code anymore. The Ghost Train was there in German for anyone to read. Did it no longer matter? Was the mystery train a secret no longer? Or was the train on August 21 not the real one at all, but just a decoy? Was the real train already hidden away in the mountains?

There was something else strange about these last two diary entries. He had written more code, but this was different. Several times the numerals appeared, but now they were separated by periods or a slash. Whatever this was, Nicu wasn't using the book cipher code anymore. This was different.

27843.47747.08012.47747.92001/48286

Paul tackled this enigma by looking up the six words that corresponded to the numbers. That didn't work. The German words were *provident manifest boy manifest concern modern.* Because of the number of pages and words per page, the second and fourth words could also be *pardon*, the third could be *wheel* and the last could be *castle*. Why did Nicu encrypt these differently? What did the four periods and the slash mark mean?

It was obvious from reading the entries that the coded numbers stood for a place. The German words preceding each use of the sequence mentioned proceeding *to*, or supervising a project *at*, or building a tunnel *under* whatever the coded sequence meant. He had only that tiny morsel of information to guide him.

He played with the words, rearranging them and using their first letters to make a new one, but it didn't work. He stared at them in hopes he'd find the meaning. Maybe Nicu had used another book to encode this entry. Paul dismissed that as unlikely. If it were true, there would have been a clue to guide whomever Nicu intended to be the one who deciphered his journal.

Paul kept at it for two hours straight. Sore and tired from sitting, he wrote the numbers and the words on a scrap of paper and took them to a nearby coffee shop. He gazed at the page, moving the numbers around in his head. Nothing made any sense, no matter what he did with them. What was Nicu trying to say?

But wait! These numbers were different from all the others - they were separated by periods and a slash. Suddenly he got it! He rushed back to try his theory.

What if the first five numbers, the sequence 27843, represented a single letter instead of a word? He turned to page 278 and counted forty-three letters. He wrote down an S. This method of decoding was more difficult than before. Because there were so many individual letters on a page, each code number could have two, maybe even three possible meanings. The number 27843 could refer to the forty-third letter on page 278, or the eight hundred forty-third letter on page 27.

He pressed on, ignoring the final sequence of numerals for now. It was unlike the rest, separated by a slash mark instead of a period. If that one was a word, it was either *modern* or *castle*. Maybe when he was finished, it would make sense.

The letters didn't help, but could this be an anagram? There were so many combinations of letters that he couldn't do this on his own. He searched the Internet and found a computer program that would sort anagrams and provide every possible solution. He entered the letters and soon had a confusing list of jabberwocky. Except for one word. There was one exciting possibility, one that could make sense. Using the last number as the word *castle*, he added the computer-generated word *peles*.

Paul had heard of Peles Castle, the most famous royal residence in Romania. Fired up, he did a quick search to find out about it.

Peles Castle was a massive 150-year-old building situated in the remote Carpathian Mountains ninety miles northwest of Bucharest. It had been taken over by the Nazis from 1943 until 1945. The family was forced to move out and the grounds were put under heavy guard, but records showed no war-related use of the huge facility. The Nazis appropriated it but did nothing with it. Why was that? Why had Hitler wanted Peles Castle but then did nothing there?

That old feeling, the familiar rush of excitement when he'd made a breakthrough, was everywhere inside him once again. Paul had solved this mystery.

There actually *had* been activity at Peles Castle. The Nazis didn't record it because it was top secret.

The lonely mountain retreat was a perfect location to build a tunnel that would hide a train.

At the same time he was on fire with the thrill of discovery, he had to face a problem. He couldn't do everything himself. He had to have help.

CHAPTER THIRTY-SEVEN

The Reich is building a secret tunnel for the Ghost Train.

Those first tantalizing words Paul decoded had fueled the passion he'd felt so many times before. The anticipation of a discovery, the adrenalin-rushing possibility of treasure, the enthusiastic desire to focus on nothing but this - all of this put Paul on an emotional rocket to the moon. He couldn't focus on the numbers any longer. He couldn't concentrate on the diary. He couldn't think about anything except a castle in the countryside, a tunnel beneath it, and a 1940s freight train with thirteen loaded boxcars sitting on a track deep inside the hidden passage.

The decoding process was critical; there had to be far more information about the Ghost Train in Nicu's cryptic numerals. There could be instructions and clues that he'd require. But there was a major logistical issue. Paul had glanced at every page in the diary, counting over a hundred that contained numbers. Some pages had a lot, some only a few. The fact was, this was no simple deciphering project. Untangling each number would take days - days he didn't have.

The time was up. He had to let the minister know exactly what he'd found. He couldn't keep this information to himself even a few more days, despite how much easier it would have made things. Once Herr Deutsch became aware of what Paul knew, this cat could never be put back into the bag. Things would be out of his control. There would be jurisdictional considerations. The Ghost Train was a Nazi issue, but Nicu's diary revealed that it was sitting under a castle in Romania. Two governments would be vying for control, publicity and the inevitable fifteen minutes of fame that would accompany the announcement.

He had to wait one more day to call Herr Deutsch so he could get his problem solved. That afternoon Paul flew to Amsterdam, and by evening he was standing outside Adriana's new flat, carry-on bag in hand.

Adriana was preparing dinner in the comfortable apartment she'd lived in for only three days. Using cash from the black card, she'd set up a bank account and rented her new place. That little card was remarkable - whenever she ran low, she simply went to an ATM and got more. Unless someone ever asked questions, she was in a perfect situation. She intended to keep a low profile. When her doorbell rang, it gave her a chill. No one was supposed to know she was here.

Through the closed door she shouted, "Yes?"

She heard a familiar voice. "Hello, Adriana."

It didn't surprise her he was here, because she really hadn't been trying to hide. She had used her new name to rent the flat, and he knew that name. She simply didn't think he'd come back, and part of her didn't want him here. After the stormy ending to their last encounter, she had doubted she would hear from him again. And perhaps that was best, she had decided.

When she opened the door, her gypsy eyes were fiery. "I'm not Adriana anymore. What do you want?"

"Nice to see you too," he replied cordially. "May I come in?"

Saying nothing, she turned and walked into a cozy living room with a fire burning in a tiny grate. He shut the front door, dropped his bag and said, "Long time no see."

She snarled a sarcastic reply. "Yeah, what's it been - a week? Can't live without me?"

"I need your help."

"*You? You* need someone else's help? Bullshit, you self-sufficient asshole! You've never needed anyone's help in your life!" She was yelling and her face was turning bright red.

Calmly he said it again. "I need your help, Adriana."

His demeanor rankled her and she screamed, "I told you I'm not Adriana! Adriana's dead! Gone! I'm Carey - Carey Apostol. Get it?"

"Carey . . ."

"No, Paul! I don't want anything to do with you! I can't. I trusted you enough that I ended up in bed with you. I believed what you told me, but all you really wanted from me was that damned book. I hope it was worth it. You're a bastard and I hate you . . ." She couldn't hold back any longer. She dissolved in tears.

He walked to her without a word and took her in his arms, enveloping her body as she tried to push back.

"Stop it!" She squirmed, trying to beat his chest as he held her arms tightly. She looked up at him, her face contorted in anger, and he kissed her. Her half-hearted struggle lasted only a moment before he felt her change. Suddenly she kissed him back, deeply and passionately, over and over. She put her arms around him and clung for dear life.

"Don't do this to me," she whispered. "Don't hurt me again."

"I won't," he promised as she led him to her bedroom.

CHAPTER THIRTY-EIGHT

Carey loved Paul Silver. She was emotionally conflicted in the same way as she'd been with Nicu, but she truly did love Paul. She had loved him since that day they met. Love: it was an unusual concept, one she hadn't ever really experienced before. For several years, love had equated to sweaty sex with strangers for ten minutes at a time in the back room of her little shop. More recently love had meant the reluctant feelings she had for the monster who had given her both bloodstained gold and a new life.

This time it had been different. She had quickly fallen for this rugged, handsome adventurer, and she had believed everything he told her, which admittedly hadn't been much. When she watched the fight in her hotel room, she knew Paul Silver was a totally different person. He could be a brutal, methodical man, one comfortable with violence and a man who knew how to inflict pain on others. The sudden metamorphosis had petrified her. She had recoiled, realizing how stupid it had been to trust someone she had just met. She felt betrayed and she retaliated by rejecting him.

Paul's arrival on her doorstep took her by surprise. Part of her wanted to jump into his arms, but she was afraid. She had no idea what he wanted, and she couldn't allow herself to fall back into the same behavior. She had to be careful.

Her caution and her good intentions had lasted for a grand total of ten minutes.

Their lovemaking took on a carnal wildness that had surprised them both. As he brought her passion to heights she'd never experienced, she began to act like a ravenous creature. She literally wanted to consume him. She clawed, she bit, she squeezed him in sensitive places until he cried out for her to stop. She loved every second of it, and obviously so did he. Paul had responded with a fierceness that would have been close to cruelty, had they not both been so intensely craving every moment of the experience.

Exhausted, they lay together on the sweat-drenched sheets. Paul laughingly asked her if she'd been trying to kill him.

"You're the savage in this equation," she responded with a chuckle of her own.

"I don't think so. Want to see the marks you left on me?" He raised his arm to reveal a red welt.

"Crybaby. You loved it."

"Of course I did. It's because I was making love with you for the first time."

"Really? I don't think so . . ."

"The other time? That was Adriana. She's gone now. This was my first sexual encounter with Carey Apostol, you sultry hellcat!"

She guffawed. "Wait a minute! That was Carey's first experience too! Does that make me a virgin?"

"Whatever you say," he countered. "I don't think there are many virgins who know how to do the things you just did."

"You never know! We gypsies are a strange breed."

They carried on until at last she hopped out of bed and ran into the shower.

An hour later over an al fresco Italian lunch, Paul told her why he needed her help. He explained he had the diary; Philippe had told him it was in a train locker. As she listened, she wondered how much pain Philippe had endured by the time he confessed where he'd hidden the

214

diary. She forced the thought from her mind. She wanted Paul to be a good person, not a sadistic killer.

Paul told her he needed help decoding the diary. Using her made perfect sense, he explained. The book's potential secrets made it risky to involve outsiders, and she understood Nicu and the diary's background already. He explained how the other book was the key. There really was a train - a Ghost Train - hidden in a tunnel in Romania, he told her. Supposedly it held the greatest treasures of Nazi Germany. If Nicu's diary were true, and if no one had found the train for seventy years, then the train was still sitting there.

She could see the excitement burning in his eyes as he related everything he'd learned. He really did enjoy the adventures, and if he was right, this one could top them all. She'd read a little of the diary that first night she had it, and now his enthusiasm was rubbing off.

"Do you know exactly where the train is?"

"Not exactly," he responded, deftly skirting the truth. He didn't want to reveal everything just yet to a girl he didn't know that well. And truthfully, he knew it was at Peles Castle but not *exactly* where.

"I have to go to Berlin. This thing is too big - too potentially explosive - to keep it to myself. I'm obligated to inform the Ministry."

She jested, "I'm glad sex with me was more important than going to Berlin!"

Paul snickered at that.

"I'm counting on your help. It's going to take days and it's going to be tedious, but we have to learn what Nicu was hiding. I've made a copy of the diary to leave with you, and I brought Hitler's book."

She was hooked. She wanted to help him already, and his enthusiasm was so infectious that Carey readily agreed. Back at the flat he showed her how to use *Mein Kampf* to decode the numbers. Finally he said, "Okay, you know everything now. It's nearly four p.m. If I go to the airport, I can fly to Berlin tonight and meet the minister tomorrow morning."

"But you'll be leaving your decoding expert here all alone with no payment for her services," she purred, squeezing his thigh with her hand. "There are flights in the morning, and you'll still see the minister before noon. Call him and set it all up. You have ten minutes. I'll meet you in the bedroom for my payment."

The next morning Paul flew to Berlin and gave his friend Franz Deutsch, Germany's Minister of the Interior, the electrifying revelation. The minister was practically hysterical, hardly able to contain his delight. He immediately called his counterpart in the Romanian government, a man whom he had met at conferences over the years. Being a cabinet-level official in Germany, the economic superpower of Europe, Deutsch would typically have dealt from a position of strength with the far less powerful Romanian official. Politics being the animal it was, the German minister deftly steered Romania's Minister of Internal Affairs into believing the decisions they agreed upon were his.

Peles Castle unquestionably was within Romanian borders. Claim to whatever was found there would be the purview of Romania's government, and any decisions would by right come from that country's minister. Herr Deutsch masterfully steered his friend, using phrases such as, "shouldn't we," "don't you think," "wouldn't this be best," and the like.

Germany had a claim too, he smoothly offered. If the train were real, then it was German, put there by the Nazis and filled with stolen property that must be dealt with. "I will defer to your wishes, of course," he continued without effort, "and I think a joint press conference should be held once we know for sure. You are going to be famous soon, Mr. Minister. Don't you think it makes perfect sense that we go there first and see it for ourselves before making the announcement? Pictures and solid information will be far more dramatic than innuendo and hearsay. If that's your suggestion, Mr. Minister, I'm prepared to meet you. Would tomorrow or the next day work?"

GHOST TRAIN

They worked out a plan for three days from now. Herr Deutsch said he and two others would fly to Bucharest airport. The Romanian minister would meet them with a limousine for the short trip to Sinaia. They also agreed to dispatch twenty soldiers from each of their countries a day early. They would go to work at the site when the ministers arrived.

The German minister was a smooth manipulator, skilled in guiding others to do his bidding. By the time the call ended, his counterpart actually believed it was he who had talked the German into visiting the site without informing their respective prime ministers. In fact, it was the other way around. There was no political danger for Herr Deutsch to keep the train private from his superiors because it wasn't on German soil. What Deutsch had to do was to be sure the Romanian didn't tell his bosses. Deutsch wanted to see this exciting discovery before the Romanian government got involved. If the train was there, Romania could assert a claim of ownership and lock down the area. Whatever the outcome, the German minister knew this site could soon be the most closely guarded place in Europe.

CHAPTER THIRTY-NINE

The more time Carey spent decoding the numbers, the more fascinating the task became. As she worked, she simply wrote down one decoded word after another without stopping to read sentences. When her eyes got tired and her brain began to go numb, she would pause for a cup of tea and read what she'd written so far. Those were the crazy, delightful times when she saw what Nicu was up to.

It was noon and time to stop for lunch. She'd been at this for four hours, and suddenly something dawned on her. She hadn't used heroin today! She hadn't wanted it. She hadn't even given it a thought. That buoyed her spirits even more, knowing that she was on a different high, one driven by unlocking the incredible secrets of Nicu Lepescu.

She knew a little already; she'd read the last two entries of the diary. Paul admitted he'd read them too. So much of what was encoded in early 1944 was openly written in German words by late August. The end of the war was imminent, Nicu had to have known.

"Since you've read the end, I have a question," she said. "Did you notice that the code was different there? There are periods and a slash separating the numbers. Did you work on that at all? I haven't, since I'm going straight through from the first, but I just wondered if you could save me some time at the end."

Of course Paul knew the answer. It was Peles Castle. But he kept it a secret, still not ready to entrust everything to this girl he hardly knew. She didn't need to know where the train was right now. It made no difference for the work she was doing.

"Keep going as you are. I want you to go through it chronologically. I'll work on those last entries."

Today was the second day of Carey's mind-numbing decoding of numerals. She was nearly three months into the diary, almost finished with March, 1944. There were five months to go. The two of them spoke every evening; during yesterday's call, she'd told him about the coded entries beginning on January 2, Nicu's first day as stationmaster, and continuing into the next month.

Paul had already deciphered the first sentence.

The Reich is building a secret tunnel for the Ghost Train.

She told him that on New Year's Day 1944, Reichsmarschall Göring himself had flown from Berlin to Bucharest for the sole purpose of meeting with Nicu Lepescu, the new stationmaster.

"Wait a minute! Are you serious?" Paul burst out. "What's that all about? Even though by now he's no longer Hitler's golden boy, he's still a top-ranking officer in the Reich, a very important and very busy man. The war is going really badly by now, but a top Nazi takes time on a holiday to fly to Bucharest just to meet the new stationmaster? What the hell did he do that for? It makes no sense."

"Hold on tight and you're going to be surprised!" she proclaimed.

The diary was full of boasts and self-confidence. *Göring was effusive in his praise of my work,* Nicu wrote. While at Auschwitz Nicu had been assigned two important projects - the extension of a rail line to bring prisoners closer to the camp and the repair of one of the crematoria that had been taken out of service. He accomplished them in record time and with an impressive attention to detail, he dutifully records Göring having said.

"Maybe that was true," Adriana added. " Göring's about to hire him for the biggest project of all!"

GHOST TRAIN

The Reichsmarschall explained he had come because he wanted Nicu to oversee a top-secret project. Nicu had demonstrated both his skill at management and his unwavering dedication to the Reich. Göring gave him only minimal information about the job. *He said I would be told more as the project unfolded and I needed to know more*, Nicu had written. The operation was so secret it didn't even have a name.

Carey stopped a moment. "On a related subject, when you looked through the stationmaster's log, did you happen to see if some of the daily entries were in a different handwriting?"

He'd seen it but hadn't given it any thought.

"What do you gather from that?"

"Nicu wasn't there on those days. Someone else - maybe a deputy - made the entries instead. The first was on January 3, two days after Göring's visit. Nicu went somewhere - a place in the mountains he never mentions by name - and met a crew of workers he would be supervising. To keep things secret, Nicu says, he would continue serving as stationmaster and no one would be the wiser. He'd make periodic trips to this place, which must have been close by since he was never gone overnight. There were several lieutenants who reported to Nicu and who were responsible for keeping over a thousand workers busy. From his notes at the end of the diary they were mostly Jews, I'd say."

Absolutely, Paul reflected without comment. He thought about how easily Nicu could have made a day trip to check on the progress of his important project. It was only eighty-five miles away. He could be off in the morning and back by dusk.

She told him more. Nicu wrote about his frequent visits to this nearby place. The workers were building train tracks and removing dirt for some type of huge tunnel. "It was going to be over six hundred feet long," she exclaimed. "This was quite a job!"

At last she said, "When I quit for today, I was into late March. The project has been underway for nearly two months and Nicu has been going there at least once a week. He thinks they're maybe a third of the way toward finishing."

They ended today's call with wishes for luck and a promise to talk tomorrow.

Yesterday after she finished the notes from March 28, Carey had stopped. The next entry would take far more time because it was page after page of numerals. This morning she sat at the table and tackled it with mixed emotions. She knew it would be tedious, but she couldn't wait for the results. Today's decryption would take her all morning, maybe longer. The good news was that it had taken Nicu equally long to encrypt it. She wanted to know just what he'd considered so secret.

Around noon she stopped for lunch and read the pages of words she'd decoded. When she finished, she treated herself to a glass of wine, since she had finally learned where all those gold bars had come from.

CHAPTER FORTY

Carey could hardly wait for this evening's call. After the successful morning, she had kept pushing through the process until she reached midsummer 1944. At the end of the afternoon, she poured another glass of wine and waited for him to call.

She had reaped one unbelievably positive result from Paul's project. She hadn't had a fix in three days. Even better, she didn't want one. After a bit of retrospective self-analysis, she admitted she'd spent most of her adult life doing absolutely nothing productive. Her days had been filled with mindless drivel. She had played away her university days with Philippe, then told fortunes, screwed men in the back room, and spent months chatting with Nicu about whatever he wanted to talk about. What she needed was structure and meaning in her life. Heroin had come close to being her god, she knew, but now she had a purpose.

Paul Silver had come along just in time. She still barely knew him. He was an enigma, but for some inexplicable reason she believed he was her answer. She was in love with this man, in adult love for the first time. She struggled to understand why she felt this way but gave it up. There was no value in analyzing it. Simply put, there was a physical, mental and emotional attraction - a chemistry - that she could neither explain nor deny.

She had no idea how he really felt about her. She had no idea about anything involving this complex man who scared her and made her fulfilled all at the same time. Heroin had given her a thrill, a coursing wave of euphoria and a feeling of peace and self-worth. But Paul Silver was a million times more addictive than heroin. With him, she needed nothing else.

But she didn't *have* him. There would be a time to talk about that, she hoped. There *had* to be. She was powerless to let him go unless he thrust her away.

On the other side, Paul was at a crossroads. He either had to trust her completely or not at all. Soon enough she was going to find out he knew more than he'd told her. He continued to keep secrets from her, but suddenly he was feeling remorseful about it.

Damn. Why am I doing this? I promised myself it wouldn't happen again.

If he and the minister took a crew to Peles Castle tomorrow and began a full-scale search, it would ultimately end up on the news. When Carey saw it, she'd know he lied to her. He really didn't owe her answers; she was simply helping him out by decoding the diary. But there was more to it than that. They'd had sex, sure. He'd had sex with a hundred others. He was certain she had too. Sex on its own meant nothing. But his time with her had been different.

What was it about her? As much as he pretended not to know what was happening, there was no mistaking the feelings. Deep in the Guatemalan jungle when Hailey Knox had left him, he shut a door in his heart and promised it would be closed forever. Never again would he deal with the baggage that came with love.

And yet here it was. This wasn't something he wanted. It wasn't something he thought was right for him. Quite the contrary. He wanted nothing to do with it. But he wanted Carey Apostol. He didn't know anything about who she really was, her background or her life. But it didn't matter.

That door inside his heart was open again. He couldn't fight it.

GHOST TRAIN

He had to tell her everything. If that drove her away, then that was how it would be. He was going to trust someone for the first time since Philippe betrayed him.

She eagerly answered his call.

"I was about to give up! How did the day go?" she asked, trying to be nice by letting him go first when all she wanted was to tell him what she'd learned today.

"It was good. I'm working with my friend Hans Steffen, the director of the historical museum. He'll be accompanying the minister and me tomorrow when we go look for the train."

"Really? That is news! How do you know where to look?"

"There's a little piece of the puzzle I haven't been totally forthcoming about," he confessed. "I know where the train is, Carey."

He explained what the last numbers meant, the ones with periods and a slash. Nicu had encoded them as single characters, not words. When decrypted, the string of numerals became an anagram with only one possible meaning: Peles Castle.

"The castle's only eighty-five miles from Bucharest. I'm certain that's where the tunnel was built. We're meeting a work crew there tomorrow."

At first she was incensed that he deliberately kept this information from her. She was angry and wanted to lash back with a sharp rebuke. She stopped for a moment. *Why do this? He doesn't have to tell me anything. Don't make a major issue out of it.*

She'd been silent so long that he finally said, "Are you upset with me? I'm sorry . . ."

"Don't be sorry. I understand completely and I'm not upset. I'm glad you're telling me now. Peles Castle is in Sinaia. My parents took me there once when I was a child. It's a beautiful place in the mountains. And very remote. I agree it's a perfect hiding place. Tomorrow's going to be an exciting day!"

He could sense there was a smile on her face as she continued. "I thought I had something important to tell *you,*

225

but now I'd rather listen than talk. Tell me more; then I have news for you too!"

Paul told her everything about his research. He said he would be lost without the diary, and he told her how much he appreciated her help.

She was ecstatic at what secrets might still lie hidden in the old man's diary, and she was committed to giving Paul the answers he needed. She made a promise.

"The last thing I decoded was from mid-July. There are only five weeks left in the diary and only a few pages with massive blocks of numerals. Starting now I'll work straight through for as long as it takes to finish the whole thing. Who knows what else he encrypted? By tomorrow morning I'll be finished."

"Perfect," he told her. "Now it's your turn. You said you had something important you wanted to tell me. I'm hoping it's about the decrypting you did today!

She related what Nicu had written on March 29th. "The uncoded part of that day's entry introduces a Lieutenant Schlosser, who was a Nazi storm trooper like Nicu. Schlosser's the man in charge of what Nicu calls an elite team who are guarding the huge storeroom at the station. Once the words stop and the code begins, this gets really interesting."

Nicu didn't reveal how the two came to partner up in a criminal enterprise, but she explained how things worked. Each day around five, he and Schlosser rewarded the team of soldiers with a trip to a beer garden around the corner and a couple of rounds of drinks paid for by the two generous officers. Nicu and the lieutenant would even stay on duty to guard the storeroom. It appeared to be a magnanimous gesture, but really it was a clever ploy to get the men away from their posts for an hour every afternoon.

There was so much stored in the massive room that an inventory would be impossible, the two must have realized as they hatched their plan. The Nazis shipped priceless objects and gold bullion so quickly and in such huge amounts that records were impossible. The shipments were simply categorized by type - gold, paintings and so forth. There was never a specific amount or a detailed description. Nicu and Lieutenant Schlosser began stealing gold bars. Each man took one or two every day. Some days, Nicu wrote, he took three. He also stole jewelry now and then, remarking on how there were buckets of it sitting everywhere in those days. She had found no clue as to where Nicu hid what he stole, she told Paul.

"You know that Nicu gave me twenty-three bars. Do you also recall what I told you he said? He said I could have them because there was much, much more for his greedy grandchildren. If he took a bar a day between March 29 and August 21, that's maybe a hundred and fifty. And he admits they took more than one bar on some days. Just think, Paul! Somewhere there's got to be a cache of gold still hidden, don't you think? You not only have a train to look for, you have millions in gold bars that Nicu stole!"

"Amazing! Great detective work. This gets more unbelievable every time we talk!"

He said he'd call her at eight in the morning to get an update. She ate a light dinner and went straight back to work. Dawn was breaking as she finished. With only a couple of hours until he'd be calling, she set her alarm and crawled into bed.

Paul hadn't told her about torturing Philippe and sending him out into the streets a ruined man with a broken body. She knew Paul had gotten Philippe's diary from the train station locker, but that was all she knew. She had no idea there had been six million dollars in bearer bonds in that locker too. Paul had the bonds, but could there be more gold than what they'd already found?

As he packed for the trip tomorrow, his mind raced with calculations. Nicu stole gold every day. If "every day" meant weekdays, and he had done it every day for twenty weeks, then there had been around a hundred days of thefts. If weekends were included, or if he had taken two or three bars a day, there was more gold somewhere. Paul had accounted for 192 bars - 23 that Nicu gave Carey and 169 Philippe had taken from the Vienna safety deposit box. Carey thought there might be more, and Paul began to think so too. The two safety deposit box keys in Nicu's personal effects had made recovery of those first 192 bars a simple task. But where would he have hidden more?

Nicu had spent a few years after the war as a free man, followed by two decades in prison. When he was released in 1971, he never held a job, but he had sufficient wealth to buy an apartment building and anything else he needed. He also had 192 gold bars stuck away in two banks. Where could more be?

Suddenly he knew! He knew where Nicu could have stashed his loot! Paul sat at his laptop, sent a couple of emails, and set a business transaction in motion. Although he was wealthy, he usually didn't blow a million dollars on a hunch. It wasn't money down the drain, he rationalized. Whether the gold was there or not, he'd own an asset.

CHAPTER FORTY-ONE

The minister's call to Romania concluded on a positive note and he turned to Paul. "Hans Steffen has been waiting all this time outside my office," he said. "I'm sure he's about to explode wondering what we're doing in here! Let's bring him in."

Steffen joined them, patting Paul on the back as he took a chair. The minister said, "Paul's made a miraculous discovery, Hans. He thinks he knows the location of the Ghost Train. It's in a tunnel, he believes. I'm sending a crew of workmen to the site, and the Romanian minister is doing the same. We're going to see if the train really is there!"

"It's in a tunnel?" Hans was incredulous. "There's a *tunnel*? Where's the site, Minister? Apologies for my rudeness, but I can hardly wait to learn more! This is so exciting!"

The minister gestured for Paul to continue.

Without going into detail, Paul said he'd located the stationmaster's diary, which was replete with coded entries. Once he broke the code, he learned Nicu had been selected by Reichsmarschall Göring to oversee construction of a secret tunnel at Peles Castle, a tunnel outfitted with a very long train track.

Hans interrupted enthusiastically. "Peles Castle, eh? Sounds fascinating! Where exactly is that?"

Paul laughed. The man was like an eager child bursting to know more. "It's in Sinaia, a ski town not far from Bucharest. The castle's remote and isolated, and the Nazis seized it in 1943 for an undisclosed purpose. The most fascinating part of this is how it all ties back to Nicu's master log. Hans, you recall the stationmaster ledger from 1944 that we found hidden in the bunker. Do you know why Göring had it sent there?

Almost overcome by all this, Hans wiped his brow and answered, "I think I do! You found the Ghost Train in that book! Hitler hid the book to keep the train secret, to make sure no one found the riches he hid away for the future rebuilding of Germany!"

The minister smiled as he watched the animated conversation playing out across his desk. It was good to see his subordinate so fired up about the project, and in fact, he was excited too. If it were actually there, it would be one of the world's major discoveries, a good thing both for his country and for himself.

Paul continued, "The entry for August 21 perfectly matched my findings from the diary. Massive quantities of artwork, statuary and gold had been accumulating at Bucharest station for several weeks. Now that the war was ending, it was time. On August 21, a thirteen-car train arrived in Bucharest empty and departed fully loaded, each car brimful of priceless objects and bullion. Within mere hours Romania would no longer be part of the Axis, and Reichsmarschall Göring snatched away the booty just in time.

"That train was destined for Sinaia, a little town known solely for its winter sports activities," Paul concluded with a flourish. "It's a strange place to take billions of dollars in treasure, don't you think? And here's the coup de grace, gentlemen. The train went to Sinaia that day, but it never returned! I think I know why. It's still there!"

The minister toyed with Hans. "I'm thinking of going to the site. Do you know anyone else I should include on the trip?"

"Sir," Hans stammered, his head bowed. "I'd be honored . . . and Paul! Paul, of course!"

"Have no fear, my good man! Both of you must come!" Deutsch exclaimed with a beaming smile. "I wouldn't allow you to miss this opportunity. Without your efforts we wouldn't be at this critical juncture. We'll leave from the municipal airport sharply at ten tomorrow morning. Meet me at the government terminal and plan to stay a few days. I may need to fly back, but if we find something, you'll remain as my on-site representatives."

Paul got very little sleep that night. He kept waking up, anticipating tomorrow with an enthusiasm he hadn't felt since that time in Guatemala, where he'd found a treasure but lost a woman he loved.

At eight the next morning, he called Carey to learn if she'd found any last secrets from Nicu's diary.

"Good morning," she murmured, glancing at the clock. She'd slept through her alarm, but it was okay. It was truly a good morning, she thought lazily as she held her cell phone in one hand and stretched her arms and legs as much as she could. *He's going to like this!* she thought.

"I'm hoping you have more news for me. What time did you get to bed?"

"A couple of hours ago. But I finished, and now I have something exciting to tell you!" She yawned and sighed. "Hold on a sec while I grab an energy drink."

In the entry for August 20, the day before the Ghost Train arrived, Nicu had written that the tunnel wasn't entirely finished, but Göring ordered him to stop. He'd described massive doors into the main tunnel and three hundred meters of track. She reminded Paul of words he clearly remembered reading. He waited patiently for her to move the story along.

"You may not remember," she continued, "but his last words for August 20 were his hope that his project, his secret place, would be the resting place for the future of Nazi Germany. After that were five pages of numbers."

Paul smiled. "And so it appears at last we get to the point!"

She laughed too. "I'm half asleep. You have to give me a break!"

"I have two hours until I meet the minister. You have my undivided attention and all the breaks you need!"

"How about this for some news. Those five pages describe how the workers hid the huge doors to the tunnel."

She consulted her notes and explained exactly what to look for at the castle. She had so much detailed information he asked for a copy of the notes, and soon he had an email. He studied them closely in his taxi to the airport. He was wildly enthused about the trip.

Let the adventure begin!

CHAPTER FORTY-TWO

The three men flew to Bucharest in a comfortable Lear jet, the thousand-mile trip taking a little over two hours. As a driver took them to Sinaia, the Romanian minister explained the interesting legal situation involving Peles Castle, which he explained was now a popular tourist attraction. Each year thousands visited the beautiful grounds and toured the nineteenth-century buildings.

"The government controls the site under a lease from the family of King Michael I, the same monarch who rescued Romania from the Axis in the 1944 coup. Since the war, the castle has belonged to the state, so one might ask why the government needs to lease something it already owns. It's a complex situation. In 2006 the government announced plans to return ownership of the castle to the royal family, but up until now there have only been extended negotiations. Today, a formal lease is the means by which the government of Romania has the right of entry onto the property, even though the government owns it!"

Paul considered how complex the situation would become if they found treasure there. Would the royal family own it? Was Peles Castle their property, since ownership hadn't yet been formally transferred? That would be interesting. He said nothing; it wasn't his place to bring up a sensitive issue with a man he'd just met. Nevertheless, he knew if the train really was hidden below the castle, the ownership issue would escalate into a big deal very quickly.

Forty soldiers, twenty from each country, sat in the shade of tall pine trees at picnic tables intended for tourists. Two transport trucks and a small backhoe on a trailer were parked nearby. The men stubbed out cigarettes and stood at attention as the limousine pulled up. A pair of lieutenants saluted their respective ministers and were told to wait for orders.

Since the grounds were so extensive, the minister had arranged for a six-passenger golf cart and he was handed a walkie-talkie. Paul knew where to look, so he was designated the driver. They piled in and headed west through acres of beautifully manicured lawn, turning northward as they circled a steep hill atop which the massive castle stood. Its spires rose as if to touch the gray clouds above. Paul was looking for a landmark. He drove past an outcropping of rocks that jutted from the earth at the base of the hill, turned around and came back to them. From this place the castle was far, far above them, at least two hundred feet up a very steep incline, one that would have been a strenuous climb even for a seasoned hiker.

"Please call the soldiers," he asked Herr Deutsch as everyone got out. They chatted as they waited for the men to arrive. There was adventure in the air, and each of them caught the excitement in his own way. Soon the trucks and backhoe showed up.

"From Nicu's coded directions, I believe we should search here," he said. "We're looking for what he describes as 'massive doors into the main tunnel under Peles Castle.' They were covered by tons of dirt and marked by an outcropping of rocks designed to appear natural but, in fact, placed here deliberately." He pointed to the rocks projecting from the hillside. "I'm hoping that place is the one he described; it's the only one I've seen."

For nearly two hours the forty soldiers supplemented the efforts of the backhoe operator, digging with shovels as he removed massive quantities of dirt. Now there was a deep cut nearly fifteen feet high and extending ten feet into the hillside. The dirt removed by the machine was piled nearby, and more was being added every few minutes. So far they'd found nothing but rich soil.

The driver moved the machine back into the cut, lowered its bucket and sliced neatly into the wall of dirt before him. There was a noisy clang as the backhoe struck something solid. Paul, Hans and the ministers were sitting in the golf cart nearby and jumped as they heard the sound. They ran to the narrow cut but couldn't see anything in front of the backhoe because it filled the space completely.

"What is it?" the Romanian minister asked.

The driver shut off the noisy machine and replied, "I hit something. Probably metal."

"Keep going!"

He started the motor, filled the bucket with dirt and backed out to unload it. The four of them went in to look. There was nothing but soil.

As the operator shoveled more dirt, they heard metal strike against metal several times. The driver backed out again, shut off the machine and reported, "It's big. I moved the bucket up and down, side to side. Whatever's there seems to be made entirely of metal and it's very wide. Very tall too."

"It appears the old Nazi's directions might be accurate, Paul," Minister Deutsch said, beaming. "And gentlemen," he said to the others, "I think we may be about to witness history."

But today wouldn't be historically significant. When the sun began to set, it grew so dark inside the deep cut the backhoe operator couldn't continue. The Romanian minister promised to have construction lights set up by daybreak, in hopes of lighting the dark tunnel tomorrow. Some of the troops remained to guard the site while the rest were sent home for the night.

The four adventurers met for dinner in the rustic dining room of their hotel. There was an atmosphere of anticipation - high hopes, impatience and jovial discussion. They had cocktails and a wonderful meal; then they adjourned to the lounge, where a roaring fire awaited them.

"There's something we must do," the Romanian minister said as they settled in. "Has any of you had Dvin, the famous Armenian cognac?"

They hadn't.

"There's a reason we must have a glass or two," he replied with a smile as he signaled the waiter and placed the order. "This brandy is perfect for tonight's after-dinner drink among the four of us. Winston Churchill was a noted connoisseur of cognac, and Dvin was his favorite. The story is that the prime minister tried it at the Tehran Conference in 1943, thought it was the best thing he'd ever tasted, and drank a bottle a day until his death."

Paul was surprised. "A bottle a day? I've heard of his love of fine cigars, but that's one hell of a lot of brandy!"

"Yes, and it was impossible to get in England. When Josef Stalin heard of Churchill's passion for it, he personally arranged for the prime minister to always have a supply on hand. Does anyone recall the saying attributed to Churchill, when he was asked the secret of his long life?"

Hans Steffen replied, "Wasn't it something like, 'don't be late for lunch, smoke Havana cigars and drink good cognac?'"

"That's almost it. Actually the last part was 'drink Armenian cognac.' He considered our Eastern European brandies to be the best in the world."

"Obviously," Paul smirked. "He drank a bottle of it a day! My God, the man's liver must have been in terrible shape!"

They raised their snifters, and the German minister said, "To success, to the Allied forces who liberated Europe during the war, and to the memory of thousands who perished at the hands of the Nazis. May our treasure hunt tomorrow be fruitful, and may it honor those who died."

Glasses clinked and Dvin cognac went down the hatch. The consensus was it was the best they'd ever had. They thanked the minister for thinking of this very appropriate idea.

"How about I buy the next round?" Paul offered. That suggestion was met with enthusiastic approval.

They were the only guests left by the time the last drop was finished. The bartender bid them good night, and they retired upstairs, each of them dreaming of success tomorrow.

CHAPTER FORTY-THREE

Hoping a rewarding day awaited, they met up with the soldiers at Peles Castle at seven a.m. Soon the backhoe was belching and snorting smoke as the driver took out more bucketsful of soil. The almost constant sound of metal striking metal kept them on edge and excited. An hour after he began, the operator backed his machine out of the cut and turned it off.

"There's a solid wall blocking the entire passage," he reported. "I can't do any more."

The soldiers went in with shovels and finished the job. Since there was now a battery of huge lights shining into the deep cut, the four men could see the outline of a pair of doors. When the troops had finished clearing, Paul, Hans and the ministers took their place, standing in front of a steel barrier fifteen feet wide and nearly that tall. It consisted of two sides that would swing open. Enormous hinges were on the outside edges, and in the middle was a heavy chain and a bulky padlock.

The men stood in silence, unable to put their emotions into words. They were awed by the sheer magnitude - the ultimate importance to the world - of what might lie just on the other side of this door.

"My God, this is it," Hans Steffen whispered at last as a tear ran down his cheek. "It's big enough for a train. It is, isn't it? Amazing!"

Finally Herr Deutsch broke the reverie. "Shall we continue, gentlemen?"

The soldiers took picks and a sledgehammer to the lock and chain, and within minutes the encumbrances were gone. The Romanian minister ordered them to open the doors. After seventy years, the going was slow. The bulky hinges wouldn't budge at first, and the decision was made to hook a chain to one door, then to the backhoe, and use the machine to pull the door open.

Just as they were getting everything in place, a cheery female voice from behind them said, "Good morning, everyone!"

They looked around and the Romanian minister muttered, "Shit! What the hell is she doing here?"

Two people stood just outside the cut where they were working. One was an attractive brunette and the other, a young man, held a camera on his shoulder.

"Stop everything and give me a moment," he whispered to the others. Walking out to the newcomers, he said cordially, "Good morning. How may I help you?"

"We hear there's big news here. The word is that you've found something very important, something from World War II." She pointed to the cut. "You've done a lot of digging, haven't you? Do you mind if we shoot some footage while you work?"

The minister replied smoothly, "This is a restricted site, Miss Vasile. Once we are prepared to release information, I'll be sure my office contacts you."

"Of course, Minister," she answered. "Since the castle is public grounds, I'm sure you wouldn't mind if we stand out here and film for a bit. We have the right, you know."

He remained completely civil although his response was firm and crisp. "I'm afraid this is official government business. Surely you don't wish to interfere? I'm going to ask you politely to let us continue our work. Once there is something to talk about, I'm sure we will be seeing each other again." He turned to the lieutenant who was in charge of the Romanian troops. "Would you please escort Miss Vasile and her associate back to the castle?"

Once they were gone, he motioned the others away from the soldiers to a place where they could talk privately.

Paul asked, "What was that all about? How do you know her?"

"Everyone in Romania knows her. That's Nicoleta Vasile. She's the news anchor for TVR, the Romanian national television network. I'd bet one of the soldiers went home last night and told his friends about the huge iron door they uncovered. It doesn't take long for word to get around in a small country like ours. She must have driven up here from Bucharest this morning."

The German minister was concerned. "She made a point about this being public property. How can we continue if she has the legal right to be here?"

"This isn't Germany." The Romanian laughed. "Sometimes I wish we were more civilized, but instead much that happens in my country is a throwback to the Communist days. For us at this moment it is a good thing. Freedom of the press doesn't mean the same thing here as it does in the West. Nicole Vasile works for the same government that I do. And I outrank her. I can keep her away from here for today, but I can't keep her from broadcasting a story about something happening at Peles Castle. At six p.m. tonight our project will be a secret no longer."

Paul, Hans and Herr Deutsch went back to the door while the Romanian minister gave orders to his lieutenant. There would be security at this site starting this afternoon.

The backhoe operator tugged and pulled, the heavy machine struggling as the taut chain failed to budge the door. He tried again, then a third time. At last they heard a heavy groan and the door shuddered. It had been almost imperceptible, but the door had moved slightly.

"Again!" Hans yelled to the operator.

This time the groan became a rumble. The machine moved backwards as the door swung on its hinges. Now there was a two-foot gash in the middle of the huge steel barrier. The door was open!

Paul had anticipated this moment for so long he imagined himself rushing up to see what was inside. Instead he felt an unusual reverence. It wasn't his place to go first anyway - that privilege was reserved for the two governmental officials. They walked to the door, slipped through the slash of darkness, and were gone for over a minute. When they stepped back out, they switched off the cell phones they'd obviously used for light.

Hans and Paul rushed to Herr Deutsch as the Romanian shouted at his men to reposition the lights. Two of the soldiers carried the heavy stand into the tunnel. When they came out, everyone could see the amazement on their faces.

Deutsch extended his hand to Paul and exclaimed, "You did it. You found it, Paul."

"Do you mean . . ."

"I mean yes. Yes, there's a train sitting in there, still on its track. We could only see the last boxcar; the engine's obviously on the other end." He held out his phone to show Paul and Hans a picture. He'd shot the side of a dusty freight car, a huge swastika emblazoned on its side.

Once the lights were in place, the Romanian minister said jovially, "What are you standing here for? Don't you want to see it too?"

For the first time Paul Silver saw what he'd been daydreaming about for months. They walked down one side, then the other of the thirteen boxcars and the ancient 1940s locomotive that had pulled them into this tunnel.

The minister ordered Peles Castle closed to visitors, called for reinforcements, and posted armed guards at the main entrance. The four of them drove into Sinaia for lunch, leaving the remaining soldiers to maintain tight perimeter security until more troops arrived. They discussed what would happen next.

"It's your call," Herr Deutsch told his Romanian counterpart, "but may I throw out some ideas for you to consider?"

"By all means. What are you thinking?"

"If this were in my country, I would open one or two freight cars just to confirm the train is what we think it is. If we find this really is the Ghost Train, I would seal the tunnel and erect a stronger barrier to protect the entrance. I would keep it heavily guarded and I'd request an archaeological conservatory team to examine and catalog everything on the train. It's not my place to interfere," he continued, "but my country has excellent resources in this regard, and I will be pleased to offer the best people we have should you require them."

The Romanian explained that although he was grateful for the offer, he must speak with his prime minister immediately. He knew the matter would then be out of his hands. He was a simple cabinet-level official in a third-world government, a participant in a discovery that could have worldwide impact.

"And by all means," he continued with a burst of enthusiasm, "after what the four of us have been through, we will certainly open one or two of the cars before I make that call to the prime minister! It would be foolish to call without knowing what's there!"

That statement put a renewed fire into each of them, and within the hour they were standing in the tunnel.

"Which car shall we open?" the Romanian minister asked. "They're identical. Shall we pick one? We are four adventurers. I choose the fourth car from the engine!"

Not wanting to subject the discovery to more publicity than absolutely necessary, the minister selected his most trusted soldier, the lieutenant, to break the chains on the boxcar door. His sledgehammer made easy work of it. Dismissing the soldier, the minister gathered them around and said, "Let's all give it a shove." The door rolled easily on its tracks, and they looked inside.

The car they'd chosen had two different loads inside it. Gold bars were stacked halfway up the side of the car on both ends, apparently to equalize the weight. On top of the bars and in the middle of the boxcar there were slatted crates. They could see framed artwork inside. They chose a random crate, pulled it out and removed the slats. As dusty and grimy as it was, the bright yellows, greens and blues of Van Gogh still shone through.

"It's *The Painter on the Road to Tarascan*," Paul murmured as he brushed away some dirt. "He painted it in 1888, and it hung in the Magdeburg museum. When the Allies bombed Magdeburg, the museum caught on fire and this painting was believed lost. But here it is." He choked up. "What else will we find? What else has been missing all this time that will at last be revealed?"

They opened five more crates, each containing paintings of greater or lesser importance than the Van Gogh they'd seen first. While they worked, Herr Deutsch was in the boxcar, moving crates here and there and counting the gold bars. The others left him to that task, but when he emerged, they were eager to know what he'd found out.

"There are ten thousand one-kilo bars in this freight car alone," he reported. "May we check one more car just to be sure?"

As the others broke the chain on the next car, Paul entered figures into his phone calculator. "That car contains roughly three hundred seventy-five million dollars in gold, not counting the value of the artwork."

They opened the sliding boxcar door of the second car, glanced inside, and shut it again without touching anything. The Romanian minister thought it would be better to leave the rest to the conservators. The cargo in this one looked identical to the other car. It was reasonable to assume it held the same number of gold bars.

Paul made one more set of calculations, then announced, "If we presume each of these thirteen cars has the same amount of gold as the one we counted, we're looking at a total value of almost five billion dollars. I think the need for heightened security just went through the roof, gentlemen. Mr. Minister, I suggest you get the heavy artillery in place immediately."

CHAPTER FORTY-FOUR

Six Months Later

Philippe Lepescu limped along a dark East London street until he arrived on a familiar doorstep. He rang the bell twice and stood by an intercom mounted near the entryway. A male voice in a clipped British accent came on and said, "May I help you?"

"I'm here to see the doctor. Six-four-three is my number."

The door swung open. A fat, balding man in a stained undershirt and torn boxer shorts stood in the hallway.

"Come in, Philippe! Come in!"

Philippe followed the man to an office at the back of the house. Philippe knew exactly where to go since he was coming here more and more frequently these days. The man sat at his desk and said, "OxyContin. That's what you're after, if I recall correctly."

"Right," Philippe panted. He squirmed, standing first on one foot and then the other, like a person needing to use the bathroom. "Fast. I need it fast."

"Of course, my good man. I can see you're experiencing withdrawal. But you know what comes first."

Philippe threw ten fifty-pound notes down on the desk. As the doctor counted out ten tablets, Philippe grabbed two and stuck them in his mouth.

"My word!" the fat man exclaimed. "You shouldn't be taking two at once!"

"Just give me the fucking pills, *Doctor,*" he said, spitting out the man's title with a sneer. "Leave the rest to me."

Philippe walked the rainy streets until he calmed down. The Bad Man was out all the time now, and Philippe had to be careful. He would curse randomly at people who passed him on the sidewalk. He would kick at a stray dog, trying to hurt the defenseless animal. Nothing made any difference to him anymore, and it was simply a matter of time until something awful was going to happen. Philippe Lepescu was a walking powder keg, and his sole motive for continuing this miserable life was to destroy Paul Silver.

Although he still dragged his left leg with every step, his limp became a little less pronounced as the pills took effect. He seethed as he thought about this little present Paul had given him. Just the thought of it made him want to lash out at the very next person he met.

He stopped into a pub he'd never visited before and ordered a pint. He constantly had to find new pubs nowadays. The Bad Man was never good company. Now that he was always out in the open, Philippe had been banned from all the places he used to enjoy. There were the fights, the screaming matches, the smashed bottles. More than once the police had been called, but he always ran away before they arrived.

This pub visit went better than most because for once the Bad Man was quiet. Philippe got a little upset when the bartender failed to notice he needed a second drink quickly enough, but he forced himself to be calm. He wanted that next pint of ale more than he wanted the satisfaction of creating mayhem.

When he finally fell into bed, tonight became the same as all the others. Throughout the endless night he screamed and kicked as sharp slivers of pain jolted him awake every half hour or so. When he did sleep, he dreamed violent dreams: vast scenes where the Bad Man was free to play as much as he wanted. Most people would call them nightmares, Philippe would occasionally reflect. But the dreams of gang rapes, suicide bombings and mass executions - always with him as the perpetrator - were simply *his* dreams ever since the day Paul Silver took away his manhood and his life.

He had one mission now. Every move he made, every thought in his head, was directed at one solitary goal. Paul Silver would pay.

CHAPTER FORTY-FIVE

The exciting discovery of a hidden train in Romania led the world news headlines for a week. Every evening newscasters reported thrilling events of the day as the conservators moved car by car through the Ghost Train. The fascinating discoveries of church relics, artwork and gold bullion astonished everyone. As much as Paul abhorred publicity, he couldn't stay out of the limelight this time. He was one of four men who had found the Ghost Train. He left the interviews to the others, but his name and picture appeared every time there was a story.

On the night the discovery was announced, Philippe had been sitting in his new favorite bar, watching the TV across the room. When he saw Paul's picture, he got off his barstool and limped over to listen. "Shit!" he screamed as he heard what his enemy had found. "Shit!"

He kicked one barstool over and then threw another across the room. The bartender rushed around and grabbed Philippe by the arms, dragging him to the door and tossing him into the street.

"I warned you last time, you crazy bastard! Don't ever come back here!"

As Philippe walked home, the Bad Man taunted him over and over. "You *are* a crazy bastard. Let me kill Paul, you crazy bastard!"

You win, Philippe said at last. *You can kill him. Just stop taunting me.*

_____

On the afternoon they found the train Paul's first call had been to Carey. She could sense his excitement as he described the Ghost Train and its priceless cargo.

"What's next, Mr. Adventurer?" she quipped.

"I hate publicity. I have to get away, somewhere small enough I can blend in with the crowd and stop all this craziness. Meet me tomorrow at the Naples airport. Pack for a week's stay and run away with me!"

He was waiting in baggage claim the next afternoon when she came through the security doors. He hugged her tightly and said, "You're the best thing I've seen in a long, long time!" They kissed passionately and held each other close. His driver loaded the suitcases, and soon they were speeding down the scenic mountain highway that ringed the Bay of Napoli. They went through a long, dark tunnel and emerged to see an overhead sign that made Paul smile.

Welcome to Sorrento.

He hadn't been here in years, and this was her first visit. They unpacked in their suite at the exclusive Excelsior Vittoria Hotel and threw open the patio doors. They could hear waves lapping against the shoreline far below them. The water was serene, and the sight of Mount Vesuvius towering over Naples on the opposite side of the bay was breathtaking.

"I love this place," he said as he stood behind her, his arms wrapped around her body.

"I love *you*, Paul," she whispered. He turned her around and kissed her deeply. Then suddenly he broke away and walked inside.

"What's wrong?" she cried, running in behind him. "If I said something wrong . . ."

"You didn't say anything wrong. You said something *right*. It's me. I can't love anyone. As much as I want to do this, I can't. I shouldn't have brought you here."

She sat on the bed, racked with convulsive sobs. "I don't understand. Ever since you met me at the airport today, I thought you felt the same way about me as I've come to feel about you. You're all I want, Paul. You're all I need from now on. I've done some bad things in my life, but all I want is you."

"God knows I've done bad things too, much worse than you. I'm no good at this, Carey. I'm no good at love. Whenever I try, something bad happens either to me or to the person I love. So I gave it up. I can't love you. It just won't work."

"Yes, it will. Dammit, I won't let you go. I won't let this happen. Do you love me, Paul? Do you? Say it if you do."

"I don't want to hurt you . . ."

"Say it!"

Suddenly he was the one sobbing. He sat next to her and said, "I love you, Carey. I've loved you for a long time. I love you, but I'm afraid."

Smiling now, she put her arms around his neck and kissed him. "I can deal with that. As long as we love each other, we have nothing to be afraid of. You're mine now. You might as well get used to that idea!"

CHAPTER FORTY-SIX

Dressed completely in black and wearing a ski mask, the Bad Man waited patiently in a grove of trees at the top of a huge cliff. The Bay of Naples stretched endlessly below him on this breathtakingly beautiful day. Less than a hundred feet to his left the expansive terraces of the aristocratic Excelsior Vittoria Hotel snaked around a mountain. Ten stories below lay the Sorrento boat docks. A ferry making the quick trip to Capri pulled away, cutting smoothly through the azure sea as an inbound one took its place.

He had checked the high-powered rifle twenty times already, but he gave it a last once-over. It was ready and so was he. He cradled it gently on his arm, watching as passengers disembarked. He had sat here for hours, waiting for one particular couple.

At last he saw them. They looked so happy, he thought with a smirk. She had her arm around him, and his jacket was thrown around his shoulders in typical Italian fashion. They looked like a pair of lovers without a care in the world as they walked along the dock toward the elevator. The Bad Man sneered as he followed them with his eyes, making sure they entered the car. He hadn't been this excited in years. In moments he would kill again. What exhilaration!

Yesterday he had limped across the veranda to that same elevator and ridden it down and back, noting how many minutes the trip took. The top of the elevator opened onto the Excelsior Vittoria's terrace, and its shaft hugged the mountain a hundred feet to the dock below. It was the only way to get to the ferries without traversing a steep narrow staircase, but the only people allowed to use it were the wealthy tourists who were staying at this elegant establishment.

He had stealthily followed the couple to the hotel. He had even rented a room himself yesterday, but he didn't use it. All he needed was to have a room key. He wanted access to the elevator. It was an essential part of his plan, so he waited. He watched the couple leave the grounds for lunch in Sorrento before venturing out onto the terrace. He couldn't risk their seeing him. That would have ruined everything.

Now at last it was time. In a minute the elevator doors would open onto the hotel's veranda. Carey would step out holding her sweetheart's arm and he would pull the trigger. Right before the bitch's eyes, her lover, Paul Silver, would die. He raised the rifle, peered into the scope and steadied the gun on a tree limb. As the doors slid open, the Bad Man tightened his finger on the trigger. It was time for retribution.

A single shot rang out, its report echoing against the mountainside. Paul heard it and threw her back into the elevator - back to safety. He watched as a body tumbled from a grove of trees next to the hotel. It plummeted to the ground far below, slamming into one of the huge rocks that lined a small beach adjacent to the docks. A rifle tumbled down after the figure, landing ten feet from the body.

As they rode the elevator down to see what had happened, Milosh Lepescu sat high above them, still holding his long gun. He'd followed his brother here, waited nearby and finally realized what was about to happen. He saw a man and woman step out of the elevator, and he watched his brother position the rifle. He immediately realized that Philippe was about to commit a murder.

GHOST TRAIN

Milosh had followed Philippe here in order to kill him. When he saw him raise the rifle, Milosh acted quickly. He wouldn't let his evil brother hurt anyone else. Seconds before Philippe pulled the trigger, Milosh pulled his. He watched Philippe's body spiral down to the pavement below, followed by his rifle. Milosh was satisfied at last. He had finally stood up to his little brother and he had finally acted like a man.

He calmly wiped his gun clean, set it in the bushes, and walked two blocks to the Sorrento town square. More satisfied and at ease than he'd been in years, he strolled the narrow lanes, window-shopping with the hundreds of other tourists who hadn't a care in the world. He felt a sense of accomplishment, something he hadn't felt in many, many years.

Finally ending up at the square, he watched the police activity down the road where Philippe had waited to kill the couple. He was safe. No one could possibly tie him to anything and he had no reason to hide. He chose the least busy of a dozen outdoor cafés, took a seat and ordered an espresso. As the waiter turned away, he called him back. "I've changed my mind. Let's make it a champagne. I'm in the mood to celebrate."

CHAPTER FORTY-SEVEN

Anticipating a romantic interlude in their hotel room after the ferry ride back from a morning on the Isle of Capri, Carey and Paul had walked hand in hand to the elevator going from the dock to the hotel's terrace. When the doors opened at the top, there was a sharp crack that Paul recognized instantly. He pushed her roughly back into the car, stood outside for a moment, and then jumped in with her. He pushed the button to go back down to the docks.

"What's happening?" she screamed.

"I heard a gunshot, and a body fell from the mountain next to the hotel. I want to see if we can help."

They found an inert human form sprawled face down on the rocks next to the bay. An automatic rifle lay nearby. She began to scream as other people who had seen the event ran toward them. Paul held her tightly and then let her go as a security guard approached.

Paul explained what had happened, and the guard used his radio to call the police. He took Paul's name in case the authorities wanted to get his statement and allowed them to leave. They went back up to the hotel terrace and walked to their room.

She was distraught. "God, Paul. What happened to that man?"

"I'd have said it was a jumper except for the rifle. I have no idea. Maybe we'll hear something later on."

Their earlier interest in romance was certainly out of mind for the time being. Frazzled, they showered and decided to walk across the street to have lunch at one of the outdoor cafés. The waiter seated them at a front table where they could people-watch and try to get their minds off what they'd experienced. As he ordered wine, they heard a man at the next table tell his waiter, "I've changed my mind. Let's make it a champagne. I'm in the mood to celebrate."

"I think anyone who is lucky enough to be sitting in the Sorrento Town Square right now should be in the mood to celebrate," Carey murmured as she nestled closer to Paul. She was glad to be right here with him, and she felt protected and safe. She put the grisly scene on the dock behind her and savored the moment with him.

Paul glanced at the next table, gave a thumbs-up and a smile, and the man grinned back with a wave. Paul thought he looked vaguely familiar, but he couldn't recall having met him. He'd probably seen the man another day right here in the square, he presumed.

When Paul and Carey got their wine and the stranger at the next table had his champagne, they turned and raised their glasses, joining him in a toast. They toasted the man's celebration, whatever it was. As they turned away, Milosh laughed to himself and took the first drink of champagne. *Those strangers have no idea they just toasted my success in killing my own brother!*

A week in Sorrento was like a week in heaven, Carey thought as she dozed in bed on their final morning in paradise. She had told him everything about Nicu, including the strange black card he'd given her and how it worked. *No more secrets,* she'd told herself, knowing that was a one-sided promise. There were things about him she might never know. But she was okay with that. All she wanted was Paul.

One more thing she confessed with pride was that her need for heroin was a thing of the past. It had been replaced with a newfound zest for living. She had enough money to be comfortable from now on, and she was in the best place she'd ever been. Paul promised to be there for her.

"You'd better not make that promise without meaning it," she said only half-jokingly. "I intend to hold you to it."

Yesterday Paul told her he had to go to Bucharest to tie up one loose end. He hadn't mentioned what that was, but she knew he would tell her when he was ready. She still often wondered exactly how much more there was to learn about this intriguing man, but she was prepared to settle down and learn everything. She drifted into slumber again then dreamily awoke when the door buzzer rang.

While she was sleeping, Paul had checked the local news on his phone, searching for the story about a man falling to his death in Sorrento. What he found astonished him. A Swiss citizen, Philippe Lepescu, had fallen from the cliff after being shot. A rifle with Lepescu's fingerprints was on the ground beside him and it had not been fired. Another rifle, the murder weapon, was found in some bushes adjoining the famous Excelsior Vittoria Hotel. That weapon had no fingerprints. The police had no motive, no suspects, and were asking anyone with information to come forward.

Paul opened up the patio doors, and the waiter rolled the room service cart onto their terrace. It was their last meal in this idyllic place, and as always, he was arranging nice things for her even while she slumbered.

He stuck his head into the room and said, "Get up, sleepyhead! It's time for our farewell breakfast!"

She dragged herself into the bathroom and came out wearing the plush hotel bathrobe. He was in his shorts and T-shirt, drinking coffee at the table on their patio.

"What's our plan for today? How much time do I have?"

Paul glanced at his watch. "Plenty. In two hours our driver will take us back to Naples. From there we'll fly to Bucharest. We'll be there by 1:30 this afternoon and spend the night. That's as far ahead as I've planned." He smiled. She knew how unlike him that was. Paul Silver planned everything. If he really hadn't thought about the future past tomorrow, maybe she was getting somewhere. Maybe she was loosening him up, putting a little of her gypsy spirit in this businessman-adventurer.

As she ate, a thought came to her. "There's no way we can fly from Naples to Bucharest in three hours. Won't we have to change planes somewhere, like Rome or Vienna?"

"Leave it all in my hands," he replied with a grin.

Their driver dropped them at Naples's private aircraft terminal, where a six-passenger Gulfstream jet sat waiting. *Will the surprises never end?* she said to herself as the plane lifted into the sky.

Paul had one final hunch, one remaining million-dollar loose end to tie up. He dodged her questions as their taxi drove them through Bucharest's busy streets. When they reached their destination, she looked out and said, "What the hell is this all about?"

They were parked in front of the building where Nicu Lepescu had lived.

Paul ushered her into the lobby; a man in a coat and tie stood waiting.

"Mr. Silver?"

Paul nodded and the man said, "Did you bring the authorization from the owners?"

He took a folded paper from his pocket and handed it over. The man glanced at it and put it in his pocket. "There's your package," he said, pointing to a box on the floor. He handed Paul a large ring of keys, advised him they would unlock every door in the building, and left.

"Okay, it's confession time," she said brightly. "Want to tell me exactly what's going on? What was that paper you gave him, the authorization from the owners? And how the hell did you get him to let you have keys to everything?"

"That paper was a letter from the corporation that owns this building, giving me the right to search it."

"How in the world did you get them to allow that?" she said with a grin.

"I've kept one little secret from you," he admitted with a grin.

"*One* little secret? Somehow I doubt that," she quipped. "But please continue!"

He explained how he'd calculated the number of gold bars Nicu must have stolen while he was stationmaster. Nicu had hidden 192 bars in two safety deposit boxes, but like her, Paul believed there were more. "I used one of my companies to buy this building," he declared.

"Stop for a minute! *You bought this building?* Are you serious? Why?"

"I was getting to the good part," he continued. "If Nicu had more gold to hide, and if Nicu owned this seven-story building, why wouldn't he have hidden it here? He almost never left his flat, you told me, so it was a perfect hiding place. No one would be the wiser. Nicu's grandchildren put the building on the market, and when I came up with my hunch, I bought it. Now I can see for myself. If there's something here, then great. If there isn't, I still have a marketable piece of real estate I only paid four million lei for."

Only *four million lei! A million US dollars! He had bought a building just to see if a hunch was correct!* She had a new respect for how seriously wealthy this man really was. The private jet ride was only the beginning to understanding what real money could do for someone. Now her boyfriend owned Nicu's building. *Crazy.*

Paul opened the box the estate agent had left. He pulled out some tools and a sophisticated piece of handheld equipment, which he explained was a metal detector. Hopefully it would come in handy this afternoon, he said with excitement in his voice. "Let's get started."

It seemed surreal as they entered the empty apartment that had been Nicu's home. She had spent much of the last three years in these spacious rooms, and now they were bare and cold. She looked around as he immediately went to work. His target would be inside walls, he told her, places where there might have been a closet or room that could have been sealed up and painted over. He set the machine to search for precious metals and ignore common elements such as iron and steel, and he began to move the detector up and down one wall after another.

It was almost dark when he called it a day. They checked into a nearby hotel, had an early dinner and were in bed by ten. They hit it early the next morning. He was finished with Nicu's apartment, so he moved to the only other vacant one in the building. It was also the only other apartment on Nicu's floor. The estate agent had told him this apartment hadn't been rented in years. For some reason Nicu kept it empty, perhaps for storage, the man surmised.

"Maybe he kept it empty for another reason entirely," Paul told Carey with a sly wink.

He'd offered to leave her at the hotel this morning, but she wanted to be with him. She sat on the floor and read a book as he methodically ran the sensor up and down. He was in another room when she heard loud chirping noises. She jumped up and ran to where he was.

"Did you find something?"

"Maybe. This is the first hit I've had since we got here." He ran the detector across the wall again and got more chirps. "Pull the wallpaper off right there!" he yelled.

She stripped the faded paper. Behind it was the unmistakable outline of a door. Paul took a hammer and furiously dug it into the drywall. It took only minutes before they were standing in front of what had once been a walk-in closet.

There was nothing in it except four wooden crates, each about two feet square. They were sitting in a corner.

The hammer made quick work of the first crate's lid. They pulled it off and saw that their hunches had been correct. There was more gold after all. A lot more.

Laughing like kids, they sat on the floor and emptied that box. In it were thirty-six bars. A quick lift of three more lids confirmed each box held the same thing. There were a hundred and forty-four bars total.

"Shit," she said with a grin. "Old Nicu stole a hell of a lot more than he admitted in his diary."

"I had a hunch he did," Paul replied. "He was making sure his future was secure. And he did it. He served his time and lived a comfortable life for a hundred and five years. Comfortable, I suppose, but I'd wager he wasn't happy until you came along."

"Don't keep me in suspense," she blurted, admitting with a giggle, "I couldn't do the math on my measly twenty-three bars. How much money are we looking at here?"

Paul pulled out his smartphone and entered some numbers. "In US dollars, around five million, give or take."

This whole thing simply took her breath away. She could barely speak. "What do we do with it?"

"Happy birthday," he replied.

"It's not my birthday. My birthday's not until September 17th!"

"Consider it an early birthday present. It's yours, Carey. I have plenty. We'll take the jet to Linz and use your black card to convert the gold to cash in your account."

Just like always, the man she was going to spend the rest of her life with surprised her once again.

"I love you, Paul Silver."

He kissed her passionately. "Ditto, Apostol. Let's get this stuff loaded up and get on with our lives!"

———

It would be years before ownership rights to the Ghost Train were resolved. By then both the Romanian and German ministers would have long since retired. Human rights organizations asserted claims to the stolen treasures on behalf of the millions who had died in the Holocaust. Romania claimed an interest since the bounty was found at Peles Castle. So did the royal family. Germany asserted its claim as well since many of the items the train carried had been stolen in Germany. The art, sculpture and relics were more simply dealt with. Many could easily be traced back to the institutions or families who had owned them prior to the war.

Ultimately each of those claimants would be awarded a share, with families of the Holocaust victims receiving the most. Billions of dollars of stolen property at last was returned to those from whom the Nazis had taken everything. Now there would be no treasure to build a neo-Nazi Germany. There would be no Fourth Reich, no rising phoenix. Hitler's reign of horror was over at last.

Thank you!

Thanks for reading Ghost Train. If you liked it and have a few minutes **I'd really appreciate a brief review on Amazon, Goodreads or both.** Even a line or two makes a tremendous difference so thanks in advance for your help!

Please join me on:
Facebook
http://on.fb.me/187NRRP

Twitter
@BThompsonBooks

HOW ABOUT A FREE BOOK?

Bill Thompson's award-winning first novel,
***The Bethlehem Scroll*, can be yours free.**

**Just go to
billthompsonbooks.com,
enter your email address and click
"Subscribe."**

You'll receive advance notice of future book releases and other great offers.

Made in the USA
Middletown, DE
17 September 2018